D0119725

A DARK, DIVIDED SELF

Also by A.J. Cross

The Dr Kate Hanson mysteries

GONE IN SECONDS
ART OF DECEPTION
A LITTLE DEATH *
SOMETHING EVIL COMES *
COLD, COLD HEART *

The Will Traynor forensic mysteries

DARK TRUTHS *
DEVIL IN THE DETAIL *

* *available from Severn House*

A DARK,
DIVIDED SELF

A.J. Cross

**SEVERN
HOUSE**

First world edition published in Great Britain in 2021 and the USA in 2022
by Severn House, an imprint of Canongate Books Ltd,
14 High Street, Edinburgh EH1 1TE.

Trade paperback edition first published in Great Britain and the USA in 2022
by Severn House, an imprint of Canongate Books Ltd.

severnhouse.com

British Library Cataloguing-in-Publication Data
A CIP catalogue record for this title is available from the British Library.

ISBN-13: 978-0-7278-5036-2 (cased)
ISBN-13: 978-1-4483-0729-6 (trade paper)
ISBN-13: 978-1-4483-0728-9 (e-book)

All Severn House titles are printed on acid-free paper.

Typeset by Palimpsest Book Production Ltd.,
Falkirk, Stirlingshire, Scotland.
Printed and bound in Great Britain by
TJ Books, Padstow, Cornwall.

PROLOGUE

Monday, 12 November 2018.

Erica Trent hurried out of the building, her tutor's words reverberating inside her head. Merging with other pedestrians, mostly students, coming and going along the main campus road, Erica was feeling decidedly up. Her tutor had been very positive about the quality of her work: if Erica maintained this high quality throughout her course, she would be well on her way to a first-class degree. Which was exactly what Erica expected. Anything less was not an option. Her tutor had also given her some advice that she planned to follow. She quickened her pace, keen to get back to her bedsit and the assignment waiting for her, hoping that the two male students new to the house were out and the place quiet. She grinned. Her tutor was right. Things needed to change.

Checking the time on her phone, she left the main campus road and upped her pace. A sudden, bone-cold northerly wind struck her face, lifting and swirling her hair. Grabbing it with both hands, tucking it inside her scarf, she headed in the direction of her bedsit in a distant row of tall, brooding, multi-occupancy houses. She pulled the scarf over her head against sudden, heavy spots of rain.

Leaving the road, she walked onto an open area of grass, lined with trees to her right, beyond them a narrow strip of land used by students for illicit parking. She had gone a few metres when a male voice sounded from somewhere in that direction.

'Excuse me, miss? . . . *Wait*, please.'

Responding to the tone as much as the words, she turned. A tall, dark-haired man was approaching her, holding up identification. This wasn't unusual given the current situation. She waited. He came closer, smiled.

'My apologies if I startled you.' Recalling her tutor's advice, thinking what a nice smile he had, she also smiled.

'Not at all.'

'I'm Detective Sergeant Daniel Hunter.' His voice was pleasant with a subtle accent. Scottish, maybe? She gave a quick nod.

'Actually, I think I may have seen you around the campus with other officers.'

'More than likely. We've significantly increased our presence here in recent weeks.' He looked ahead then back to her. 'I'm heading this way, too.' They fell into step together. She glanced at him.

'It's terrible what's happening. Do the police have any ideas as to who—?'

'Not yet, but we're doing all we can to track down possible witnesses.' He looked at her. 'Have you been spoken to, yet?' She shook her head. 'In that case, could you spare a few minutes to answer some questions?' A refusal citing pressure of work didn't strike Erica as the right thing to do in the circumstances.

'Of course.'

His steps matching hers, her bookbag brushing his side, he pointed at her scarf with its pattern of tiny gold stars.

'That's nice.'

She smiled, her tutor's words from barely twenty minutes before still inside her head. Yes, Erica was on target to achieve a first-class degree, but she might do well to consider her life balance. The tutor had followed that up with advice along the lines that Erica needed to relax, perhaps become a little more sociable, that all work and almost no play was probably not the best way to live. Erica gave Detective Hunter a quick glance. Mid-twenties or so? A second glance, this time at his hands. Well-kempt. No ring. What if she suggested answering his questions inside that warm little coffee shop close to where she lived? A small, first step to extending her social life. He was pointing to the trees on their right.

'My car is parked just over there. I need to get my schedule of witness questions. Wait here, please.' She watched him walk away from her.

'*Witness* questions? I'm sorry, but I didn't know any of those girls so I probably won't be able to help—' He looked back at her with a quick, reassuring smile.

'You'd be surprised at how much people *do* recall. Like you said, it is terrible what's happened and the only way for us to stop it happening again is for people familiar with the area to help us.' She nodded.

'Now you put it like that, of course I'll help in any way I can, but I still don't think I can be of much help . . .'

He had reached the line of trees. She waited, telling herself that when he came back with his list, she would get straight to the coffee invitation. She watched him head towards a just-visible vehicle. On another strong gust of wind, the trees parted and she saw him open a rear door, lean inside then emerge, folder in hand and walk back to her.

'This will take no time at all.' She took a quick breath.

'I've just thought – there's a really nice coffee shop not far from here.' She pointed in the direction of the distant houses, interspersed with little shops. 'It's nice, really warm and not crowded at this time of the evening. Could we do it there?' He smiled.

'That sounds like a great idea. Just to give you an idea of how difficult the questions are, this first one is the most challenging: What is your name?' She grinned back at him.

'Erica Trent.'

He patted his pockets with one hand, then the other. 'I think that was my phone. It must be in the car. I'd better respond. It might be a colleague.'

She followed him a short way as he walked back to it, opened the driver's door, looked around the interior, then called to him, 'Can't you find it?'

He straightened, turned to her with a quiet laugh.

'Like most men, I have trouble finding most things.' He held up a phone. 'Got it!' A sudden wind caught her hair. He frowned upwards at the swaying trees.

'Stand over here where it's sheltered while I return the call. It won't take a minute and then we'll get that coffee. On one condition.' He placed his hand against his chest. '*My* treat.'

Erica smiled, thinking how easy it had been to make this first social contact. Something she would do once every day from now on.

'Agreed.'

'Experience tells me that you'll make an excellent witness, Erica.'

An hour later, they were inside his car as it moved smoothly along. He glanced across at her.

'Tell me, Erica, now that we've got to know each other, how

do you view the world? What I mean is, what's your view of it generally? No, let me guess from what you've told me so far. You see it as . . . a kindly, fair place in which to live. A place in which, if we do right to others, we can expect a similar response. How did I do?' He sent her another glance.

'I feel a certain responsibility towards you, you know. I have to tell you that, from my own experience, the world is truly a very dark place. Which actually doesn't matter. Because I know how to make it work by keeping to my own rules of engagement. By the way, they're also a little on the dark side. Although you've probably guessed that by now?' He picked up muffled sounds as she stirred.

'You get it now, don't you?' His eyes fixed on the road as his vehicle ate it up, he whispered, 'Welcome to my world, Erica.'

Hours later, with the merest hint of a new day visible, he breathed deeply. He looked down at her, carefully removed a leaf from her face.

'I'll be back soon, but don't worry. I promise that you won't be lonely.' He stood, walked away to his car. Reaching it, he looked up, seeing mostly darkness.

'Thanks, my old friend.'

ONE

Propped on pillows, Jess Meredith studied the broad shoulders and still-slim waist as Will Traynor came out of the shower. This was something she anticipated whenever she had a late start. She watched as he gave himself a vigorous towel-dry then wrapped the towel around his waist, all done without vanity. He lifted both arms to dry his short, fair hair. She looked at the scar on his side, thinking how much he had changed since they had first met, when he was still consumed with grief at his wife's murder some years before.

She tracked the familiar morning routine, listened to the buzz of the razor, his eyes fixed on the mirror in front of him, knowing he was already in work-mode. Postgraduate students competed to get onto the courses he taught. He repaid their keenness by delivering high-quality lectures and tutorials. She watched him pat on a splash of aftershave. He looked at her through the mirror and grinned, moved across the room, reached for the fresh, white shirt hanging from the wardrobe door.

'Busy day ahead?' she asked.

'Some students are coming in to discuss vacation assignments and there's a lot of research waiting for me.'

'That's a coincidence. There are one or two areas here which require some in-depth study.' The towel dropped. Smiling, he returned the shirt to its hanger, came to her, reached for the soft brown-gold curls, lowered his face to hers.

'How about you tell me about them?'

Same day. 6.38 p.m.

Chloe Judd brought her car to a halt for what felt like the hundredth time that day and took a deep breath. She looked across at the little house in the middle of the terraced row. Her heart squeezed. It happened every time she saw it. Her new home. *Hers.* A one-bedroom house built in 1910, its second bedroom converted to a bathroom. She shook her head in disbelief. *Chloe Judd, property owner.* She loved every brick and tile. Knew how lucky she was to have it. She also knew the years of debt it represented. But it was foot-on-the-property-ladder debt, she reminded herself.

Getting out of the car, she walked around it, opened the passenger door and heaved two boxes from the seat. Carrying them through the little gate and up the short path to the front door, she put them down and inserted her key, aware of subtle movement to her right. The curtain at the bay window of the house on the other side of the low dividing wall fell slowly back into place. She had yet to meet any of her neighbours.

Unlocking the door, she carried the boxes inside and felt the door close behind her, experiencing yet again the rush of pride in the shadowy, high-ceilinged hall, the dark red-and-blue tiled floor, the stairs to one side. She hefted the boxes and followed the long passageway leading directly ahead to the kitchen.

Dumping the boxes on the floor, she took a deep breath. Taking her earbuds out of her pocket, she scrolled through the playlist, searching for the perfect unpacking music. She had been here all of the previous day. One medium-sized van had been enough to convey her furniture in a single journey. One more by car had brought all of her personal belongings. Her old bedsit was empty now, save for the items which weren't hers, awaiting its new tenant. Over the past few days, Judd had arranged and rearranged her few basic items of furniture until they were to her liking, brought flowers for her one vase, cleaned all of the paintwork, done the same to the comparatively modern bathroom and the empty kitchen cupboards, inside and out. This evening she was moving in.

Singing along with Eminem – yeah, OK, mainstream now, but to Judd's thinking still the coolest – she opened boxes, carried items to cupboards, delighting in the practical decision-making required. She stretched up to place her three dinner plates on the top shelf. On second thought, she moved them to the lower shelf, placing two cereal bowls next to them, recalling another job she needed to do and soon: measure the large bay window in the sitting room for curtains. The thought brought with it a wisp of anxiety. Large window. Big expense. Behind her, the kitchen door drifted slowly open.

'You left your car door open, Chlo! . . . Where do you want these? . . . *Chlo?*'

A man pushed his way into the kitchen. Lowering the two boxes to the floor, he flexed his back and shoulders. Still getting no response, he sighed, walked across to her and tapped her shoulder. She yelped, vaulted against a nearby worksurface, dropping a small plate. It hit the tiles and shattered. She whirled on him.

'*Jonesy*, you bloody *idiot*! Don't sneak up like that! Women *hate* it!' He grinned.

'Not in *my* personal experience. The front door was open and I gave you a shout. Who did you think it was? Some low-life after your body or your money, not necessarily in that order?'

He watched her get her breathing under control then pointed to the boxes he had brought in.

'Where do you want these? They feel like they're full of paving slabs.' They knelt either side, unpacking various items.

'This is a really great house, Chlo.' She narrowed her eyes at him. Jonesy was a joker.

'Are you being serious?'

''Course, I am! This whole place has a good vibe.' She looked back at him.

'That's exactly how I feel about the place.'

He stood, reached into a pocket of his fleece. 'Before I forget, here's your spare key.' He grinned at her, winked. 'Or, shall I keep it?' She reached out, took it from him, looked around the kitchen.

'Listen, I've got instant coffee, some milk, bread, cheese. I'll track down some mugs.' She saw him glance at his watch. 'OK. I get the drift. You've got plans and you're thinking you're on a promise.'

'I wish. Change of shift. I'm on earlies tomorrow.' He looked at her. 'You're all right being here on your own?'

'In my own house, not having to listen to rubbish music or worse coming from other bedsits? Get real.'

'OK, I'll leave you to it.' She watched him walk away towards the hall, called after him, 'Thanks for all your help, Jonesy. You're a good mate!'

He turned, looked back to her.

'How about I come back here after I finish tomorrow? Bring some food, some wine, yeah? What do you say?'

She liked Jonesy, but only as a mate. She knew he was a player.

'Thanks, but I've got loads to do and only the next few days to do it.'

'OK, I'll leave you to it, you and your nosey neighbour who gave me a once-over just now.' He nodded in the direction of the party wall.

She stood, went to the kitchen door, a finger to her lips, whispered, 'Who did you *see*? A him, a her? . . . A they?'

He shook his head.

'Just a curtain-twitch.'

She watched him continue along the hall.

'Thanks again, Jonesy. Give the door a firm pull!'

She heard the sound of it closing, listened to it echo throughout the house.

Some hours later, tired, her back and legs aching, she headed upstairs, running her hand lightly over the smooth mahogany banister, waylaid by a sudden memory of her foster mother as she was before she got ill. She breathed deeply. If it weren't for Moira, she wouldn't be here in this house—

A sudden, loud thump made her flinch, her head jerking to the shared wall centimetres away, her still-unseen neighbour somewhere on its other side.

Please. I can put up with nosey. What I don't want is noisy.

But hearing only silence, she continued upstairs. She had always lived with other people or in bedsits. Living entirely alone in a whole house, even a small one, would probably take some getting used to.

Same day. 10.50 p.m.

The doors of the small inner-city police station flew open, bringing both lounging officers to their feet, tension soaring as two men in cycling helmets, dressed entirely in black, bustled inside, one supporting a sobbing, shoeless woman, the other manoeuvring two racing bicycles.

'Hey! You can't bring those in here!' One of the officers pointed at the bicycles.

'We're not leaving them outside. They're worth three grand each. This woman needs some help.'

Sergeant Jacques, the senior of the two officers, came towards them, frowning.

'We're closing in five minutes. If you've knocked her down, she needs A & E—'

'We didn't. Push that chair over here so I can put her down.'

The desk chair was moved and the cyclist gently lowered the woman onto it. She looked up at both officers, her long dark hair damp, hanging over her face, her eyes huge, her mouth, hands and legs quivering.

'I can't believe it. He was going to *kill* me. I *swear* he was going to kill me!' The senior officer turned to his colleague, mouthed *Domestic*, then turned back to her.

'Who was going to kill you?'

'One of your officers! His name is Huntley, or something. He works *here*. In terrorism.'

The two officers exchanged another look. The one who had spoken shook his head.

'There's nobody of that name who works here. And this is a small station. We don't work on that kind of—'

'*This* is where he was bringing me!'

Hearing the hysterical edge in her voice, he crouched down, still keeping his distance. If she was as adrift as she sounded, he was taking no risks. He looked at her properly for the first time, seeing beyond her fear and upset. It was obvious now to Jacques how much younger she was than he had initially assumed. At most, she was in her late teens.

'What's your name?'

'. . . Driscoll. Carly Driscoll.' She began to sob. He looked up at the two cyclists.

'What do you know about this?'

'Next to nothing. We were on our bikes, heading home when we saw her—'

'Where, exactly?' They looked at each other.

'On a road that runs off Broad Street then on in this direction—'

'Who else did you see?'

'Just her, running towards us, waving her arms and screaming. She almost brought me off my bike.'

The officer glanced back to the woman. She was quiet now, except for an occasional, explosive sob. She looked too young for domestic issues but you never knew these days. His suspicions moving in the direction of some kind of mental health problem, he clicked his fingers at his colleague, making a 'writing' gesture as he sat down and slowly wheeled his chair closer to hers.

'Is it OK if I call you Carly?' She nodded, her face paper-white. 'Carly, I'm Sergeant Robert Jacques. Can you tell us what happened?' She looked down at her hands.

'There was this man . . . and I . . .' She looked up at him, her hand at her mouth. 'I . . . feel sick.' Jacques was on his feet, his eyes fixed on the cyclists.

'We're the only two officers on duty here—'

'*Please* . . .' Seeing her struggle to stand, he jerked his head at the cyclists.

'Come on! You help her up and I'll show you where the bathroom is.'

He led the way, holding the door open as one of the cyclists helped her inside. They both came out, Jacques closing the door behind them. His colleague stood nearby, arms folded.

'Still think it's a domestic?' he whispered. Jacques frowned, hearing a cough, followed by a retching sound, followed by a rush of water.

'Buggered if I know—'

The door opened. Driscoll emerged, her face empty of colour except for deep grey shadows beneath her eyes. She was led back to the main office and her chair.

'Feeling better?' She didn't look it but she seemed calmer.

'A bit, now I've washed my face and hands. Can I have some water please?'

Jacques went to a low cupboard, brought out a glass, inspected it, filled it with water, brought it to her, uneasy now about having allowed her access to washing facilities, wondering if it was a back-of-the-net own goal waiting to bite him on the backside sometime in the future.

She took a long, slow drink, wiped her mouth with the back of her hand. He noticed that her nails looked neat, except for a couple which were ragged.

'Do you feel up to telling us what happened?'

'I was in Broad Street for a concert at Symphony Hall with a couple of friends. They came by taxi. I had my car. I parked in—' She frowned. 'I don't know the name of the road but it's no distance from there. I've parked there loads of times. After the concert finished it was pouring with rain. I'd forgotten my umbrella so I said goodbye to my friends and ran back to where I'd parked . . . I'd almost reached my car when – this man just appeared.' She paused, looking shaky again.

'He said he was a police officer, that his name was . . . Huntley, something like that. You must know him.' Jacques and his colleague exchanged quick glances. 'He said he worked in terrorism, that he had colleagues with him who were starting to close off the top of road where I'd just come from.' She looked up at Jacques. 'I didn't actually see anybody doing that. There was nobody about except him.' Her head dropped down.

'I just don't get it,' she whispered.

'Tell us all of it, Carly, all of the details you remember. My colleague here will write it all down.' They waited.

'He said my car had been tampered with. That *really* upset me. It's my first ever car and— He said they knew the identity of the man who did it. That they had arrested him. He said he would take me to his station, *this* one, which wasn't far, just along the road I was parked on, to see if I could identify him. I told him I hadn't seen anybody but he said not to worry about it. I said OK. I've driven past here loads of times, and I just assumed from what he said this was the place he meant. The way he was with me, the way he looked and sounded, I just agreed.'

She lowered her face to her hands, tears coming again. Jacques waited, a picture of what had happened to this young woman now forming.

'What you've said so far has been written down. Is there anything else you remember?' he asked. There was a long pause. 'What did this man look like?' He waited some more, then added, 'Is it possible he's somebody you've seen before?'

She looked up at Jacques, her eyes huge.

'I didn't know him! I never saw him before,' she cried, her voice rising. She closed her eyes, gripped her hands together. 'He was just *there*, like I said.'

'Can you describe him?'

Pushing her fingers through her hair, looking exhausted now, she said, 'He was tall. Dark haired . . . That's it.'

'Can you take us through the detail of what actually happened?' She frowned, trying to remember.

'He walked me to his car. It wasn't a police car. I didn't think anything of it, except that maybe he was undercover. He opened the door for me—' Her head came up. 'That's something I noticed. How polite he was. And his voice. He was well-spoken. If he had looked or sounded rough, I would never have gone with him—'

'What happened after you got into his car?' She looked away, stared at the floor.

'He started driving and talking just normally, you know, asking about my evening. He said something about his team chasing somebody but it was all top secret . . . and then, after a while he got really quiet and . . . he pulled into some entrance to a warehouse or something and . . . stopped the car. He just sat there, not looking at me, not saying anything. I asked him why he'd stopped because I knew this police station was a bit further along the road. He didn't answer. That's when I knew that something was *really* wrong. I reached for the door and—' her words sped, 'he grabbed hold of both my arms. I was struggling to get free, he was trying to get some sort of plastic thing on my wrists. That's when I knew I *had* to get away from him, had to *fight* him, which is when he got angry, *so* angry, shouting at me to stop struggling but I just *knew* that if I did, he was going to kill me!' She stopped, out of breath and words. Jacques looked up, saw the cyclists' shocked faces, then back to her.

'OK, take your time. Then, what?' She brushed away tears.

'I was screaming, trying to kick him, but there wasn't enough room inside the car, so I used my hands, my fists on him and . . . I can't remember, it's all jumbled up, but somehow the car door just opened. I fell out onto some grass at the edge of the road and—' She took a wavering breath, looked up at the two cyclists.

'I saw them coming along and I got up and started running as fast as I could to them, just . . . hysterical.' Both cyclists nodded.

'Can you say anything else about this man?' asked Jacques. 'You've said he was tall, dark haired.' She looked down at her hands.

'I . . . he was nice-looking. He had neat hair. Dark hair. Sorry. I already said that.'

'Tell us about his car.'

'It was a Mini. I'm not sure about the colour. It might have been brown. It was shiny, like it was new. Or clean.'

Jacques turned to the cyclists. 'You saw it?'

They nodded.

'Only for a few seconds as he drove off,' said one. 'Our attention was on her—'

'Colour? Registration?'

'We didn't get a reg. It was some dark colour, possibly red. It was really shifting, the last we saw it.'

Jacques looked back to Driscoll. 'This man. Do you recall anything else about him?'

'Tall, dark haired . . .' She shook her head. 'Sorry. My dad is around six feet so I'd say he was similar . . . but slim . . . That's it.' Her voice quavered. 'I want to go home.'

He reached for his desk phone.

'You need a hospital check—'

'I told you I'm not hurt. I want to go *home* . . . I've lost my shoes.'

A few hours later, Carly Driscoll had been collected by her parents, having refused medical assistance a second time. Jacques had dispatched his colleague to follow the cyclists to where they had first seen the young woman. He was now at the computer, watching words steadily fill the screen. The violence in what she had described carried clear implications that the incident was sexually motivated. This station was a real backwater. Jacques had heard a few witness accounts in his time, but this one struck him as believable. It needed other eyes on it.

The main door opened. His colleague was back, a pair of black, high-heeled shoes in his gloved hand. Jacques looked at them, added a few words to his report, reread it and pressed SEND.

'Put her shoes in the internal post bag.' He switched off the computer, reached for his coat, his colleague doing the same.

It was headquarters' problem now.

TWO

Sunday, 7 April. 6.45 a.m.

The man was waiting, voices and radio-static drifting to him on the mild air. Keeping his dog on a short leash, his eyes moved slowly over the heavily wooded slope covered in thick ferns and some half-choked, budding bluebells. He was thinking about what he'd seen. He wouldn't forget it in a hurry.

He thought of his mother, seven years dead, wondering if that's what she looked like now? He was also thinking about money. He looked around, quickly raised his phone, took another couple of shots and just as quickly pocketed it, starting at a voice some distance away.

'*Hey, you!*'

Two red-faced, heavy-set officers in short sleeves were heading up the steep incline in his direction, one holding a roll of blue-and-white tape, the other pointing at him.

'I told you to wait over there!'

'How long will I be hanging about here? I've got a farm to run.' Looking unimpressed, the officer without tape demanded his details, wrote them in his notebook, ending with a sharp stab of his pen.

'Farm workers are early risers. What time did you get here?'

'Around quarter to six, why?'

'A regular here, are you?'

'You must be joking. Nobody in their right minds comes here to walk. Look at it!' He turned, jabbed his finger at a spot some way off. 'I was way over there when the dog took off so I followed his barks here—'

'Did you see anybody else?'

'Not alive, if that's what you're wondering—'

'What about any other morning?'

'I just told you, we don't come here.'

'We?' The officer frowned.

The man nodded at the dog who was looking up at them, tongue lolling. 'If I had seen anybody, it wouldn't have been whoever left that over there, would it?'

'What makes you say that?' The officer's eyes settled on his.

'It's obvious. It's been here years.' He gazed beyond the officer, his eyes narrowing on a small woman in white. 'What's she up to?'

Ignoring the question, the officer looked down at his notes. 'OK, Mr Fincher, we know where to get hold of you if we need to. You can go, but watch where you're walking. See that tree stump?' Fincher looked in the direction the officer was indicating. 'Walk to it, turn sharp left and carry on up there, got it? You'll find another officer at the top who'll escort you off the site.'

'I should've started my job half an hour ago, not hanging around here,' Fincher muttered. Looking disgruntled, he gave the dog's lead a tug and headed towards the stump.

Sending a quick backward glance to several official-looking figures, he saw that the small figure in white was now kneeling, almost concealed by tall ferns. She had to be looking at what he had seen. Why would any woman, anybody, want that for a job?

He quickened his pace, one hand clasping the dog's lead, the other around his phone inside his pocket, a small smiling forming. He had some phone calls to make.

Her hair damp to her forehead, pathologist Dr Connie Chong was thinking among other things of the unseasonably warm weather and how long it might last. Voices and static drifting on the air were now mixed with staccato clicks as she and her pathology assistant waited for the forensic officers to finish taking their crime scene photographs.

Seeing a couple of their hands raise, she returned to where she had been and crouched again, absorbing every visible detail of what was lying in front of her. She had noted the particular vigour of this patch of vegetation as soon as she saw it. Had guessed the cause of its flourishing: by-products of decomposition, nitrogen and phosphates leeching into the ground, feeding the soil around and beneath, that same vegetation returning the favour by producing vigorous growth which had in time provided heavy concealment. A natural cycle, disrupted now, its secret revealed.

What was here was anything but natural. Fresh green creeper tendrils had wound themselves around the length of the spinal column and partially obscured what was obviously a pelvis. She ticked a mental list. Female. Hearing Igor's camera whir, she looked up and around at the steep slope and mass of groundcover. This was no straightforward recovery task. There was going to be a lot of scatter, all of which needed locating. The whole area would require a meticulous search. She stood, and headed down the slope with her assistant, their coveralls swishing, tall, dark firs crowding them. He glanced at her.

'Not exactly my idea of picturesque countryside.' They walked on, both aware of the temperature increasing.

'As always, where would we be without dogwalkers, Igor?'

'Working in headquarters' air conditioning on cases still waiting for us, blissfully unaware of this—'

'Don't.'

'Just supplying the facts, ma'am.'

She gazed back to where they had been.

'"Shallow grave" hardly describes it. Whoever she was, there was no attempt at concealment. She was simply dumped for nature to do whatever it could.'

'She?'

'No question.'

They headed to a single red flag within more long grasses and leaf litter. Chong crouched, gently parted the grass, her eyes taking in the brownish-yellow skull and what had probably been two rows of excellent dentition. Igor took a series of shots.

'Looks to me like a roll-down.' he said.

'I agree. Dislodged by animals and probably helped further on its way by the recent lack of rain and soil dryness.'

She studied the thick build-up of leaf litter surrounding the skull, then looked up the hill to where they had seen the other remains. Igor continued capturing the scene in full colour. He paused midway in his routine.

'What's your general thinking so far?'

'Homicide victim about covers it, after which animals got really busy doing what they do, carrying away evidence. We're going to be here for a while.'

Chong raised her hand to two scenes-of-crime officers moving up the slope towards them. As they arrived, she gestured to the area of ground before them, then upwards to the location of the skeletal remains.

'All the vegetation immediately around and between these two deposits requires a careful search. Flag anything which looks to be small bones. There's no indication of clothing, which doesn't mean there wasn't any when she was left here so you're also looking for buttons, pieces of metal, bits of zip, cloth, jewellery. Better get started.'

The sun was well past its highest point, multiple red flags now in position, the vegetation surrounding them carefully removed. Chong looked down at the partial skeleton now fully revealed, her eyes moving over an almost-complete ribcage, pelvis, a portion of spinal column and an array of what looked to be tiny, pale pebbles. His feet planted wide, Igor leant forward, camera poised. It clicked and whirred.

Pointing a small trowel at the remains, she said, 'Whoever left her here literally dumped her.' Her eyes moved back over the extensive, thick woods then downwards. 'Which doesn't mean it was careless. Maybe, whoever it was knew this was a good place to do just that and save unnecessary energy. Possibly somebody familiar with these kinds of rural places. Or with this one in particular.' She pointed to a narrow, indistinct trail, another to their right.

'Animal tracks. I don't see anything which suggests an actual pathway through the nettles, thick weed and tree roots. Her killer must have realized that the chance of anybody stumbling across her after he left was very small. He was right. The condition of her remains suggests that she's been here a long time.'

'We're talking years?' asked Igor.

'Could be.' She pointed to the tiny, grouped pebbles.

'I'll take a sample of DNA from one of those foot bones once you've finished doing your thing.'

She waited as Igor continued recording every aspect of what was before them. He stopped, nodded and Chong reached out her gloved hand to one of the tiny bones. After several minutes she had sufficient material for lab testing. She held up the clear plastic vial, gave it a small shake, squinted at its contents.

'I'm anticipating a speedy result.'

'And you also believe in the tooth fairy.'

'Who doesn't?'

She labelled and dated the small vial, handed it to him, looked up at the head of forensics and four of his officers waiting nearby and raised her hand.

'You can start freeing-and-recording, Adam.'

Directing his officers into position, Adam approached her.

'I've heard a whisper that Bernard Watts' name is on this. What do you think his response will be, given his plans?'

'I have absolutely no idea,' said she, her attention on the printed form she was completing.

They worked on, the air gradually cooling as each small bone was photographed in situ, carefully freed and lifted out, photographed again, meticulously recorded on a drawn site map, covered in bubble wrap and labelled, along with insect samples, then placed inside small plastic containers.

Chong's phone vibrated inside her suit. She pulled at the zip, reached inside the TYVEK, looked at the screen.

'Now, *that's* what I call quick service.' She looked up as Igor and the officers nearby stopped what they were doing.

'We have a DNA result. She's already in the system as a MISPER and quite a few miles from home.'

THREE

Same day. 3.50 p.m.

Detective Chief Inspector Bernard Watts was heading to Superintendent Brophy's office, aware that something significant had occurred in the last few hours. He knew it from Chong's terse words over the phone early that morning, had felt it as he walked inside headquarters. Over these last few days of his leave, he had been optimistic about his request for early retirement, backed by Brophy's assurances that it would happen. Brophy had phoned him forty minutes ago to inform him that his request had been refused and that he wanted to see him. Watts was trying out words for how he was feeling. 'Gutted' about covered it. He also had a feeling that his mood wasn't about to improve.

Entering Brophy's office, Watts found Will Traynor already there. They raised a hand to each other. Brophy spoke.

'Come in, Bernard. Close the door, please.' Watts sat. Brophy gave him a series of quick glances.

'I understand that Dr Chong has more or less brought you up to speed about the situation we've got. I'll add what I know, which isn't much. Take a look.' He slid an A3 sheet across the desk. Watts frowned at it. As maps go, it was light on detail. He passed it to Traynor.

'That's an area known as Brampton, four miles beyond the city boundary.' Brophy pointed. 'Part of it is Forestry Commission land and it's of interest to us because it's where human remains have been found. Dr Chong estimates that they've been there approximately three years. Local officers were initially involved but they don't have the numbers or the forensic expertise required, so it's ours now.' He looked from Traynor to Watts. 'The remains have been identified.'

'Quick work,' said Watts. 'Name?'

'Amy Peters.'

Watts and Traynor exchanged glances. Back in 2016, that name had had limited newsworthiness beyond the city of Manchester from which she had disappeared. By late 2018, that situation had changed. Amy Peters was not the only young woman missing from the city. There were now four others. Numbers always attract media attention, as do the physical characteristics of the victims. These were young, attractive students. Interest started to spiral nation-wide, sparking 'Reclaim-the-night' protest marches by students in various cities. Watts had heard enough. He wanted this case about as much as he wanted to be here.

'Dr Chong is still working on the post-mortem, so I have no details to give you. I've made a request to Manchester University for help from forensic psychologist Dr Julian Devenish.' Watts nodded his approval at this request. Julian had been a useful asset in several police investigations, including most recently the Lawrence fatal carjacking case, when he'd evaluated witness state-ments. 'I'm waiting for confirmation that he'll be granted a month's leave from his lecturing job to assist us. I'm assuming that both of you are in agreement that his knowledge of that area, the university and the investigation itself would benefit us.'

Not waiting for a response, Brophy's attention turned to Traynor. 'You and Julian worked together a few months back. As a criminologist, what do you see as the benefits of you working alongside him on this current case?'

'There's some overlap in terms of our psychological theory but I would anticipate Dr Devenish providing a focus on the mental state of this killer and the continued risk he poses, whereas I would be focused on the specifics of what was done by the killer, plus the behaviour of both killer and victims during the commission of the murders.'

Brophy transferred his attention back to Watts. 'You know Dr Devenish from way back?'

'Sir, while he was still a student at the university here, he worked with me in the Unsolved Crime Unit I headed back then. He's keen, he's trustworthy and he knows his stuff.'

Brophy watched as the criminologist stood.

'Thanks for coming in and agreeing to be part of this, Dr Traynor.' As Traynor went to the door, Watts also got to his feet.

'Bernard, a few more minutes of your time, please.'

He waited, anticipating Brophy pulling together sympathetic words about his failed request for early retirement. Particularly as Brophy's own retirement plans had been approved. He was going in the summer. Watts now had the picture: the Peters case was to be Brophy's swan song. He wanted to go out on a high.

'I supported your application because I knew it was what you wanted. I'm sorry, Bernard.' Watts believed him. He had seen the paperwork. What else was there to say? He settled for a nod.

'But there's good news. Your investigative successes have caught the attention of the brass.' He paused, waiting for a response which did not come. 'Those two complex homicides you brought to a conclusion as Senior Investigative Officer?' It was obvious where Brophy was going with this. 'You'll head the Peters' investigation. How does detective chief inspector sound?'

Like a consolation prize, thought Watts.

'Give it three years and then apply for retirement, yes?'

'Why us?' Brophy stared at him.

'We've got the body!' Brophy made it sound like a raffle prize. 'That reminds me, as and when Devenish does join the investigation, he'll be responsible for all media contact and announcements. He did a lot of it while he was involved in the Manchester investigation and he's got a professional yet pleasant way of doing it.' Watts ignored the implied criticism of his own dealings with the media. ❧

'I want an early start on this tomorrow morning, so your first job is to confirm to officers that they're part of this major investigation.' Brophy frowned in the direction of the door. 'Yes?'

Watts turned. Chloe Judd, blonde hair short at the sides, dark at the roots, the top part in a gravity-defying upsweep. Tension of the kind which had made him want early retirement surged.

Judd grinned at him and to Brophy. 'You wanted to see me, sir?'

'Yes. As of now, your leave is cancelled.'

'Sir? I'm in the middle of moving house!' Watts closed his eyes.

'You're needed here.' Brophy was sounding more like his old self. 'You're now part of a major investigation, headed by Detective Chief Inspector Watts. He's got the details.'

They left the office and headed downstairs, Judd in the lead, talking a mile a minute. Watts' head tightened.

'Promotion, Sarge, yay! What's the Bro giving us?' He told her. She stopped, turned and stared up at him.

'Shut the *door*. Julian talked about that case when he was here, remember? From what he said, it's a real dog's dinner, but its profile is a mile high!' She paused. 'What do I call you now?' He continued past her down the stairs.

'"Sarge" will do.' She sped after him.

'Are you *serious*? You need to rethink that. You don't want people taking liberties.'

'Perish the thought.'

'Come the day, I get some real promotion, I'll have everybody using my rank every time they open their mouths and if they don't, I'll know they're dissing me and there'll be *big* trouble. When the Bro said that my leave was cancelled, I'm telling you, "pissed off" just didn't cover it, but now I'm *well* up for it.' She gave him another look.

'New rank. New investigation. Julian with us again, make that *major* investigation. Is Will on it with us? What's with the face?'

'You're overlooking the likelihood of a load of aggravation between us and Manchester.'

She looked dismissive. 'You'll sort it, Sarge, like you always do. How about I make coffee to celebrate?'

He followed her into his office.

'I'd applied for early retirement.' She turned to him.

'That's just not on. What about—?'

He knew her well enough to identify the single unspoken word. He knew a bit about her early life and a wildlife programme he'd watched about young birds had clinched it. Apparently, they're clueless about what they are at birth, but it worked out all right because they fixed on the parent bird which is what got them through. Judd had been part of his team on the last two homicide cases and for each of them she was there, alongside him, like one of those young birds, starting as an eighteen-year-old rookie. Talking, usually, and when she wasn't she was taking in all of what he said and did.

The downside was what he was getting right now. The energy. The enthusiasm. The stream of opinion, added to which her continuing lack of any sense of her place within headquarters or the force hierarchy in general. It was wearing some of the time. Make that, a lot of the time. He should have drawn firm lines with her from the start, showed her where she fitted in. Too late, now. A further indication if he needed one that it was time for him to move on.

'I suspect Brophy blocked it. Which is where the promotion comes in. A way of keeping me sweet.'

'Brophy's got something right, for once. You're only, like what, fifty-eight—?'

'Fifty-*one*!'

'—so, why chuck it in?' She frowned, giving him a quick once-over. 'You're not ill?'

He sat in his usual place at the big worktable, about to say the usual things to explain why he wanted it to stop. The same things he'd told Connie Chong when they last talked about it. The long hours. The late nights. All of it true, none of it the real reason. It was about the people. The victims. The families. Too many sad stories over too many years, no matter what the outcome. It seeped into your— He rejected the word 'soul'. He'd heard more than enough of that at the schools he'd gone to. He recalled several officers from his own young days on the force who were doing the job he now had, who drank a bit too much. Ate rubbish. All dead now. At fifty-one, he wanted more from his life. When he told Chong how he felt, her advice was to talk to his doctor. He hadn't seen much of her over the last week or so. She was staying at her apartment, citing pressure of work.

'No, I'm not ill.' Judd brought black coffee to the table. 'This is going to be a massive challenge and we haven't got an "ology" between us.'

'Doesn't bother me.' She pointed at her hair. 'In case you're narked about this as well, just chill, yeah? A pixie-cut "n" quiff is all it is.' She grinned. 'No animals were harmed in its production.'

He took the coffee from her. She was an odd mix: worldly for barely twenty-one, yet surprisingly young at times, but her quickness, her determination meant that he couldn't think of a sharper officer to have on any investigation. He would put up with the rest. He glanced at her.

'Did I mention hair?'

'For once, no.' She sipped coffee, her eyes on him. 'So you've got some oldie-type plan for growing marrows?'

'It's what I want. Working on my allotment in the summer, in my shorts—' She grimaced.

'That's an image that'll take some getting rid of.'

'Judd, you're always on about your private life being your own—'

'Which it is.'

'Well, *that's* mine, or was going to be, before this case landed on me, and I don't need anybody's approval of it.' They sipped coffee in silence.

'Is Ade Jones on this investigation with us?' she asked.

'Yes.'

'Does he know?'

'No.'

'Shall I tell him?'

'No.'

The office phone rang. He reached for it, listening as he watched her waving out the window. He put down the phone.

'Jonesy's just arrived, Sarge.'

'And there's some stuff waiting at reception – which *I'll* get.'

They walked to reception, where Judd overtook him, heading for the main doors. At the reception desk, PC Reynolds was waiting for him. He held up a clear plastic internal post bag. Watts took it, gazed at black, high-heeled shoes, then back to Reynolds.

'And?' The young officer's eyes darted left and right. 'Anything *else*?'

'No, Sarge. I thought you were the best person to give it to.' Reynolds pointed through the plastic. 'There's a label on one of the shoes, see? "Carly Driscoll".'

'Never heard of her.' He handed back the shoes. 'Circulate an internal memo, ask if anybody else has—'

He glanced at Reynolds: leaning on the counter, chin on fist, eyes fixed on Judd, who was in animated conversation with Adrian Jones. Character-wise it was a puppy with designs on a Doberman. Watts' earlier frustrations now rose like a tsunami.

'*Reynolds.*' The young officer leapt.

'Sir!'

'The *memo*. But first, coffee in a large mug, *fat* milk, *three* sugars and I want it *now*!'

FOUR

Monday, 8 April. 7.32 a.m.

Inside the incident room Watts was slow-breathing. The previous evening, he had called Chong. She was already aware that he was leading the investigation. They had briefly discussed the remains recovered from the scene which were now inside one of the refrigerated drawers in the basement pathology suite. Brief, because she had little to tell him.

He slowed his breathing some more, eyed Traynor's black Labrador lying under a nearby table. Watts studied the criminologist, taking in the relaxed demeanour, wondering if that was how he himself had been when he was, what, forty or so? He looked back to the dog. Maybe he should get one? Hard on the heels of that thought came others. Dogs needed regular walks. They got wet from being in the rain and jumping into dirty water. When you took them out, you had to carry a plastic bag— His mouth tightened. Chong was right. He routinely looked for the downside and never had difficulty finding it. It wouldn't work, anyway. The cat would go mental.

The door swung open and officers who had worked with Watts on his two previous investigations filed inside, among them Judd, Kumar, Jones and Josie Miller, who was already sending Traynor avid glances. Watts waited as they found seats. Not one of them was over forty. He recalculated. None over thirty-five. Watts took three more slow, deep breaths. As SIO, it was part of his job at the outset of an investigation to instil in his team a sense of purpose, of resilience, a belief that they had what it took to get a result. What he wanted was go home. He waited until their attention was on him. Jones stood in the silence, looked round at his colleagues, then back to Watts.

'On behalf of the team, *Detective Chief Inspector* Watts—' Whoops, laughter and handclapping filled the room. Jones raised his voice. 'We couldn't have a better SIO, Sarge! If it is still "Sarge"?'

Watts batted his big hands.

'Yeah, yeah, that'll do.'

They waited, as he got to his feet, looked at each of them.

'One or two of you have already been to the Brampton site so you won't need me to tell you that this is going to be a demanding investigation. A challenge.' He glanced to his right. 'As you can see, Dr Will Traynor is working with us again.' He paused for the murmurs of approval. 'He's going to inform us with his criminological know-how.' Miller's facial expression suggested that she was more than keen to inform Traynor on anything that might interest him.

'You all remember Dr Julian Devenish from our previous investigation. He'll be with us in a day or so. He's had some involvement in the Manchester investigation – which makes him a valuable resource because I'm anticipating a delay until we receive case data from the team up there.' He let a few seconds of silence build.

'Amy Peters. The first in a series of five suspected abductions which took place up there between 2016 and 2018 and which are now presumed to be homicides.' He looked at each of them in turn.

'Amy Peters is thought to have gone missing in May 2016. I'll give you the basic, known details about her disappearance, plus the other four in the series, but first,' he reached for a single A4, 'there's a preliminary report from Dr Chong on the incomplete skeletal remains. So far, she hasn't identified any obvious cause of death. She's continuing to examine the remains, which is why she isn't here to tell you in person, but she has already flagged up the possibility, given the condition of the remains, that she might not be able to identify a specific cause.' Judd raised her hand.

'What are the chances of evidence of sexual activity being found?'

'Based on what I've said, highly unlikely.'

He turned to the smartboard, aimed a remote control. The massive screen leapt into life. They all gazed at a head shot of a smiling young woman with long, dark hair and white, even teeth.

'Amy Peters. She is our sole focus. Manchester is continuing its investigation of the other four disappearances but there'll be close liaison between our two forces in relation to Peters.' He caught Jones' headshake. 'My optimism is low that they'll hand over anything without numerous requests from us, so that's what we do. Keep requesting.' He pointed to the photograph.

'Amy Peters, twenty-one years old and about to graduate when she disappeared in May 2016. She was planning to start a master's degree there during the next academic year. At the time she disappeared she was still living in the area, working two jobs to save money, one in a city centre bookshop, the other in a bar local to the university. Her friends, fellow students, co-workers were all questioned. None reported Amy having any personal problems. Lecturers described her as dependable. An excellent student. She had a boyfriend. The view shared by those who knew her, including the boyfriend himself, was that the relationship wasn't serious. They were all spoken to. All described Amy as untroubled at the time she disappeared.' He looked back to the board.

'Her family live in Wiltshire. At the time Amy disappeared, her parents stated that they had not seen nor heard from her in the two-week period prior to the time she is believed to have been abducted.' Miller's hand came up.

'Did they consider that unusual, Sarge?'

'Not according to what I've got here. The parents described Amy as an independent person who didn't call home regularly but both were adamant that she wouldn't have left the university without at least indicating such plans to them.'

'Was there ever a confirmed date for her disappearance?' asked Traynor.

'No. The last sighting of her was during the evening of Monday, 9 May 2016. Amy didn't work on Monday evenings. She was seen by a female friend, a fellow student, at around eight thirty p.m., heading in the direction of a pub popular with students and close to the campus. Another friend confirmed seeing her inside that pub. She and Amy had two halves of lager each, after which Amy left at around nine forty-five, saying she was tired, that she had a double shift at her pub job the next day and that she was heading back to her accommodation. That friend watched her go. It was the last reported sighting of Amy. She didn't report for that double shift the following day.'

Traynor made a quick note, and asked, 'Were the five victims known to be acquainted at all?'

'No. They were following different courses and living in different locations on or around the campus.'

'Did Amy Peters or her wider family have any known connection to Birmingham?'

Watts shook his head.

'There's nothing in what Manchester has provided so far which supports that.'

'In which case,' Traynor said, looking down at his notes, 'a key question for this investigation is, why are her remains so close to this city?' He looked up at Watts. 'Any clothing or other personal artefacts with the remains?'

Watts shook his head again.

'In that case, as Amy Peters appears to be one of a series of disappearances, we'll need to consider that her killer is a trophy-taker.'

Traynor's words sent Watts' mood plummeting. What he knew of trophy-taking from other investigation was that the behaviour was a means of reinforcing homicidal fantasies, an indication of a commitment to killing. He pressed on.

'I'll give brief outlines of the other four victims in order of disappearance.'

He summoned up a photograph of a second dark-haired young woman with a wide smile.

'This is Melody Brewster. Last seen on Monday, 10 October that same year by a fellow student, which is the closest indication we have to when she disappeared. At nineteen, she's the youngest in the series, a sociology student. Family home in Peterborough. No known boyfriends. Described as a quiet, serious person.' Watts looked at his audience, their eyes fixed on the photographs.

'Claire Walsh,' he continued, pulling up the next image, 'the third woman reported missing on 10 August 2017.' He glanced at Traynor to see if 'Claire', the name of his deceased wife, had resonated. Traynor's face was devoid of expression. Seeing name-recognition on a number of faces, he pointed to the third photograph, which showed a confidant-looking woman with dark shoulder-length hair.

'Claire got most media coverage at the time, probably because she worked for a Manchester television news company. At twenty-three, she's the eldest in the series and there is a reliable date for her disappearance. She left work on Thursday, 10 August 2017 at approximately nine p.m. to cycle to her home about a mile from her office. That journey took her along a road which skirts the perimeter of the campus. There are no reported sightings of her after that. Her father rang her on her mobile phone at approximately nine forty p.m. His call was diverted to voicemail. According to the information I've received so far, when tenants in her apartment building were questioned, two of them, both female, reported last seeing Claire leave for work at around seven forty-five that morning. Her mail, delivered at around eleven a.m., was retrieved by officers from her secure mailbox that evening, unopened. Her bicycle has never been located.' Watts turned to the smartboard. The photograph, showing Claire in what looked like evening dress, was replaced by a darkened screen.

'What we have got is CCTV footage of Claire very soon after she left her office for the day.'

All eyes fixed on the lone figure, in the bottom left-hand corner of the screen.

'This cyclist was verified as Claire by an image adviser.' He pointed to the bottom edge of the footage. 'Time: 9.12 p.m. That road she's on led directly to her home about ten minutes away.'

They watched in silence as the figure moved steadily along the wide, tree-lined pavement for twenty seconds before disappearing out of shot. Watts turned to them.

'There's more. The individual you're about to see was an early person of interest.'

Attention was back on the screen. A few seconds of nothing was followed by movement, a male figure suddenly appearing on foot, walking in the same direction Claire Walsh had cycled a minute or so earlier. They watched as he also disappeared from the edge of the screen. The recording ended. One of the officers asked, 'Was he ever identified, Sarge?'

'No, and he was the only person picked up by CCTV. It was Julian Devenish who suggested that Manchester's SIO call in the image adviser. She was shown this CCTV recording and analysed that individual's appearance and movements. Unfortunately, she wasn't able to provide any detail beyond confirming that the dark clothes he was wearing had no discernible distinguishing features and the same for the dark hair. She wouldn't commit herself on height or build due to the angle of view but suggested an age estimate of late twenties to late thirties. There's no confirmation that that individual had any direct connection to Claire Walsh's disappearance, although the SIO in Manchester decided to use the image in an appeal to the public. The response was poor. What there was, was judged irrelevant by investigators.' Judd sat forward.

'Was other CCTV checked?'

'Yes, but neither Claire Walsh or any individual who looked similar to this dark-haired male was picked up by any other camera, either that evening nor the several days before or after.' Judd stared at the screen.

'Did Claire Walsh ever appear in any of the news programmes she worked on?' Watts nodded.

'I get your reasoning. That was my first question, given the nature of her work, but no. She was a behind-the-scenes production worker. No steady boyfriend. Raised in Manchester. A media graduate of Middlesex University, who went back to her home city to work.' He waited out the silence. Getting no questions, he continued.

'The fourth woman to disappear was Marella Ricci, Italian national, twenty years old, working on a BA in art history.' All eyes fixed on the photograph of the dark-haired woman.

'According to her family in Italy, Marella chose a university in the UK because she was interested in our history and architecture. She's believed to have disappeared on or around Friday, 2 March 2018. That evening she had gone with another student to a film show on campus. At around ten thirty p.m., they had coffee together at a nearby bar and, as far as could be established, that was the last sighting of her.' Traynor looked up.

'What kind of film was it and what do we know about the individual she was with?'

'According to what I've got here,' Watts scrutinized his notes, 'it was an art-house comedy, *Life is Beautiful*. No sex, no violence, and she was with a female friend. After they separated, there were no direct sighting nor CCTV which confirmed that Marella returned to her halls of residence. It looks like concerns about her absence weren't raised until the late afternoon of the following day, by which time that same friend had failed several times to make contact with Marella via her phone and alerted campus security. It seems this was the disappearance that got the Manchester team thinking that something was happening to young women up there.'

'About bloody time,' murmured Jones. 'There was a lot of general talk in the area at the time. It looks to me like there was a lot of foot-dragging going on, Sarge.' Knowing that Jones was referring to his own Stockport roots, Watts felt like agreeing with him.

'I want to get one thing straight. There'll be no blame-game on this investigation. We haven't got time for it.'

'Got a question, Sarge.' Jones' hand came up. 'Were female students ever questioned about being approached by a male with a convincing spiel?'

'From what I've read, it was followed up as a possibility. The SIO, Ray Boulter, requested an appeal via the university for all female students who had been approached by an unknown male on whatever pretext to come forward. It produced nothing.' Watts eyes moved slowly over them. 'I'm going way beyond the evidence we've got, but that suggests to me that whoever was involved in these disappearances was a smooth operator who never put a foot wrong.' He pointed at the screen and the fifth photograph, this one of another dark-haired young woman.

'The last to be reported missing was Erica Trent, a twenty-year-old science and maths student from Hampshire. She's believed to have disappeared during the evening of 12 November 2018. What we know about Erica is that she attended a six p.m. tutorial that day. Her tutor confirmed it and that Erica left her office at around seven p.m. Her understanding was that Erica was returning to her accommodation, a bedsit just off-campus. Erica had several lectures the following day but neither staff nor students who knew her recalled seeing her at any of them. Her disappearance was officially reported to the police that day, which indicates that by that time both university and police were very much aware of the risk to young women.'

Watts looked down at the dates he had listed. He was thinking what he might have done in that situation up in Manchester if he'd been the SIO, slowly becoming aware of unexplained disappearances over a two-to-three-year time frame. He had some sympathy for Boulter. Just a bit.

'It still sounds to me like that investigation was lax, nobody getting a grip on what was happening,' Jones said. Watts looked across at him.

'It's easy to criticize without being involved. We've had similar experiences when leads were short on the ground. You all know how difficult abduction-by-stranger cases can be.' He turned to his file and pulled out some papers.

'I've got a note here from Julian Devenish which gives us some insight into the situation. Julian's impression, some time prior to his being involved in the investigation, was of an extremely gradual situation developing. In his view, the student way of life contributed to what might seem to us to be a slow university/police response. Amy Peters was technically no longer a student. Both Brewster and Ricci were known to have skipped lectures in the past. Friends of Brewster's stated that she had taken up an offer of a week's work at a pizza restaurant without the faculty having any knowledge of it. Ricci had also taken time off from her studies to visit a cousin in Oxford, returning after several days and telling her tutors that she had been unwell.

'My take is that Julian wasn't greatly impressed by the investigation up there, but his view of the unfolding situation there is balanced. Yes, the police response was slow, but by the time Trent disappeared, everybody involved in the investigation had suspicions as to what they might be facing. Unfortunately, by then, they were seriously on the back foot.'

'What led them to finally recognize the likelihood that all five victims had probably been abducted?' asked Traynor. Watts shook his head.

'It wasn't evidence-led. It looks to me like it was identified as the likeliest explanation. I'm talking here without the benefit of full data from Manchester, so that's my guess. After Ricci disappeared there was growing media interest and pressure from the families, but by the time a media appeal on the cases was launched, memories had faded. It produced no leads.'

'So, what's the current position with that investigation?'

'Manchester has spent a lot of time and money in the last few months searching large areas of the campus and beyond for remains. I've seen the costs. They're eye-watering. Having found nothing, the conclusion was that all five victims were taken from the area. That investigation seems to have reached stalemate. Julian says here that during the time he was involved he contributed psychological theory, but because he was still lecturing half of his time, he felt increasingly on the side-lines. Most of his suggestions weren't actioned. He ceased his involvement around mid-2018. There's been little to no progress on any of those five disappearances until now.'

'Were any of these five women known to have personal or health problems?' asked Traynor.

'Not according to what I've read, which I'll copy to all of you. Erica Trent, the last to disappear, was described by her tutor as a bit socially isolated. During the last tutorial, she advised Erica to extend her social life. It looks like she never got a chance to do it.'

'As far as we know,' Traynor added.

'I'm thinking she disappeared sometime that evening. There were no further sightings of her after that tutorial, no CCTV images, nothing reported to university security.' Judd pointed to the on-screen photographs.

'It's pretty obvious whoever abducted them has a type: slim, long, dark hair, good teeth.' Watts nodded.

'Which describes much of the young female population.' Jones grinned.

'*And* some of the lads, Sarge.' There were a few muted laughs.

'These are the actual victim photos,' Watts said, reaching for an envelope, removing its contents. 'I've asked Adam to make enlargements so they're constantly available for reference. Until they are, fix each of these in your heads. Nothing beats a physical photo for getting a sense of somebody. Here, Jones. Put them on the whiteboard.'

Jones took them and attached each one to its smooth surface with a sharp click of a colourful magnetic cube. It made for an eye-catching display. Watts turned away, his mood lowering.

'I've got some observations on what you've said, Bernard.' All eyes turned to Traynor whose attention was on his phone. 'I've checked the days of the week suggested for the disappearances: Peters last seen on a Monday, Brewster also a Monday, Walsh on a Thursday, Ricci a Friday, Trent another Monday. We can't be certain about the exact dates, but if these young women *were* taken on those days, the big question is, why did none of these abductions occur at a weekend. Is it an indication that this individual works in Manchester during the week but is elsewhere at weekends, possibly wherever home is? Is home a place or situation from which he can't easily absent himself at weekends without questions being asked?' He looked at Watts.

'I'm also thinking about the types of employment that allow a high degree of personal freedom during the working week. He could be somebody who travels as part of his work.' Jones rubbed his hands together.

'This is what we need. A bit of analysis of the facts.' Traynor's dog stood, stretched, giving his owner a beseeching look. He patted his flank.

'OK, Boy,' he said quietly.

'Is anything else known about Erica Trent?' Judd pointed to one of the photographs. 'Hers is the most recent disappearance, so it makes sense to know as much about her as possible.'

The detectives turned to the photograph of the young woman, long dark hair framing her face, gazing out at them from clear, grey eyes. Watts walked across the room to stand next to it.

'Erica's tutor was the last known person to see her. Her understanding was that she was returning to her accommodation to do some work. There's nothing which confirms that she did and there were no confirmed sightings of Erica after she left that university building.'

Watts had not yet seen the location of Amy Peters' remains. He was thinking it was time he did.

'That's it. Those of you already working at the scene get back to it. Jones, take Reynolds with you and I'll see you there.'

'Will do. Tobes will have it sorted for us in five minutes.'

Reynolds grinned. His first name, Toby, had been a source of some low-level amusement when he first arrived at headquarters, the kind of humour common to all forces, much worse when Watts himself joined.

'Let's hope he does.' Watts looked across at Miller. 'Before you leave, Josie, get onto Manchester and emphasize that we need everything they've got on Amy Peters and I mean *everything*.' She reached for her phone.

'I'm on it, Sarge.' Watts looked to Traynor who nodded.

'I'll see you there.'

FIVE

Same day. 11 a.m.

Traynor's dog watched from the half-open window of the Aston Martin as they started climbing the steep hill, passing officers in shirtsleeves scouring the thick undergrowth around and within the trees. They went directly to the two flagged rectangles of bare earth surrounded by vigorous growth. After a brief look at them, Watts left Traynor and walked to where Chong was working at a table set up on a small area of flat ground, her attention fixed on whatever was on it. Reaching her, he saw an array of multiple small bones. She glanced up at him.

'Good morning.' She paused, then. 'We've located a few more items of bone from within the leaflitter and undergrowth.' She pointed to them. 'They've endured a fair amount of exposure to the elements and what is here isn't complete.'

He stared down at them. That first viewing was always a jolt.

'Any idea how long she's been here?'

'And, good morning to me. How am I? Fine, actually—'

'Come *on*, Connie.'

'If you're asking whether she was kept elsewhere after she was killed then brought here later, in my opinion she's been here since soon after she was killed. Which is still a problem for us because, once animals locate remains, they do the instinctual thing and carry off bits and pieces to who knows where.' She reached for one of the small bones, looked up at him. 'These were found scattered at varying distances from the skeletal remains. This whole site needs an in-depth forensic sweep.' A brief silence stretched between them. Watts was thinking of the budget implications for an area like this, which would guarantee a tussle with Brophy.

'I'm not sorry about the retirement thing, by the way.' She lowered her voice. 'It was never one of your best ideas as far as I'm concerned, but you already know that.' He followed her eyes, seeing Traynor walking towards them with Judd. He raised his hand.

'Good morning, Connie.'

She smiled, sent Watts a *See how easy that was?* look.

Watts walked to where the land fell steeply away, gazed out at a seemingly endless landscape fading into the distance. Traynor arrived at his side, pointed downwards to the just-visible narrow strip of unedged tarmac where they had parked.

'Let's start with the obvious. Amy Peters' killer had a vehicle. We've seen where he left her. It's likely he parked somewhere on that road because it gave him direct access to this site.' He glanced at Watts. 'He knows this area well.' Watts frowned down to where they had parked.

'It's barely a road.' He turned, stared upwards at the land rising beyond the two bare patches of earth which had held Amy Peters' remains.

'You're saying that he drove her here from Manchester, that he took her up there, which would have been a massive struggle with a dead weight. Unless he had somebody helping him. My question is, why abduct and kill a woman then drive eighty or so miles with her body? He would have passed endless places where he could have left her.' He shook his head.

'No. That makes no sense. Why would he risk an eighty-mile journey, during which he could have had car trouble, been stopped by police, had some kind of accident and there he is, with a dead woman in his vehicle! *That*, Traynor, is madness.'

'In my experience, what appears to be madness often isn't.'

Hearing the quiet words, he studied the criminologist's face. It was calm, giving nothing away. Traynor had encyclopaedic knowledge of deviant behaviours and those who exhibited them. Whatever else he might be thinking, he would divulge it in his own time. Watts left the issue. They carried on together, Traynor's focus still on the wider surroundings.

'His willingness to take the kinds of risks you described indicates how important it must have been to him that Amy Peters and probably his four other victims were brought here.' This was the last thing Watts wanted to hear.

'Our focus is solely on Amy Peters. Got any early ideas?' Judd was coming towards them, her brow in furrows as Traynor shrugged and continued up the steep slope. Watts called after him, 'Why would whoever killed them bring them *here*?'

Judd watched Traynor moving upwards.

'It had to be a hell of a job to get a dead weight up here, Sarge. What about an accomplice?'

'I've asked myself the same questions.'

'And?'

Traynor was now crouching close to where Amy Peters' remains were found, his eyes fixed on the slope down to the road.

'I don't have a bloody clue,' said Watts.

'There's something not right about this whole— Wait for me!'

She jogged after Watts up the steep hill to where Traynor was walking slowly around the exposed earth which had been Amy Peters' final resting place, his eyes fixed on it, using his iPad to capture images. He flipped it closed.

'There is sense in what he did.' Watts eyed him.

'Yeah? How do you know?'

'Because Amy Peters has lain here, unburied yet undiscovered for three years.'

Watts looked down at the two patches of raw earth.

'OK, Traynor, he knows this place. He'd been here, checked out this whole area. My question is still, why here?'

Judd's gaze moved from the exposed earth to the dark trees on all sides. Despite the unseasonal heat, a chill tracked its way across her shoulders, as she heard Traynor's quiet words.

'He already knew what it was like here. Secluded. Expansive tree cover. That very few people come here. That he wouldn't be seen. Or heard.' Watts frowned.

'And Manchester and the eighty-odd miles in between don't have similar places?'

They stood in silence, the sun slipping momentarily behind cloud, transforming the surrounding trees into a dark, impenetrable barrier. Traynor broke the silence.

'Leaving her here gave him what he needed.'

Watts and Judd exchanged glances, looked at him.

'What was that?' asked Judd.

'Time.'

'Time for—?'

'*Dr Chong!*'

They looked in the direction of the shout, followed Watts as he headed to where a SOCO was standing, both arms raised. Watts and Chong reached him at the same time, looked to where he was now pointing at the ground. Within the thick vegetation, barely visible unless specifically looked for, was something small and very dark. Watts pulled a latex glove from his pocket, slipped it on, crouched next to the pathologist. After it had been photographed in situ, and getting a nod from her, Watts carefully parted the tall grasses, reached for it, carefully lifting it from its resting place.

They stared down at it lying across his palm. A rectangle of dusty black, roughly eight centimetres wide. Chong took it from him, turned it over.

'Masking tape. Folded onto itself.' She lifted it closer, eyes fixed, her voice low. 'I might be wrong but this is telling me that there could be more death here.' She looked up at him, whispered, 'And, if I'm right, you and I are going to need some serious diversion and distraction to get through it.' Straightening, she said to Adam, 'I'm leaving now, so I'll take this and the small bone finds back to headquarters.'

Watts watched her go, then headed to Judd and Traynor.

'What was it, Sarge?'

'Black masking tape. Been here a good while, judging by the look of it—'

'A *gag*.'

'We don't know enough for conclusion-jumping.'

Traynor's eyes were focused on the ground.

'She wasn't buried. Have you thought why that might be, Bernard?'

Watts' eyes moved steadily over the surrounding trees and vegetation. He was thinking of the hours it would take for an in-depth search, hoping that Chong's theory about there being more death to be found here was wrong.

'Believe it or not, Traynor, that's low on my long list of things I already have to worry about.'

They returned to their vehicles, Watts' tension climbing due to the unanswered questions pulsing inside his head. He made himself breathe, watched Traynor walk to where the dog was looking out of the car window, ecstatic to see the criminologist. He watched him open the door, lean inside, his arms encircling the animal, lowering his face to it. Watts had a lot of time for Traynor. Not only for his endless knowledge of all kinds of human depravity, but also for how he had pulled himself back from what could have been the brink of personal and professional ruin following the murder of his wife more than decade ago and built himself another life. Something Watts had wanted from early retirement while he still had some. He glanced at Miller sitting in the open doorway of one of the police vehicles, looking overheated.

'What was Manchester's response when you asked for the data to be sent down?'

'They're getting it together, Sarge.'

'When?'

'They wouldn't give a timeframe. Shall I ring again?'

'Just keep an eye out for it for now, but don't let it slide.'

Same day. 1.30 p.m.

They came into headquarters, Watts unsettled by what he had seen and heard, plus the questions to which he had no answers.

He looked at his watch and left the building, returning ten minutes later carrying a grease-stained paper bag. Judd paused in the process of removing a sandwich from her lunch box.

'What's your impression of the scene, Sarge?' He sat opposite, opening the red-, white-and-blue-striped bag.

'Big. Difficult to search. Too many trees—'

'I don't like it there.'

'Email me a list of your requirements and I'll make sure that all future crime scenes meet with your approval—'

'All right, narky!' She watched him fetch a plate, transfer the contents of the bag onto it.

'You said you weren't going to the English Caff after you lost all that weight and started calling it Cholesterol Central.'

'Adil's got a special, two-egg-two-bacon deal on. *Behave.*'

She did a slow headshake.

'I just hope for your sake that Dr Chong doesn't see it.'

'My response to that, Judd, is *relevance*? Want some?'

'No, thanks. I've got smashed avocado and chickpea.'

He grunted.

The door opened and a familiar face appeared.

'Can I come in?'

'*Julian.* Look who it is, Sarge!' Judd smiled, as he came inside and dropped a large leather holdall onto the floor, a light-coloured raincoat on top of it. Watts smiled, raised his hand.

'Great to see you, Jules.' Judd stood up.

'I'll get some posh coffee going.' Julian watched her go.

'Don't go to any trouble for me. Sorry, I'm interrupting your lunch.' He took a chair opposite Watts. 'What's happening?'

'Nothing much, so far.' Watts studied the young face. 'I did the first briefing this morning. Traynor is already on it with us. I'll bring you up to date. It won't take long. This morning we went to the site where Peters' remains have been found.'

'Whereabouts is it exactly?'

'Four miles over the city boundary. It's a rolling hillside area, quite steep in places, fir trees everywhere, courtesy of the Forestry Commission. Judd's not a fan,' he added, as she brought coffee to the table.

'You need to have a look at it, Julian. Will has some pictures and video on his iPad. He's left now but Adam was taking loads of pictures this morning too. He can show you what it's like—'

'He's just driven from Manchester,' said Watts. 'Give him a break. A chance to get his feet under the table,' and to Julian, 'Got any plans for today?'

Julian looked at his watch.

'I need to drop my stuff at the apartment where I stayed last time I was here, get settled in. My dad's tenant is away again, so it's worked out well.' Watts studied him, seeing tiredness in his eyes.

'What's it been like up there?'

'The investigation?' Julian shrugged. 'I only know from a distance now, but I'm guessing Ray Boulter, the SIO, is at the edge of his professional competence. I don't mean to be uncharitable but it's probably the truth.'

'Has he made any progress?'

Julian shook his head.

'Not while I was involved. Since I've been side-lined, I can't say anyway, because he's not telling me anything. Which, come to think of it, isn't a lot different to how it was when I *was* involved.'

'Sorry to hear that.'

'I'm over it, but I admit that at the time it was frustrating. I had a lot of ideas which he mostly ignored. After a few weeks I realized that he didn't see me as part of the investigation because I still had a half-timetable of lecturing.' He shrugged. 'It felt like I was being dismissed as some kind of dilettante with nothing useful to contribute. At one stage, around the time Claire Walsh went missing, I suggested a full media appeal, He turned the idea down, except for releasing some murky CCTV footage.'

'We've seen it. What was his reason for refusing?'

'He didn't give one. In the January, following Erica Trent's disappearance, he suddenly decides it's a good idea, organized one and got nothing. By then, most people's recall for anything which might have been useful had deteriorated to nothing.' He shrugged, grinned. 'Enough! I'm down here for the next four weeks and I'm hopeful we'll make progress. Show them how it's done, Bernard? I'd love it if we sorted that whole case.' He looked at his watch. 'Listen, how about I leave you to finish your lunch, go over to the apartment and sort myself out? I can be back here pretty quickly.'

'Fine. I'd like you to be at the briefing early tomorrow morning. Will Traynor's going to be there and it'll be a good opportunity for you to see everybody again, hear first-hand what's happening, maybe even contribute some ideas?' Watts paused, a question on his mind. 'About the Manchester investigation. Was there ever a time during your involvement when a result felt like it might happen?' Julian shook his head.

'Never. There were no leads. All five women were just – gone. In fairness to Boulter, that's what tends to happen in repeat cases, but over the weeks it was increasingly obvious that he was out of ideas. The media was playing up that whole situation, giving the killer a name: 'the Phantom'. I think that had a psychological effect on Boulter. He completely lost his way and was treading water from then on.'

Watts had already come to the same conclusion. Whoever this killer was, a name like that didn't help any investigation. It merely gave whoever it was an aura of some creeping, unstoppable entity and sank morale like a brick. He wouldn't tolerate the kind of defeatism on this or any other case for which he was SIO. He didn't have to say it to his team. They knew. As Julian stood to leave, he asked, 'Can you spare another half hour or so? Dr Chong's expecting us to view the Amy Peters remains in a couple of minutes. Will's probably already down there.' His phone bleeped. He looked at it. 'A text from Traynor: *We need to consider the possibility of buried artefacts.*'

'What's that mean, exactly?' asked Judd.

'Anything belonging to Amy Peters that might still be in the ground.'

They went down to the pathology suite. Igor let them in. They joined Traynor and Adam at an examination table.

'Well-timed,' said Chong. 'Hi, Julian. Great to see you again.'

'It's good to be back.' he said, returning Traynor and Adam's nods of welcome.

Chong removed the pale green sheet, exposing the skull recovered from the scene, plus the blackened ribcage, length of spinal column and pelvis, plus the array of smaller bones, some no larger than a thumbnail. Watts looked up at his colleagues. Julian's face had drained.

'OK, Jules?'

'Yes. The young women who disappeared were always pictures on a wall. Seeing this is – too real.'

The black tape was here, now pulled out in one continuous

length, lying inside a metal dish. Watts eyed it. Definitely long enough to go around somebody's lower face. Chong reached for it, looked to Julian.

'This was recovered from the site earlier.' She pulled down a light which flooded the table. 'Once I had it open, I found this.' Their heads lowered to where she was pointing to a single, medium length hair still ensnared on the adhesive side.

'It's one of Amy Peters' own, and unfortunately for us there were no others, but if this tape was around her lower face and mouth it has more to offer in the form of a vast number of her epithelial cells. Of course, what I'm really hoping for are cells which aren't hers, plus any other trace evidence left by whoever killed her.' Julian peered at it.

Watts pointed to the skeletal remains. 'What can you tell us so far?'

Chong shook her head.

'Not much that's going to help your investigation, beyond DNA confirmation that these are Amy Peters' remains.' She pointed at the rib section. 'Identification is further supported by a small healed fracture right here, sustained by Amy during a fall on a skiing holiday several years ago. I know DNA is the business, but I still like a secondary confirmation.'

'I wasn't expecting it to be fully intact.' Traynor leant forward, hands clasped behind him, his eyes on the skull.

Chong carefully lifted it in gloved hands.

'I understand what you're saying. We get so used to blunt force trauma.' She ran her hand gently over the dome of the skull. 'I've examined the cranium using strong UV light and by touch. There is no gross, visual indication of trauma but I picked up a very slight anomaly – right here.' They looked at the small area she was indicating.

'There's a *very* slight depression just there. So slight, it's not necessarily discernible to anyone not used to handling skulls.'

'Does it tell us anything?' asked Watts.

'It could suggest the possibility that she was struck, but not sufficiently hard to cause injury,' she set down the skull, 'or it could just as easily be a natural feature of Amy Peters' skull. We all have minor physical variations. I'm mentioning it only to indi-cate the possibility that she was subdued by a light blow to the head.' She moved away from the table.

'Come and have a look at this.'

They followed her to another table and an array of tiny bones lying on pale grey paper, Watts quickly recognizing the incomplete but obvious configuration.

'Her . . . right hand?' Getting a confirmatory nod, he gave them a closer look, pointed. 'What happened here?'

Chong looked to where he was pointing.

'That small indication of damage is telling me that that index finger sustained some damage, ante-mortem. Forensic pathology is a goldmine of information about people's actions and responses. We haven't recovered all of her bones, but given what I said about the small anomaly to the skull, there's a possibility that at the time she was killed some kind of instrument was raised above her head. If that's what happened, Amy Peters either knew or sensed that a blow was coming and raised her hand, like this,' Chong positioned her right hand above and close to the top of her own head, 'to try and ward it off, protect herself.' She pointed to the tiny, crushed finger bones.

'All theoretical, but if that is the scenario, these are defence wounds.'

'Speaking of goldmines, as no items belonging to this young woman have been recovered so far, I'll be asking SOCOs to do a focused, in-depth search of the area where the remains were located, possibly including a metal detector.'

'For anything in particular?' She reached for a single A4.

'I've been sent this from Manchester. An inventory of Amy Peters' belongings. It includes a reference to a gold necklace and crucifix, a twenty-first birthday gift from her parents which they have stated Amy routinely wore.'

Watts read the inventory, the few other details. Of the other four victims, only Ricci was known to wear jewellery. In her case, a fine gold bracelet. He read on. None of the young women was known to routinely wear a watch. He gave Judd a quick glance. Sometimes she did, sometimes she didn't. This was a no-watch day. She kept track of time using her phone.

'Boulter sent you this information?'

'Among other miscellaneous items.'

'I'll phone him to tell him that dribs and drabs are no good to us and that it all comes to me.'

'How about I start an initial search for anything that's still at the scene?' asked Julian. 'I want to feel useful, Bernard, and it'll save tying up SOCO time.'

'Go on, then.' Julian grinned, tapped his right temple.

'At least, it'll get the synapses firing if I take a look at the site.'

'You haven't settled in yet—'

'Not a problem. I'll drop my stuff off and go.'

Traynor's eyes were fixed on the finger bones.

'Amy Peters was alive and she knew death was coming. She raised her hand to protect herself.' All eyes moved to him. Watts looked down at the small bones then up.

'What's your take, Jules?'

'I'm not sure yet. This is why I want to be out there searching, being useful. After working on the Manchester investigation, getting to know the lives of these women, it's tough seeing this. We all knew it wasn't going to end well for any of them, but to finally know . . .'

'Easy, lad.' Watts' attention was back on the tape. 'I'm probably pushing it here, but don't they use tape like this on the sort of equipment Claire Walsh might have come across in her production work?'

Julian looked doubtful.

'You're thinking of microphones and similar equipment which might need adjusting, keeping in place? A couple of officers visited that news set-up. According to them, there was none of that kind of equipment. If this tape was found close to Peters' remains, a link with Walsh doesn't seem to fit anyway. Walsh disappeared more than a year after Peters. OK, I'm off to view the site.' He headed for the door.

Watts looked to Chong.

'When will you have the results on any cells from the tape? Soon, I hope?'

She carefully replaced the green sheet over the bones, her tone even.

'You're clearly still intent on annoying me. I'll get to it as soon as I can.'

'It's still "need-to-know".'

'And I need to do what I do, without pressure.' As Traynor and Judd left, he turned to her, mouthed, 'Sorry.' She shrugged.

'See you later.'

Same day. 3 p.m.

Julian came onto the site, acknowledging hands raised by some officers taking a break.

'Back in the hotseat, Jules?' He grinned at them.

'Can't stay away.'

He continued up the incline, fir trees looming to his right and above him. Knowing what had occurred here, he could see why most people would find this area and its shadows uninviting. To him, it was a really good choice for anybody intent on concealing human remains.

Reaching the flags, he looked down at the area of cleared earth which had once supported then concealed those of Amy Peters. He knelt, recalling their configuration in scene photographs. He studied the raw earth, shook his head. How was it possible that an item which had lain unburied for so long had not been found before now? This killer had had the luck of the devil.

Reaching out, he gathered up a handful of earth, crumbled it, watched it fall from his hand. Here was the answer, and it wasn't luck. During a time of very dry weather, the item had become detached from what was probably just bones and had fallen through the groundcover, to be concealed yet further by earth gradually covering them as winter weather turned wet.

He searched his pockets for a glove, then thrust both hands deep into the soil. If anything was still here, he would find it. He moved his fingers seeking anomalies, totally immersed in the task.

'Dr Devenish, sir?' Startled, Julian looked up at the young officer standing over him.

'Give me an evidence bag, *quick*.'

Reynolds rooted in his pockets, took one out.

'Drop it down here next to me.'

Reynolds watched as Julian pulled his hand from the earth and gently released what he had onto the bag. Reynolds dropped to his knees.

'Holy – what's *that*?'

'Fetch a SOCO, quick!'

Reynolds leapt up and rushed down the hill. He was soon back with a SOCO officer who crouched next to Julian, gently brushing earth from the recovered item, his eyes intent.

'You're here five minutes, Jules, and you're onto something.'

Reynolds watched as the small item was held up, meagre sunlight shining on where it was resting on the SOCO's palm. Julian sat back, dispirited.

'Just a two-pound coin.'

'It looks like it was relatively new when it was dropped.' The SOCO brought it closer. 'Yep. See? Bimetallic and dated 2015.'

'Which is no help to us.'

Julian got to his feet, brushing earth from his trousers. The SOCO looked up at him.

'It had to be found so we could rule it out.'

'I like your positivity,' said Julian, his thoughts going to the young, still-missing women. 'If there are more remains here, it's likely he learnt from losing it that he had to be more careful.'

'A two-pound coin? If it's his, he probably never even missed it.' Julian gave a tired grin.

'Ignore me. I'm overthinking. Like everybody else, I want this sorted.' They walked down the incline together.

Reynolds watched them go, then turned back to stare down at the disturbed earth.

Later that afternoon, Judd was getting ready to leave when Adam Jenner came into the office.

'You're putting in the hours, Chloe.'

'Hi, Adam. If you're looking for the Three Musketeers, you've just missed them.'

He grinned, handed her a large manila file.

'I wouldn't have guessed you had such traditional literary tastes.'

'I read it when I was about seven. Before I moved on to crime.'

He laughed, then pointed at the envelope.

'The enlargements of the victims' photographs. I'll leave them with you. When you see Bernard, let him know that Julian found something at the site—'

'*No.* What?'

'Something not that relevant: a two-pound coin which predates Amy Peters' abduction, but it emphasises the need for an in-depth search of the whole site.'

'OK, I'll tell Sarge. Thanks for the photos.'

As the door closed behind him, she removed the pictures from the envelope, placed them side by side in front of her, studied each of them in turn. Five women. All of them attractive. Healthy-looking.

All of them probably dead, if what they had seen was any indication. Four of them getting a university education, the other already
established in her career. In the dull light of the office, Judd's
thoughts were back at the scene. The prickling sensation crossed
her shoulders again. Giving them a quick shrug, her attention settled
on the photograph of Amy Peters, twenty-one years old at the time
she disappeared. The same age Judd was now. She pushed them
back into the envelope, placed it on the table where Sarge usually
sat. The office had cooled, the shadows lengthening. She had had
enough for today.

Reaching for her bag and jacket, she walked to the door, stopped
and went back for the envelope.

Fifteen minutes later, she was unlocking her front door, sensing
subtle movement to her right. She looked up. A man had appeared
and was standing a few feet away from her in the small front
garden of the house next door. She gave him a quick once-over.
Forties. Dark, lank hair. A fan of beige and brown. He was regarding
her through heavy-framed glasses. Without introducing himself,
he asked, 'Have you heard about the kerfuffle, early Sunday
morning?'

Registering the slow delivery, the northern accent, she looked
to where he was pointing in the general direction of headquarters.
She now had her door fully open.

'No, sorry.'

'Had to be six a.m., possibly earlier, and on a *Sunday*! If I lived
around there, I'd have lodged a complaint. I saw it all. Black estate
car. Big van. Three or four smaller ones. Four police cars. All their
lights flashing and—'

'Nice to talk to you.' She stepped quickly inside her hall.

He leant in the direction of the wall separating their two gardens.

'My name's Dennis!'

She forced a smile, not wanting to get off on the wrong foot
with him. He extended his hand. Feeling unable to ignore it, she
stepped out, took it briefly in hers.

'Chloe.'

She was about to go back inside when he spoke again, his arms
folded across neutral wool, looking past her into the house. 'I walk
early. Every day I'm out of the house by half five, do four or five
miles then back here. A man of leisure during daylight.'

Wondering what he did when it was dark, she felt her phone

vibrate inside her bag. She reached for it, seeing him point towards the road.

'That's my car there.' She glanced at the tan-coloured estate, a fixture since she had first seen her house. 'See the orange-and-white cone next to it? That's mine. It's a nightmare round here for parking. I've got a spare you can have—'

'Sorry, Dennis, I need to take this call.'

He raised his hand.

'Go for it! I'll catch up with you later. By the way, a man knocked on your door late this afternoon—'

Inside, she leant against the closed front door and breathed. One thing she knew about Dennis. He disproved the perception that northerners were short to the point of brusque. She got out her phone again, listened to her builder's voice confirming that he would let himself in tomorrow with the key she had given him to start work on her kitchen floor.

Pushing herself away from the door, she dropped her bag and the envelope on the stairs and headed for the kitchen, taking juice from the fridge. She needed to tell what's-his-name next door that a workman would be arriving here in the morning. If she didn't, he sounded like the type to alert Neighbourhood Watch. Or worse. She pressed the cool glass to her forehead. She would put a note through his door in the morning.

Three hours later she was cross-legged on the sitting-room rug, the five photographs placed around her, word-processed details on each to one side. At twenty-three, Claire Walsh was older than Judd was now. It was still a small shock to realize that two of the victims were younger. She reached for the nearby glass of wine, sipped. All young women with plans. Working hard. Wanting to get on. *Just like me. Until some low-life saw them and decided his plans and wants were more important than theirs—*

She straightened, ears keening. The doorbell. She looked at her phone: 9 p.m. If it was Dennis, she would tell him about the builder and discourage future late-evening visits. She got up, went along the hall to the front door and pulled it open.

She stopped, the shock feeling like a physical blow to her chest. The man standing there was somebody she hadn't seen for over ten years. More like fourteen. He had to be in his late twenties now. Still vaguely recognizable. Tall. Prosperous-looking. She wouldn't ask how he had found her. She didn't care.

'What do you want?'

He held an envelope towards her. She didn't take it.

'Your foster mother's daughter sent me this and asked me to deliver it to you to sign.'

'What is it?'

'I believe it's a legal document. Something to do with your foster mother's estate.'

She stepped back. He came inside, closed the door then followed her to the sitting room. She took the envelope from him, seeing his eyes drift down to the photographs. She opened it, pulled out papers, unfolded them. As he had said, a legal document. She read quickly, getting the gist: she needed to sign it in full and final acknowledgement of receiving her beneficiary share of her foster mother's estate. She picked up a pen lying nearby, signed her name, added the date, returned it to the envelope, handed it back, all without looking at him.

'Thank you,' he said. 'Now, I'm instructed to give you this.' She frowned, took a smaller envelope. He came closer, pointed to it. 'I understand there was a balance still outstanding.' A heavy silence built between them. 'I'm really glad for you, Chloe. You deserve—'

Turning away, she headed for the hall, her hand already on the lock as he came out of the room and walked slowly towards her. He stopped next to her.

'We were all children, Chloe.'

Molten rage she hadn't known she still had rose from somewhere deep, flooding her chest, her throat. She could barely speak.

'If that's how you choose to remember it, that makes it OK for you.' She looked him straight in the eye.

'It doesn't work for me. You were all older. In your place I would have done something. Told somebody.'

'Who would have believed us? They weren't the usual social services parents.' He paused. 'And . . . it was just you.'

Just you.

The two words took her back. She was five, six years old, both parents, professionals, intelligent, confident, believable in their exchanges with authority figures such as paediatricians and teachers because they were viewed as just like *them*. Judd had understood none of it back then. That came much later, when she was, what, nine, ten, the carefully crafted illusion of 'family' by then having fallen apart. She forced air into her chest, the wave of anger threatening to stop her breathing. Her brother was speaking.

'And we haven't seen them for years.'

Shaking with anger, she spoke the words roaring into her head. 'I was *seven* years old, *seven* when it ended for me!' He looked away from her. '*I* would have *told* someone. If I was you or either of the other two, I would have told a *teacher*, a *neighbour*, anybody I thought would listen . . . that I had a little sister who was always . . . left out, while the rest of you had all that you—' Her throat was closing up.

'That she was left to fend. Get whatever she could—' Her hand pressed against her mouth to steady it, she pushed him to the front door, pulled it open.

'Get out and don't ever, *ever*—' He was now outside.

She heaved the door shut on him, went back to the sitting room and stood, shaking, unable to recall the last time it had upset her like this. She swallowed hard. *This* was the last ever time.

She looked down at the envelope, reached for it, opened it, pulled out a brief letter, then a cheque. A final settlement from the estate of a woman who had shown her at just seven years old that there was enough food, enough hot water, enough clothing – enough love to go around.

She gazed up at the huge bay window, an ache in her chest.

'Thank you, Moira,' she whispered.

SIX

Tuesday, 9 April. 6.50 a.m.

Watts pulled one of several identical white shirts from his wardrobe, aware of Chong's eyes on him.

'Have you made peace with continuing to work?'

'I have a choice?' He pulled on the shirt, began buttoning it. 'It's not about the hours.'

'I *know* what it's about, because I know *you*, but whenever there's something on your mind, which there has been for weeks, I have to piece it together because you don't *talk* to me.'

'What's the point of talking? I'm not getting early retirement and *now* I've got a high-profile homicide investigation I don't want. End of story.' She came to him.

'I thought it was a good idea to create some space between us, to spend some time at my apartment. I was wrong. I'm here. We need to talk.'

She reached for the pack of antidepressants that he hadn't yet started taking. He took them from her, dropped them into a nearby drawer.

'I'm all right,' he said, sliding his belt through its loops.

'Did I say you weren't?'

'Thanks for staying over.'

He looked down at her, momentarily lost in her eyes, the smooth golden skin, the heart-shaped face, the whole, to him, intoxicating in its beauty—

'Is that what I did? "Stay over"?'

He gave his suede shoes a quick brush, stood, reached for his jacket, pushing a tie into his pocket. Her small hand arrived on his arm. He looked down at the ring he had given her.

'You're right. There are some things that need discussing.'

'That sounds like a lot of talking, for a man who doesn't.'

Finding the office deserted, Judd went upstairs to the incident room. A relaxed-looking Traynor was there, listening to Julian in full flow.

'—And, what you just said, Will, is *exactly* what it was like up there: Day One, *this* is the plan, Day Two, the plan's changed and now, I'm being instructed to—' He looked up.

'Hi, Chloe.' Traynor raised his hand.

She didn't respond. They exchanged looks as she dumped her bag on the floor, took the enlarged photographs out of the envelope, went to the whiteboard, removed the A4 copies, replacing them, in order of disappearance, with a sharp click of the coloured plastic cubes. Traynor came to look at them. Getting out her phone, she jabbed her builder's number and waited.

'Hi, Mick. I put a note through my neighbour's door earlier— Oh, you've met him.' She nodded. 'OK. As long as he knows you're supposed to be there. See you later, maybe.' She ended the call, returning to Traynor in conversation with Julian, their eyes on the photographs.

'What you've just described is very much my own experience of supporting a large homicide investigation led by a panicked SIO. Plans and objectives change overnight and the psychologist or criminologist is expected to ditch all previous theories on how to proceed and immediately come up with an alternative. Sometimes, several.'

'Exactly. How do *you* deal with that kind of situation, Will?'

'I tell them to find another criminologist.'

'Where's Sarge?' asked Judd. Julian turned to her.

'He's with Brophy, who's probably demanding action and results.'

'That'll put him in a mood—' The door opened and Watts came inside carrying a buff folder.

'Morning.' And to Julian: 'He wants to see you now, about a media announcement. Why the face? He thinks you're "it" because of the way you handled the Manchester media. He's as good as told me he doesn't want me anywhere near it. Which suits me. His angle for the Peters homicide is that we formally request whatever data we want from Manchester by email only, so we have a record in case this "collaboration" fails. Make that '"when"'. I'm running the Amy Peters investigation on the basis that Birmingham is now ground-zero and Manchester is out of the picture, except for providing that data.' As Julian left, Watts looked to Traynor whose intent gaze was still on the photographs, then at Judd.

'Where did they come from?'

'Adam brought them down after you left.'

'This is all we've got so far on Peters.' Watts slid the folder towards her. 'I want you to start on her victimology ASAP with whatever is known about her so far. Her personality, her interests, details of the specific locality where she was living when she disappeared, the friends she had, relationships if any. Start pulling it together this morning. If there's so much as a hint as to how she might have crossed paths with her killer, I want to know about it.'

Judd opened the folder, flicking through the meagre A4s.

'Not all of this is about Peters.' She pointed at a couple of lines. 'See? A reference here to Melody Brewster, the second student to go missing. How about I start victimologies for all five? The more we know about their backgrounds, the people in their lives, the more chance we have of seeing connections and nailing whoever killed them.' She frowned at the few pages. 'Manchester's not exactly knocking itself out to give us what we need.'

'Start the process on all five, but Amy Peters is our focus.'

'I'll get on the phone to her close family, friends and whoever else is mentioned.'

'When you do, watch what you say.' She gave him a look.

'You don't want me starting with, *'Hey, there!* How's it *going*?'

'Now who's narky? Keep it formal is what I'm saying.' She studied him. She knew his moods. He was buzzing.

'You've got an investigative angle.' He nodded, looked across to Traynor.

'You asked the question, Will: why is Amy Peters here in the West Midlands? There has to be a reason good enough, important enough, for whoever killed her to bring her a high-risk eighty miles to here. The reason has to be at that site. Plus, it's making no sense to me that she's the only one he left there. I've raised with Brophy a full-scale forensic search and he's considering it.'

'How about a data check of open cases of women missing from the West Midlands who fit the Manchester victims' profile?' Julian suggested, coming back into the room.

Watts shook his head.

'We'd be inundated with names, some of them no longer missing, others who've chosen to leave for one reason or another, all of it needing follow up.'

'Julian's raised a legitimate point,' said Traynor. 'We don't know where this killer lives. We can't assume it's the North. All roads between Manchester and Birmingham run both ways. He could be living in the Midlands. A data check on violent males known to have a problem with females both here and the Manchester area could be narrowed down in terms of nature and seriousness of past offences.'

Watts was at the window, looking out at officers getting into vehicles, on their way to the site.

'I like that better. It's based on facts, rather than possibilities. It'll still generate acres of names but if we don't do that kind of basic check and it turns out he's somewhere there, I'll have all the time I want for an allotment.'

'Refine the search further,' proposed Traynor. 'Focus on violent attacks which involved similar victims to the Manchester five, including "abduction" as a key word.'

'How about I do it?' Julian said. Watts shook his head, reached for the phone.

'I'm putting Miller onto it with Reynolds who needs the experience—'

'You mean the young guy I've seen on the desk?' Julian shook his head. 'He doesn't seem that clued-up to me.'

Watts spoke into the phone, replaced it and nodded to Traynor.

'It's all sorted. Will, I want you overseeing that search. Miller going to let you have details of each name which merits further follow up.' Watts turned to Judd. 'Before you start on the victimologies, email Manchester with a formal request for any and all information relating to Amy Peters which they haven't yet sent us.' He paused. 'On second thoughts, make it a request for all they've got on *each* of the victims.'

Moving to the computer, Judd hit keys.

'Boulter isn't going to like it,' said Julian.

'He can please himself.'

'You want to check the email when it's done, Sarge?' she asked.

'No, send it.'

She did, then turned her attention back to the victimologies.

Forty minutes later, the phone rang. She reached for it.

'Hi— *Really?* He's right here— OK, I'll tell him.' She put down the phone.

'That was Adam ringing from the site. No jewellery of any kind located within the area where Peters' remains were found, but a couple of items have been recovered nearby which sound really promising. Right now, he's examining them and Dr Chong is searching the areas where they were recovered in case there's more. He's suggested we go over in, say, an hour.'

'Did Adam give any details of the items?' asked Julian.

'No.'

'I want to be part of that site visit, Bernard.'

'Later. First, I want you going through everything we've got from Manchester and adding any facts you know from your involvement.'

Same day. Mid-afternoon.

The sun was barely penetrating the expanse of dark firs when they arrived. They headed to Adam and Chong, engaged in conversation over an evidence box, looked inside at two dull-looking keys on a ring, no fob, a discoloured cardboard label tied to them, the string earth-stained.

'Where were they?' asked Watts.

Adam pointed to two yellow flags, a few metres from where Amy Peters' remains had been located, then reached inside the box. Watts pulled on a glove, took the keys from him, as Adam said, 'They could, of course, have been dropped by anybody walking here in the last several years.'

Watts studied them, looked at the label, something handwritten in pencil, faded almost to nothing. He looked up at Adam.

'This looks to me like it might have been put on by a garage.'

'Exactly my thinking.' He nodded, pointing at the label. 'See the small smears? Engine oil. I examined the writing under ultra-violet light inside the forensic van but got nothing useful. I took a picture of both keys and sent it to headquarters for comparison to those stored on our database of ignition keys.' He looked at Watts. 'We got the results back a few minutes ago. The make of car they belong to is a 2015 Fiat 500.'

'Amy Peters didn't own a car.'

'Claire Walsh did.' All eyes moved to Judd. 'A Fiat 500.'

Watts stared at her. 'How do you know that?'

'From the time I spent on the victimologies before we left to come here. We know Claire Walsh used a bicycle to travel between work and home but it just leapt out at me: a single reference to her owning a Fiat 500.'

'No flies on you, are there, Judd?' He turned to Adam. 'You said two things?'

'The other one is here.' Adam reached for a second evidence box. 'We'll be testing these for prints and DNA later, so no handling.'

They looked at the two black plastic loops, both ends fed through a small junction.

'Hand restraints?' said Judd.

'Never used them myself,' said Watts, 'but I understand they're quick to apply and remove.'

'To me, these are screaming "law enforcement",' Judd said. 'They could be the link we're looking for.'

'Not necessarily. There's any number of hand restraints and cable ties like this for sale online.'

'You're saying *anybody* can buy these things? That's plain wrong is what that is.'

'I don't make the rules, Judd.'

'You would if you were female and at risk of having them used on *you*.'

Thinking she had a point, Watts said, 'Adam, I want to see where both these items were found.'

They followed Adam to the yellow flags barely a metre from the location of Amy Peters' remains.

'The keys were under this deep leaflitter here, and,' Adam pointed, 'the restraint was here. A couple of my team have done an eye-hand search which turned up nothing else, but SOCOs are now ready to remove all groundcover in this area for an in-depth search. Let's hope we get lucky.'

Watts got out his phone, called Traynor. 'Anything of interest from the violent offender search?'

'I've followed up twelve names so far and discounted all of them.'

'I'll talk to you later about a possible big development at the scene.' He ended the call.

Adam ended his own call. 'Dr Chong wants to talk to me.'

They watched him go, Watts' eyes narrowing against a sharp glare of sun piercing the topmost branches of nearby firs. He gazed down at the whole site spread below them.

'Brophy has to know that this investigative team is nowhere near big enough for what we've got here.'

'Because of Claire Walsh's keys and the restraint? How do you think he'll take it?'

'He's mellowed a bit because he knows he's going, but depending on the number I request, he'll revert to type, starting with outright disbelief followed by point-blank refusal, a short delay then grudging agreement.' He didn't add that Brophy knew his own mind only when he was told what others were thinking.

'I'm off to have a word with the lads. See how they're getting on.'

She watched him walk down the incline, then waved at Julian who was coming up from the road. She waited till he was close enough then told him about the finds, showed him the small area from which they had been recovered, watched him slowly pace the distance between the yellow flags and the two small areas of dry-looking earth, stripped of vegetation where Amy Peters' remains had lain.

'Have you got an idea you're following up?' she asked.

'Not yet. I've spent over an hour going through the Manchester data and adding to it where I could. I'm glad to hear about the finds and your victimology has already paid off.'

'If you mean Claire Walsh, I don't see the possibility of another woman's remains being here as a "pay-off".'

'Sorry, that was carelessly said. I meant it in terms of progress.' He waited. 'Something wrong?' She looked around the site, the light just beginning to fade now.

'I'm wondering what it is about this place that made him come here. Why did he choose it?' She pressed her hand against her forehead. 'It's possible it wasn't a choice. One thing I do know is that I hate the place and I hate him. He's turned this whole area into a nightmare that nobody's going to forget.' He came towards her.

'Hey, hey, come on.' He paused. 'Want some advice?'

'Go on.'

'Avoid creating a persona for every killer and an atmosphere for every scene. It can stand in the way of making cool, professional evaluations.' She looked up at him.

'How do you know that?' He looked around the site, down to where Watts was standing, then back to her.

'It's what I learnt way back when I was a student, working on cold cases with Bernard and busy knitting up an individual to fit the crime. Once I stopped doing that, I got better at the work itself.' He smiled down at her. 'I think we've both had enough for today.'

They walked together to where Watts was talking with Adam and Kumar. They neared just as Watts was saying to Kumar, 'I want everybody inside the incident room for an update briefing at ten thirty tomorrow morning.'

'I'll spread the word, Sarge.'

Watts turned to Julian.

'Start giving some thought to what you're going to say when you address the media. Keep it non-specific. No details to be released about the keys or the hand restraints.' He turned away then back to him again. 'And *zero* reference to a connection to Claire Walsh.'

'You're the boss.'

Watts jabbed his phone, waited. 'Will, we're bringing two found items back to headquarters. I want you to see them before you leave so you can pull some ideas together about the kind of individual you think we might be dealing with.'

Watts ended the call, his head full of the next day's demands. If Brophy refused his request for more officers, Brophy himself was going to learn what aggravation felt like.

SEVEN

Wednesday, 10 April. 10 a.m.

Watts was gazing out of his office window, preoccupied with the unseasonably warm weather for April. Weather could play havoc with the kind of investigation they now had. He squinted at the sky, wanting a temperature drop of, say, eight degrees or so in the next day or two, which might make it easier on SOCOs and forensic workers. Rain was something they could do without. As Traynor's Aston Martin slid smoothly past the window and into a parking space, Watts was recalling kidding Judd about her 'just-right' Goldilocks demands of scenes. A few minutes later, his office door swung open and Traynor came inside.

'Morning, Will. Adam's team has been at the scene since five a.m. Nothing new located so far. Right now, what I need is some of your criminological insight, starting with anything you've got to say about this madman.'

'He's not mad, Bernard.'

Watts turned to him.

'We've worked together long enough for you to know that when I say "mad", it's my way of saying, "I don't get this weirdo."' He gazed at the criminologist. 'What makes him tick? A sentence will do.'

'It's complex.'

Watts sighed, checked his phone, watching Traynor walk to the door.

'Thought it might be. You're keen to get started.'

'I want to make some changes to the incident room.'

Watts was there as more officers filed inside looking hesitant. All of the worktables had been arranged into a large rectangle facing inwards. Traynor's reasoning to Watts was that it removed the emphasis on hierarchy and increased the likelihood of a sharing of ideas. Watts had wanted to say that, with the exception of Judd, the notion of hierarchy was firmly embedded in all members of his team. He hadn't. He was now watching them exchange glances, searching for a discernible head of the table and not finding it. Eventually, Judd sat next to Julian, then Miller, Jones, Kumar and, finally, Reynolds. Once they had chosen seats, Watts and Traynor also sat. In the absence of the several officers still on search and recovery duties at the site, these were what Watts considered the nucleus of his investigative team.

Chong arrived a few minutes later, followed by Adam and finally Brophy. Watts waited as they took seats. He had decided against an earlier one-to-one meeting with Brophy because Brophy was already aware of developments. Now he was going to hear the details, without an opportunity to resist or drag his feet on a decision about additional personnel. That decision had to be made. Brophy had to make it. Watts looked around at them.

'You already know about the masking tape found at the site. I'm still waiting for forensics on that. Most of you are aware of two further items recovered yesterday: keys to a 2015 Fiat 500 and plastic hand-restraints. Claire Walsh owned a Fiat 500. I emailed SIO Boulter yesterday and got his response this morning confirming the keys belonged to Claire Walsh's vehicle. It changes this investigation.' He saw Brophy's face set, looks being exchanged.

'Amy Peters' homicide is still our focus but the finding of the hand restraints and keys indicates a need for a comprehensive search of that whole area of land. It also means that we can anticipate Claire Walsh is somewhere within that site. I'm extending this investigation.'

Brophy's head shot up. 'On whose authority?'

'Mine, sir, as SIO. There's enough evidence now for that whole site to be subjected to a thorough excavation.'

'Officers are already searching it,' snapped Brophy, 'and the investigation is still limited to the Amy Peters homicide.'

Not for the first time, Watts wondered what kinds of aptitudes had enabled Brophy to rise effortlessly through the ranks. Probably good at paperwork.

'Sir, this new physical evidence places Claire Walsh at that site. We need to extend the remit of this investigation—'

'That's my decision,' barked Brophy. 'Leave it to me.'

Watts let his sudden anger subside. They both knew that Brophy didn't have much choice. He turned his attention to Julian.

'Will is going to give us his views on this killer based on what's been found, but first, Julian's going to talk us through the kind of individual he thinks we're looking for, having been part of the Manchester investigation. Their combined ideas are going to give us focus, help identify suspects as and when we have them. OK, Jules.'

Julian looked around at the faces looking back at him, all receptive except for Jones whose face was closed, eyes lowered.

'At this stage, I have some very basic biographical characteristics which should give a sense of the guy who's responsible for the abductions and the murder of Amy Peters. I estimate his likely age range to be mid-thirties to mid-forties, his intellect probably modest-normal, with an IQ range somewhere between eighty to one hundred. In terms of work, I would anticipate it being manual. We know he's extremely mobile which increases the risk he poses. Given the distance between here and Manchester, it's very likely that driving is an integral aspect of his job. possibly in some kind of product distribution or selling. There is no indication of violence on Amy Peters' remains but a likely scenario is abduction followed by either physical or sexual violence, possibly both, which in turn indicates a likely antisocial personality type. Given the condition of Amy Peters' remains, we lack confirmation of physical or sexual violence. My overall impression from what we know so far suggests that her killer is impulsive and a risk-taker.'

Watts waited, allowing officers to make quick notes, then looked to Traynor.

'Thanks, Julian. Want to give us your take, Will?'

Traynor nodded, glanced around at the faces now looking back at him.

'This isn't a situation where I talk and everyone listens. I welcome questions, ideas, comments or observations. Whenever there are two experts involved, there's the potential for some

divergence of opinion, which is no bad thing. I'm in total agreement with Julian that we're looking for an antisocial male, although
I would envisage his having sufficient social skills to conceal that
aspect of himself. The little we know of his attack on Amy Peters
leads me to anticipate extreme anger, yet other aspects of his
behaviour cause me to question his having impulse-control
problems.' Hearing this, Jones smirked in Julian's direction.

Traynor continued. 'The hand restraints found at the site indicate
foresight, planning. The finding of Claire Walsh's car keys suggests
the possibility that he takes mementos from his victims, possibly
revisiting that site over time. From what we know of the Manchester
cases and what we've seen at the site, I would anticipate that he's
already known to the police but not necessarily recently or for
violence.' He looked across at Julian.

'In terms of age, I would estimate he's in his mid-twenties to
mid-thirties, his IQ somewhere between 110 and 129. Not genius-
level, but pretty smart. In consequence, he probably has a level of
awareness of his own psychopathology and is untroubled by it.
Having said that, I would anticipate his expending considerable
energy concealing it when he thinks it's judicious to do so. These
have all the hallmarks of sexual homicide, which suggests that
he is likely to have sexually offended against females, although
not to the degree seen at the site. I would anticipate sexual violence
to be an integral part of his thinking and behaviour.' Traynor
paused, looked around at each of them.

'If that aspect of my description is accurate, it would need to
be borne in mind once we begin to identify potential persons of
interest or suspects. What I'm saying is, don't anticipate him being
recognizable for what he really is. Don't hope for a quick or
easy arrest.' He looked to Watts, who nodded.

'As you said, Will, we shouldn't expect a quick fix, nor
for any two experts to produce the exact same profile. Treat them
as a guide.' He looked around the faces. 'Most of us have seen
what he's done to one woman. The big challenge for us is to
see *him*. To understand what makes him do what he does, what
makes him tick.' Julian leant forward. 'Something you want to
add, Julian?'

'Yes. I can offer a basic intro to his psychopathology—'

A loud sigh took everyone's attention to Jones sitting low on
his chair, arms folded. He looked to Watts. 'Sarge, what we need

is stuff which will make him recognizable, as and when he's there in front of us. If he ever is.'

'As the investigation progresses,' Julian responded, 'we'll doubtless gain more information which will help us identify persons of interest, particularly those already known to the police. We'll have their social and other reports, their offence histories, so that we're forearmed when we do talk to them, to help us decide which if any might be promoted to suspect—'

'It looks to me like right now there's not a lot of agreement between you and Will—'

'Leave it, Jones.' Watts looked to Julian. 'Thanks for the insights so far. Much appreciated.' And to the team, 'A five-minute break and a chance to take in what you've heard.'

They stood, some heading for coffee makings, others to the water cooler, Brophy for the door. Watts quickly followed.

'*Sir?*'

Brophy stopped, turned. 'You need to consider what I said in there about search personnel.'

'Which is exactly what I am doing.' He turned and walked away.

Watts returned to the incident room, his eyes on Jones. He went directly to Traynor, keeping his voice low. 'I'm not pushing, Traynor – well, I am – if you've got ideas that you're keeping to yourself, it's time to share them.'

'Speculations are probably not helpful, right now.'

'I need you to give them something they'll see they can work with. Something to make whoever destroyed five young women sound *real*, rather than hypothetical.'

Officers were returning to their seats. He and Traynor joined them. The room fell silent. Traynor looked at each of them.

'Prior to my work as a criminologist, I qualified as a forensic psychologist.' Julian's head came up, interested. 'That involved working with a long procession of adults, mostly male, who had been found guilty of acts of extreme violence and cruelty towards others. I learnt a lot from working with them as to why such offenders do what they do.' He took in the faces looking back at him.

'It's possible that what I'm about to say may not directly relate to the individual at the centre of this investigation but what I'm hoping is that it might generally convey the type of individual I believe he is. What I'm offering is an outline drawn from psychological theory, plus my own direct, professional experience as a criminologist. The individual we're searching for may have all or few of the features I'm about to describe.' He paused, looked at them.

'You've probably guessed that we're dealing with a highly deviant individual. He's vicious and he's cruel.' Tension climbed inside the room. 'That's all we can be certain of at this stage of the investigation, but it's enough to tell us that, whoever and wherever he is, this killer is deadly. Part of that deadliness lies in his being highly socially skilled. If he weren't, it's unlikely he could abduct five intelligent, healthy young women without anyone seeing or hearing anything.' Miller caught Traynor's eye and he nodded at her to speak.

'Will, if he's that good at hiding his real self and we come into contact with him, how likely is it that we'll know he's the one we're looking for?'

'I understand you want some specifics, Josie. Unfortunately, I can't give them because recognizing this individual for what he really is will be entirely dependent on the situation he is in and his perception of it. If he feels fully in control of what is happening, he is likely to maintain his "normal" face. Only at those times he perceives himself under threat might he display his negative qualities.'

Miller looked quizzically at her colleagues, then back to Traynor. 'You're saying that as soon as we have a person of interest or a suspect, we get him in and start putting on the pressure?'

Traynor shook his head.

'No. In the situation you're suggesting, it's highly likely that the individual I am describing would feel more than equal to presenting himself well.'

'The more I hear, the less I get what he's about,' Jones interrupted. 'He sounds to me like he's two different people.'

Traynor slow-nodded.

'That's a good summation. He lives a dual existence. He's capable of very different presentations which enables him to interact normally while concealing his extreme deviance and negativity. He's had a lot of practice. It won't surprise anyone here when I suggest he has had some very damaging early life experiences. In situations where he believes he is in complete control, say during a police interview, he would almost certainly maintain his socially skilled façade, supported by his above-average intellect.' Jones shot a look in Julian's direction.

'He's had years to perfect that façade,' Traynor continued. 'so he's extremely adept at concealing the maelstrom of negativity behind it.'

He gazed around at the downbeat faces. They had to know what he knew. They needed that level of honesty.

'I doubt he'll be found on databases of serious offenders. He's too clever. Too cunning.'

Jones rubbed at his short hair, shook his head.

'He's abducted *five* women, probably killed all of them,' he mused. 'How has he managed to get to this point without somebody even suspecting he has these problems? He must have one *hell* of an act going for him.' Traynor nodded approval at Jones' insight.

'Well put. That's exactly what he has. Stopping him requires an awareness of what he truly is and his developmental journey towards it. If he does come to our attention, don't look to uncover all of that in a single interview.' Traynor leant forward for emphasis. 'You need to understand his developmental journey. I would anticipate a history of voyeuristic behaviour, possibly from late childhood, certainly from his early teens, probably lowkey, confined to peeping at females within his home environment, which was either not noticed or, if it were, it was disregarded by adult family members who had little understanding of it.'

'The creepy *bastard*.' Jones looked around at his colleagues. 'Don't know about you lot, but what Will's just said makes me think his bloody family is no better than *him*.' Julian snorted and shook his head.

'*That* indicates such a simplistic engagement with what I'm saying, it's almost laughable.' Jones rounded on him.

'And you're one of the experts here and you couldn't even get his age range right—!'

'Jones!' Watts glared at him.

'There is no "right",' said Traynor. 'Julian and I have similar knowledge and training but none of what we're saying is set in stone. Right now, I'm offering my professional opinion on this individual's early behaviour. It would have progressed over time, possibly accompanied by alcohol or drugs as he got older. At that stage, he would have extended his behaviour into neighbourhoods familiar to him, watching unknown females inside their own homes.' Judd looked up from her notetaking.

'The way you describe it, Will, it sounds like it's a kind of routine thing he's following. He's doing the same stuff wherever he is.'

'It is a recognized, deviant pathway. We find it time and again in such offenders.' Julian shook his head.

'Will, if you're suggesting that he was watching the five victims in their own homes in Manchester as part of his preparations for abduction and homicide, there's a real problem with that. One of my tasks in the investigation was to check the physical situations in which each of those women was living at the time she disappeared. Claire Walsh had a third-floor apartment. Amy Peters had a first-floor bedsit. So did Erica Trent. The others were living in halls, none of them on the ground floor. He wouldn't have been able to watch them within their homes.'

'In which case,' Traynor carried on, unfazed, 'he would have adapted his behaviour, started watching them as they moved through their usual daily and evening activities, gathering information about their routines.' He stood, moved to the five photographs, pointing to each one.

'It is evident that he has an extremely well-developed criteria for what interests him.'

The team now focused on the photographs of the five women, Judd thinking that there was something to be said for being five-two at a push and short-haired. She heard Jones' voice.

'So, one of our jobs is to look at stalkers who've attracted some police attention during the previous half-decade or more.' He frowned at Julian. 'Why didn't that lot in Manchester do it?'

'I suggested it,' said Julian. 'but they chose not to listen.'

'*Jesus.*' Jones dropped his pen onto the table in front of him and sat back, arms folded.

'Take it easy, Jones.'

'Face it, Sarge, we've got *five* homicides and we're nowhere on this case because that lot up there couldn't get their backsides into gear. Which now leaves us searching for some weird git who disappears like some bloody ghost into the woodwork.'

'We can learn a lot about him from what he does,' Traynor picked up the thread again, 'because there's a lot of available research relating to stalkers. They rarely stop, so it's extremely likely that stalking is still part of his M.O.' Judd's head came up. She stared at him.

'Erica Trent was the last to disappear, after which, nothing. You're saying he's still out there, scoping for potential victims.'

'Almost certainly. He's a planner. He takes his time. We see that in the gaps between the homicides. He's patient. He feels at home in the kinds of places young women choose to frequent. Those are his hunting grounds. He fits in. It's one reason I've suggested a twenties–thirties age range. If he were older, he would probably be remembered for looking out of place. When he's in those environments, he's likely to drink alcohol.' Traynor paused.

'Remember what I said earlier, about his level of personal concealment: the strain of maintaining that façade would be considerable. It needs to be considered that he may choose to live alone, but he may also be extremely good at compartmentalizing his behaviours. In which case, it's difficult to predict his personal situation.'

'Surely, alcohol or drug use would compromise his planning abilities?' said Julian. 'Or mark him out as somebody most females would stay clear of?'

'I'm not suggesting he presents as intoxicated,' said Traynor. 'He is likely to drink to a level which relaxes him without compromising those abilities.'

'Sir?' Reynolds raised his hand tentatively. 'How, why, did he change from voyeur to stalker to killer?'

'That's a really good question. It's about crossing lines. Psychological lines.' Traynor paused, considering. 'The first line he crossed would have been from watching females within his family to watching unknown women in the general environment. At some point, he decided to follow those women: he's moved from voyeur to stalker, a second line is crossed. It's possible that during one of those early stalking forays he found himself in an area which was quiet and he made physical contact: a third, significant line is crossed.'

Jones stared at Traynor.

'What you're saying, Will, it sounds like he's been at it for *years.*'

'Yes, and you're wondering how it's possible that nobody has picked up on him before? The answer is in what we've already discussed: his physical presentation, his intellect, plus the fact that he's highly motivated. He *likes* what he does.'

Traynor paused again, weighing what he was going to say next. They had to be in no doubt that this killer was a challenge but not invincible. Once that kind of thinking seeped into an investigation it drifted, like a tanker from its moorings. Impossible to stop or redirect. He had seen it first-hand in the investigation tasked with finding his wife's killer. All of them good, hardworking officers who were gradually overwhelmed.

'This team has all it needs to stop him. I've described his likely development. It's possible that he made a mistake somewhere along that early journey, perhaps during that first physical contact with a female. If she reported it, it is somewhere in the system, although not necessarily recorded as either sexual or violent. A national search for that offence might pay off. If he's made one mistake, he's capable of making others.'

'What are our chances of catching him, Will?' Jones asked.

'They're good, if we follow every lead we get. Stay optimistic. The nature of repeat homicide-by-stranger is that leads are often slow arriving. We keep in mind that a high proportion of repeat killers *are* caught.' He didn't add that for some cases a solution did not come easily. Or, at all. He didn't need to. They already knew it.

'You've met people like this, Will?' asked Kumar. 'Worked with them?'

'Yes, frequently.'

Traynor was lost for a moment, thinking of one he had never met and probably never would now. The one who took away his wife.

'Forget fictional portrayals of psychopaths, or what you see in the news. None of the repeat killers I've met was like those depictions.' They listened to him in silence. 'Unfortunately, they're super newsworthy. For however long it takes to bring this case to a resolution, we have to accept that the media will be there, creating some demonic persona, not in an attempt at explanation, but rather to sensationalize and demonize in equal measure. It sells news. Whatever is written or said about him will have little relevance to his true self.'

He was suddenly tired. He could give them more. He could provide the likely reason for the lack of concealment of Amy Peters and why her killer chose that Brampton site, but they had enough to think about. What he had given them had taken its toll on him, forced his thoughts back to his own experience. Something he mostly managed to keep distanced. He heard Judd's voice.

'What Will's just said about his likely first attempted assault on a woman going wrong: if it exists, we have to find it, Sarge.'

'I'll start the search, Will,' said Miller, 'if you give me some search guidance.'

'Query all UK cases in, say, the last fifteen years. Key words: stranger attack, young, female, struck from behind, minor injury.' He waited as she wrote. 'Anticipate a high volume of results. Focus on victims who described their attacker as smelling of alcohol. Eliminate victims with any prior history of domestic violence to avoid confusion with attacks by a violent partner. Yes, Julian?'

'Sorry, Will, but I can't see how you can be so sure of any of this.' Watts shot Julian a warning look, wondering if Traynor's theorizing had put the young psychologist's nose out of joint.

'I'm not sure. This isn't a blueprint. Right now, I'm calling on theoretical knowledge which you'll have recognized, plus my own observations of this case and also my professional experience.' Watts decided to bring the briefing to a close.

'I'd like to thank Will for his insights, and Julian. They've given us a lot to consider, plus some possibilities to check out.' He glanced at Adam, who was looking at his phone.

'Anything coming in?'

'Only what I was anticipating. Two of my officers have sent the drone over the whole site but the results are poor because of the surrounding heavy tree cover.'

'Got any other search ideas?'

'Ground penetrating radar, but it's time-consuming, particularly on a sloping, wooded terrain full of tree roots.'

'Leave it with me,' said Watts.

Adam and Chong left the room and Miller went to her computer. Julian joined Traynor.

'That was really impressive, Will. I didn't know that you'd qualified as a forensic psychologist.'

'A long time ago.' Traynor turned away, sliding his papers into his backpack. 'I need to leave. I don't like to keep my students waiting.'

Julian watched him go, turned to Watts.

'Do you think I offended him by what I said earlier, about being sure?'

Watts shook his head. Traynor was tough. He knew that his theoretical expertise hadn't helped him find his wife's killer and by God, he'd tried.

'No, lad. This investigation has probably touched a nerve around a previous case.'

Watts and Judd left the incident room, but Julian remained, his attention fixed on the computer screen in front of him, barely aware of voices some distance away.

'Thanks to Will, we know what we're up against now.' Jones stretched his arms, let them drop. 'We've got a sex-crazed killer on the loose!'

Officers exchanged grins. One of them said, 'Know anybody who fits the "sex-crazed" bit, Jonesy?'

'Don't know what you mean, but I'm telling you Chloe's looking—' His next words caused some laughter. Julian got slowly to his feet and approached the group.

'That's inappropriate.' Jones' attention was fixed on his screen.

'I wasn't talking to you, Posh Boy, but here's some advice: it's time you forgot your prep school or wherever else you went and joined the real world.'

Julian was across the room in seconds, Miller leaping to her feet and placing herself between them.

'Hey! You two! Cut it out!'

'If the comment I just heard is typical of you, you're a lout!' said Julian. Jones was now on his feet.

Miller said, 'Cool it, both of you!' Julian pointed.

'What he just said about Chloe was disrespectful—'

'No, it *wasn't*.' Jones, a head shorter, faced him up. 'Chloe and me, we're mates and don't *you* forget it!' Kumar was now at Jones' side, his voice low.

'Come on, Ade. Leave it, yeah?'

Jones moved to the other side of the room where he sat with his back to Julian. Miller looked across to Julian and shrugged.

Same day. 7.10 p.m.

Traynor came into his house, hearing music from an upper floor. Dropping his backpack inside his office, he headed for the large kitchen and peered out the wide open, floor-to-ceiling windows.

He watched his partner Jess move around in the lights on the deck, her red-blonde curls tied back. A sudden rush of anxiety at her being there at dusk sent him outside. Seeing him, her mouth widened into a smile. He took the laden tray from her and they came into the kitchen.

'Emelia had a couple of friends here earlier.' She watched as he put down the tray, came to him, her eyes moving slowly over his face.

'Hard day?'

'Mmm . . . What about yours?'

She had left the house before him. Having sold the local newspaper she owned when they first met, she still helped out there. He reached up, lifted a stray curl from her face, gently tucked it among the others. It sprang out again.

'It was good. I enjoy going in occasionally, now that it's no longer my responsibility.' She grinned. 'I'm becoming feckless and I don't care.'

She moved to the tall fridge freezer.

'Wine?'

'Please.' He followed her. 'What if I told you that I'm . . . ravenous?' A look passed between them.

'Well, I just might have something for you—'

'Hi, Dad!' His daughter came into the kitchen, her long hair loose on her shoulders.

'Hey, Em.'

She kissed his cheek, gave him an evaluative look. 'You look tired.'

'I'm fine.'

'Have you got any money?'

'Yes, thank you.' She grinned as he reached into his pocket, brought out his wallet. She took the money from him.

'I'll give it back.' He smiled at Jess.

'That would be a first.'

'I *promise*.' She reached for her keys. 'Thanks for feeding my friends earlier, Jess. See you both later!' They listened to the front door close, the car engine start. Jess glanced across at him. His face had that shadowed look it used to have, before they got together.

'You are OK?'

'Yes. Glad to be home.'

She came to him, reached up, put her arms around him, felt him press his face against her neck. She whispered, 'I think it's time we explored your hunger, Will.'

EIGHT

Thursday, 11 April. 7.30 a.m.

Chong's finger tracked her list of tasks for the day, all of them urgent. Drawing a decisive circle around one of them, she went upstairs, took the key from the officer on duty, signed her name in the book, went directly to the Exhibits Room and unlocked the door. Inside it was cool, the temperature regulated. She walked directly to the distant left-hand corner where shelves met at a ninety-degree angle. Searching the most accessible shelf at eye level, not finding what she was looking for, she knelt, checking the lower shelves. Pulling a small stepladder closer, she searched the two topmost shelves. Stepping down, she surveyed the entire room, got out her phone.

'Give me its location again, Igor.'

'Back wall, left-hand side, middle shelf.'

'That's what I thought. I'm looking at it. It isn't here.'

There was a short silence.

'I'll come up.'

Following an hour of exhaustive searching, the black tape had still not been located. They stood in the middle of the room.

'I'll check the log book,' said Chong. 'It could have been removed in error and whoever did so, forgot to return it.' To her own ears it was possible, if unlikely.

She left Igor and headed back to the duty officer. He lifted the book onto the desk. She took it, opened it, found the relevant page. Igor joined her as she ran her finger down the list of handwritten dates, stopping at the one she was looking for. Her finger moved to the right and the detail written there. *Item: black masking tape 50 mm wide. Recovery location: Forestry Commission site, Brampton. Case: Peters, A. Homicide.* She followed the line to its stated location in the Exhibits Room, tracked back details to the person named as having logged it in: Dr J. Devenish. No details of it being signed out. Igor was looking over her shoulder.

'Warn me when you decide to tell DCI Watts and I'll make sure I'm far, far away.'

She took out her phone, tapped a number.

'Consider yourself warned.' She turned away from him.

'It's me. Come down to the Exhibits Room – yes, *now*.'

Moments later, Watts' eyes were moving over shelves filled with labelled evidence boxes and plastic bags. 'How sure are you that it's not here?'

'I checked all of those shelves on the back wall,' she pointed, 'and Igor and I have gone through everything else. It isn't here. You're welcome to do your own search.'

Watts turned to Jones and Kumar waiting outside the room.

'In here, both of you, gloves on.' As they came inside, he said, 'I want a systematic check of every single item in here. You're looking for Exhibit Number 4359, description: black masking tape. Let me know as soon as you've tracked it down.'

Same day. 10.40 a.m.

The black tape had not been located. Watts was now checking the Exhibits book for a third time, looking for a detail which would tell him who had most recently been inside that room. His finger stopped at a name. Heading up to the incident room, he opened the door and leant inside. Most of his officers were at the site.

'Reynolds!' Startled, the young officer looked up.

'Sarge?'

'My office. *Now*.'

Watts already had the book open in front of him as Reynolds came inside. He turned it around, pushed it towards him, pointed.

'See this entry?' Reynolds looked at it. 'It shows the date and time when a key piece of evidence in the Amy Peters homicide was placed inside the Exhibits Room by Dr Devenish, yes?' Reynolds nodded again, watched Watts' finger move slowly downwards.

'And here's the name of the next visitor to that room.' Reynolds tracked the line of details, stopping at his own name. He looked up at Watts.

'I was told to put the Fiat keys and the hand restraints in there, see—?'

'Who told you to do that?'

'Dr Chong— no, actually it was Igor who gave them to me and told me to do it.'

'And you placed both of those items in that room.' Reynolds nodded again. 'Then what did you do?'

'I wrote the details in this book, then left it with whoever was on duty.'

'You never went into that room again?'

'No, Sarge.'

'And, as you left it, you locked the door?'

'Yes . . .' A wave of colour rushed the young face. '. . . I'm pretty sure I did.'

Watts was not surprised at the young officer's uncertainty. Locking a door was such an automatic action, it was unlikely that Reynolds would specifically remember doing it. Which meant that there was still a problem. A big one. If Reynolds had not locked that door, it created multiple possibilities as to what might have happened to the tape and neither Watts nor any of his officers had the time to chase them up and probably not get a definitive answer. And that was only the half of it.

'OK. Get back to what you were doing.'

'Sir.'

He watched Reynolds go, knowing that he should alert Brophy to a potential chain-of-evidence issue. He also knew that he wouldn't. Not yet, anyway. Reynolds was young, thrilled to be part of the investigation and he needed the experience. What Reynolds could do without was Brophy getting onto him just as he was starting to feel his feet. It was a grey area, anyway. It was very possible Reynolds had locked that door. Trouble was, Brophy didn't do grey. The tape might turn up. Hard on that thought, came Brophy's likely reaction to evidence 'turning up'. It was similar to Watts' own: it meant a potential compromise of evidence which applied not only to the Peters investigation but all others represented by exhibits in that room. He looked up to see Julian coming inside.

'Just the person. Are you busy, Jules?'

'I was. I've just made a third phone call to Manchester requesting the information we've already asked for and I'm hoping it will arrive in the next hour or so. Why?'

Watts eyed him as he sat.

'You all right?'

'I'm fine, apart from having a head cold and the temperature already hitting twenty-four degrees when I left the site an hour or so ago. You want me to do something?'

'Yes. I've formally requested CCTV recordings from the Forestry Commission of roads within a one-mile radius of the Brampton site. I'm expecting that information sometime today. When it arrives, I want you to start going through it, looking for youngish, dark-haired males on foot around that area, plus vehicles moving around it or parked.'

'I'll do it,' Julian said, looking doubtful. 'But three years is a long time to keep recordings and I didn't notice cameras anywhere close to the site.'

'I still want you to go through whatever they do send. Recordings sometimes escape being used again and we all know about killers revisiting a scene. Let me know what you come up with.'

'I'll get onto it as soon as it arrives.'

'Good lad. I want you to make a note of anything you think might be relevant.' He paused. 'Do you remember logging the black masking tape into the Exhibits Room?'

'Yes, why?'

'Just asking.' Julian turned to leave. 'Hang on a minute, Jules. Have a seat.' Watts regarded him. He didn't look his usual self.

'Early days I know, but how's it going here for you, generally?'

Julian bowed his head, ran a hand over his short, blond hair. They made eye contact.

'You've heard something.'

'Yes. You and Ade Jones facing each other up.' Julian sighed, sat back.

'It's— Jones said something about Chloe which I didn't like.'

'And?'

'I don't know . . .' He shrugged. 'After the Manchester investigation I was very keen to be part of this one. I hadn't realized it, but I think I lost confidence while I was part of the one up there.' He looked up at Watts. 'I never really was a part of it, you know.'

He shrugged, got to his feet.

'That's about it. I'll try and be more chilled out now I'm here. If it's OK with you, I'll take some stuff back to the apartment to go through.'

'You do that, son.'

He watched him go. When Miller had told him about the scene in the incident room, he had had trouble visualizing it, let alone believing it, yet he trusted Miller. Boulter came into his head. Watts' face hardened. His own limited contact with the man made it easy to visualize him having a negative reaction to Julian. He thought of asking Traynor's advice, got out his phone, tapped his number, almost immediately stopped the call. If Julian found out what he had been about to do, he wouldn't be happy about it. And, anyway, he didn't need Watts or anybody fighting his corner for him. He was an adult now. Manchester had provided him with what was probably his first bad experience of police work. It had knocked his confidence. He had to find his own way to get over it. Watts decided he'd keep an eye on him. And on Jones. The desk phone rang. He reached for it.

'Yeah?'

'Sarge, a woman is in reception, wanting to report an unknown male in a car who engaged her two young daughters in conversation as they walked along a road close to where they live. She's got the daughters with her—'

'Pass it to somebody who's not part of the Peters' investigation.'

'I think you might want to talk to her yourself, Sarge. From what she's said, the incident happened very close to the Forestry Commission site.'

Watts thought about it.

'I'll come down.'

He headed for the door as Judd came inside.

'Morning, Sarge—'

'With me, Judd. Bring three witness statement forms, in case we need them.'

NINE

'Where are they?' he asked the female civilian worker on desk duty.

'A slow turn to your left and you'll see them. A

woman and two teenage girls.' She indicated towards them, her voice low. He glanced round, then back.

'We'll talk to them in the small interview room.' He went to it and stepped inside, Judd at his heels.

'Something happened, Sarge?' He gave an almost imperceptible nod towards the waiting woman in the reception area.

'She's here to report an adult male in a car accosting her two daughters late yesterday afternoon.'

'Low-life. Why us?'

'Because of where it happened on a road very close to the Forestry Commission site.' Judd looked across at them sharply. 'I want to hear what they've got to tell us about it.'

'You think it might be connected to the Peters investigation?'

'No idea, but if it is, he's totally reckless, which isn't the impression I've got of him.'

'Or, he's got massive mental health issues.'

'We're here to establish that it's irrelevant to the Brampton site, following which we hand it to somebody else to follow up.' He glanced again at the woman and the two young girls.

'I'll lead. We take it nice and casual, listen with our ordinary faces on to what the mother's got to say. I want you to talk to the daughters. I'll go and fetch them.'

Judd watched as he spoke to the mother, saw her and her daughters stand, follow him to the room and inside. All three were strikingly similar, all very attractive with long dark hair. Once they were seated, Watts turned to the mother, his tone relaxed yet business-like.

'We appreciate you coming in to talk to us. I'm Detective Chief Inspector Bernard Watts. This is Police Constable Chloe Judd,' Judd nodded to them.

'Constable Judd has the fastest pen so she's going to take some notes, starting with your names.' Pen poised Judd sent them a smile. The mother was still looking anxious but returned the smile. Judd noted white, even teeth.

'I'm Alicia Fielding. These are my daughters, Olivia, who's almost eighteen, and Mia, who is thirteen.' Watts nodded to them.

'Mrs Fielding, did you witness this incident yourself?' Her smile faded.

'No, but I trust what my daughters have told me.'

'How about you set the scene as it were? Tell us what you do know?'

Judd began some swift, detailed notetaking. At ten past six the previous evening, getting on for dusk, the younger of the daughters had asked to go to a local shop a short distance from the family's house. Olivia was on exam study leave, had worked hard most of the day and their mother suggested the girls go to the shop together. She looked at Watts, emphasizing the shortness of the distance from their house to the shop and the likely presence of at least one or two neighbours in their front gardens, even at that hour. On the girls' return, she said she had been shocked on hearing her daughters' accounts of a man in a car stopping to talk to them. She had quickly decided that the police should know about it and had called the local station, following which she was advised to report it to headquarters.

Watts gave Judd a swift glance, guessing that her thinking was much the same as his: somebody at that station had made the geographical link between what was being reported by the mother and the ongoing murder investigation in that area.

'We appreciate you reporting it,' said Watts. 'I'm hoping that with PC Judd's help, Olivia and Mia can tell us everything that happened from the time they left the house.' Both girls smiled at Judd, who smiled back at them. More white teeth.

'DCI Watts has introduced me but in case it was a lot to take in, my name is Chloe. What we'd like now is for one of you to describe to us exactly what happened in your own words.' Olivia raised her hand.

'I'll do that.'

'What about *me*?'

Olivia grinned at her young sister.

'You can listen to what I say and if I forget something you can say it.' She looked back to Judd.

'We walked to the shop together. Mia wanted ice cream and I needed a pen. Like Mom just said, it's not far from our house. We bought what we wanted and started walking back to the house. That's when I heard a car coming along. It was behind us. It's not a busy road—'

'I heard it too!'

Olivia smiled, eye-rolled.

'We were eating ice cream and just walking along and talking, and it passed by then stopped a short way ahead of us.' She suddenly faltered. Judd nodded encouragement. 'We had to walk past it to get home. We didn't think anything of it, actually. We just carried on walking. When we got level with it, the driver called to us.'

'Where was he when he called to you?'

'Still inside the car.'

'How did he do that, Olivia?'

'The passenger window went down and he kind of leant across the passenger seat towards us—'

'He had a moustache.'

'*Mia.*'

'He did!' Judd smiled.

'OK, let's see if I've got it right. This man has stopped his car and he's leant across the passenger seat to the open window to speak to you through that window.' Olivia nodded. 'What happened next?'

'He asked us for directions to Canterbury Road. I told him, there isn't one and he said, "Show me."' Judd's interest piqued, knowing Sarge had to be feeling the same.

'He asked you to *show* him the location of a road you had already told him didn't exist?'

Olivia pushed back her hair.

'Yes. It didn't make sense. He was talking really quickly, like he was in a rush or something. He'd got a big map and it was unfolded and he was pointing to it, and that's when – I don't know, I suddenly felt something wasn't right. Mia had gone closer to the car and—'

'Only a *bit* closer.'

'He, kind of, gestured to the passenger door, as if to say "Get in" and I pulled her back. Then we ran for home. When we got in, I told Mom because she's always going on about what to do and not to do when we're out and about.'

'You hear some worrying things, so I do warn them to be cautious.' Mrs Fielding looked at Judd, then Watts, for validation.

Judd focused on the girls.

'Did you see anyone, any cars, on your way to the shop?'

'No,' said Olivia. Mia shook her head.

'You didn't see this man's car at all when you were walking there?'

'No.'

'Was there anyone inside the shop when you arrived?'

'Only the man who owns it.' Olivia looked at her mother. 'What's his name again?'

'Bill Robson. He's owned that shop for years. He's a near neighbour of ours.'

'What about houses on the other side of the road you were walking along?'

Olivia shook her head.

'There aren't any. There's just a fence and some trees along the road and after that it's—'

'Just grass and stuff,' said Mia, 'and a *really* steep hill and we go to the top where there's like loads of trees and we sledge down when there's snow.' Judd didn't need to look at Sarge to know where his thinking was going. Her sister frowned.

'They don't need to know that kind of stuff, Mia.'

'Can you describe what this man's car looked like?' Judd asked. They looked at each other, then back to Judd.

'It was small,' said Mia. 'Dark red.'

'It was a Mini,' said Olivia. Judd wrote quickly.

'Was there anything in particular that you noticed about it?'

They looked at each other again, responded in unison. 'No.'

'Olivia, let's go back to when this man spoke to you. You said you felt uneasy.' Olivia nodded. 'Could you give us some idea why you felt like that?'

'It's hard to put into words—'

'It was the *map*.' Judd smiled at the younger sister.

'The map?'

'Yes. He, sort of, waved it and held it at the window, like he wanted us to go up really close to look at it, but why did he want us to do that?' Tension spiked inside the small room. 'He'd already asked for directions to the road and Olivia had told him it didn't exist. He had the map, so obviously he'd looked at it and seen it wasn't there, so why was he still asking about it?' Seconds slid by. 'I thought he was weird.'

'Can you describe this man for us?' asked Judd. 'Olivia?'

'Not young,' said Olivia. 'Probably in his late twenties, maybe, thirty-ish, something like that, with dark hair. I'm not sure about anything else. Like Mia said, he had a moustache. I can't describe his clothes. I didn't see them.'

'He had some kind of light-coloured coat on,' said Mia. 'I just saw the collar and sleeves.'

'When he spoke, did you notice anything about his voice?' The two girls exchanged glances, shook their heads.

'Did he sound like he was local?'

'I'm not sure,' said Olivia, frowning. 'He just spoke quietly.'

The statements completed and having shown Mrs Fielding and her daughters out, Judd returned to the interview room.

'That young Mia is a bright spark,' said Watts.

'She is, and you're thinking the same as me.' Getting no response, she added, 'The elder sister in particular looks like the Manchester victims.'

'I've already said, that's how a lot of young females look—'

'Oh, come *on*, Sarge. A bloke in a car, up to no good and *where*? Just the other side of the Forestry Commission land. He's already abducted young women in Manchester and he knows his way around the West Midlands.' She looked down at the notes she had made.

'He needs finding, whoever he is. If he *is* anything to do with our investigation, he must have confidence to spare. He wanted both girls inside that car, yet how the *hell* did he think he was going to control them, once he had them?' She looked across at him. 'It doesn't bear thinking about, but was he going to use one as a sort of hostage so he could get the other to do whatever he said?'

Watts was on his feet.

'I want to see exactly where this happened.'

They went up to the near-deserted incident room, brought the map onto the smartboard, Judd quickly locating the road along which Olivia Fielding and her sister had encountered the man in the dark red Mini.

'This is where the shop is and around here is where the Fielding family lives. Remember what they said about a fence, trees along the opposite side of the road, a steep hill?' Judd ran her finger along the road, then upwards, over an expanse of space to a heavily wooded area. She looked up at him, whispered, 'It's no distance away, Sarge.'

'I see it.'

'What if it was him?

'"Him", who?'

'You *know* who. The dark-haired male on the Manchester CCTV footage.'

Watts moved from the smartboard.

'You mean the bloke Traynor has described as clever? If he has got all his chairs upstairs, why would he risk trying to pick up young females barely a mile from where he left Amy Peters and within close proximity to a full-on police investigation?' He paused. 'And while you're looking for an answer, try guessing how many dark-haired males there are in Manchester, add it to the number you think we've got down here and let me know what you come up with.'

'You're saying there's zero connection.'

'I'm considering what we've been told and not rushing to connections and conclusions.'

Judd looked up as Julian came into the incident room.

'Hi, Jules. You look like you've had enough.'

'It's just the start of a cold.' He shrugged, smiled. And to Watts, 'I'm still waiting on the case data from Manchester, but I've been through every single bit of Forestry Commission CCTV footage from around that site. Not that there's much.' He sat heavily. 'I checked further than the one-mile radius. Still nothing. It's not an area that attracts people, but if you want, I'll go through it again with Josie in case I missed something—' Watts was on his feet.

'No need. I know you're thorough.' Judd and Julian watched as Watts left the room. Julian looked at her, brows raised. She shook her head.

'He's starting to feel the pressure of the case and now he's got a woman local to that area whose two young daughters have reported a man trying to entice them into his car.' He stared at her.

'You're not serious?'

'I am. It might be completely unrelated but I've got a feeling about it.' She smiled at him. 'I've also got some paracetamol in my bag. You look like you could use a couple.'

He held out his hand.

'OK, Nurse Chloe.' She grinned, took the pack from her bag and held it out to him. He took it, his hand brushing hers. Her phone buzzed in her pocket. She took it out, read the text.

'Sarge, telling me to stop nattering and get down to his office. I'd better go.'

She found him going through search data relating to the site. He looked up at her.

'Remember the dog-walking farm manager, who reported finding Amy Peters' remains? It says here that one of the officers at the scene that morning thought he saw him using his phone to take pictures barely a couple of metres from the remains—'

'No!'

'—and he data-checked him. He's got form for violence against a female partner.'

'Where is he now?'

'Jonesy and Kumar are bringing him in.' He glanced at his watch. 'They'll be here in twenty minutes.'

Judd got busy typing up her notes of the Fieldings' account of the man who accosted the two sisters. She watched words fill the page, shook her head.

'The world is full of perverts.'

The click-clack of computer keys started up again. Watts watched her, his own fingers tracking the lines on his forehead.

'This case just goes on and on and what am I doing? Sitting here, waiting for something solid that'll really progress it.' He looked across at Judd, fingers flying. 'I doubt a farmworker with a dog will do it. What I want is a real lead.'

'We've been on this case no time.'

'I'm not letting this investigation go the same way as Manchester's. I'm thinking about all the theoretical stuff Will has given us. That's the kind of detail that could well help us unravel the case if we stay sharp.' He sat back. 'I've just thought of something one of my old grannies used to say: *Keep your eyes to business, Bernard. Eyes to business!*' The typing continued without pause.

'What's that mean?'

'It means, we stay focused on all that we *see*, and whatever turns up to be read.'

Judd glanced up at him.

'This wouldn't be the old granny who told you you'd never amount to anything because you were short when you were ten? *Rude* is what that is, *and* she was no judge of anything, if you want my opinion.' He nodded.

'I was already five foot eleven at fourteen but I think she had a point—' The desk phone rang. He answered it.

'We're on our way.' And to Judd, 'The farm manager has arrived.'

TEN

Same day. Noon.

Watts was seated sideways, face averted from the man sitting across the table from him. Fincher interested Watts but he was having trouble seeing him as a five-times killer with a sound knowledge of Manchester and the social smoothness to abduct young women. Yet he knew cases where individuals who turned out to be guilty were initially ruled out for not fitting expectations, one or two going on to kill again. Hadn't Traynor said that they wouldn't know this killer if his immediate situation wasn't rattling him.

'Again.'

The man sighed.

'I've *told* you. I started early, took the dog, walked from where I live to that place, found what you know I found and reported it. If I'd known it would cause me this much hassle, I'd have kept my mouth shut and gone straight home.'

Watts slow-nodded.

'Why were you out so early?'

Fincher rolled his eyes.

'You know all of this. I manage one of the farms near there. I know that whole area well and—'

'Tell us what you did there that morning.'

'What are you getting at?' Fincher's face hardened. He looked from Watts to Judd who was swiftly writing. He pointed. 'What's *she* up to?'

Watts turned on his chair, faced him. His initial impression of Fincher had been that of a typical agricultural worker, a bit rough around the edges. His eyes moved slowly over him. He wasn't that rough. Yes, his clothes were well-worn, what you might expect from what he did for a living, but the jacket he had on was a Barbour, the rest of his clothes worn-looking but of good quality. It was obvious from being in the room with him for the last ten minutes or so that he was clean, as was his dark, longish hair.

Watts' eyes moved over the weathered face, beginning to question his original age estimate of fifty.

'Answer the question. What did you do there?'

Fincher avoided Watts' gaze.

'I don't like your tone.'

'Not many people do. I don't care. Tell me every single thing *you* did at *that* site *that* morning. *All* of it.' Fincher looked petulant.

'Is this a police state? I took the dog out for its morning walk, got to that place, saw what I saw and reported it, there and then. End of story.'

'Was that the only time you used your phone.'

'Yes.'

Inside his head, Watts was doing a steady count. He reached twenty.

'You're *really* starting to irritate me, Fincher. You used your phone more than once.'

'Who says?'

'One of my officers.'

'He's a liar.'

'There is a liar in all of this and I'm looking at him.' Fincher transferred his gaze to Judd, his eyes narrowing.

'I've got a farm to run. I don't have time for sitting about here being accused of stuff I know nothing about!' Judd held his gaze. He looked away. 'All I did was help the police, or so I thought, and now all this!'

'Have you always been so helpful to the police?'

Fincher's attention was fixed on the table between them.

'I don't know what you're getting at. I don't have anything to do with the police—'

Judd slid a sheet of paper across the table towards him. He looked at it, looked at her, his face reddening.

'Got anything to say about that?' asked Watts. Fincher said nothing. Watts reached for it.

'Let's have a look, shall we?' He nodded. 'Interesting. Three callouts to your place last year from your wife—'

'Common law,' snapped Fincher.

'—the first reporting that you had hit her on the head with a heavy soup ladle, the second that you had attempted to strangle her and the third that you threatened her with a billhook.' He glanced at Judd.

'A type of scythe, small, hand-held, nasty-looking. What do you say, Mr Fincher?'

'I say it was none of the police's business then and it *still* isn't. Did she press charges? No. she *didn't*, because she's a liar.'

'Is she still living with you?'

'No.' After a few seconds' silence, he said, 'She lives the other side of Brampton.'

'Give me her contact details.' Watts waited as Judd wrote them down, then asked, 'Got your phone with you?' He waited out the short silence. 'On the table now, or I arrest you.'

The only sound in the room was Fincher's heavy breathing. He reached into his jacket pocket, pulled out the phone, put it on the table.

'See?' said Watts. 'There's always an easy way for most things.' He pointed to it. 'Show me the photos.'

'. . . What?'

'You heard. You used that phone to take pictures at the Forestry Commission site. I want to know what got your interest. Show me.' He waited out more silence. 'I'm not known for my patience and it's *fast* running out.'

Fincher gave him an evaluative look.

'I took a couple of photos, so what? I was hoping to sell them to the papers. The press is all over what's going on there.'

'Get any takers?'

'I haven't had a chance, have I?'

'I want to see them.'

Fincher reached for the phone, dragged it towards him, tapped it. Watts took it from him, looked at two photographs of the spot where Amy Peters' hard-to-make-out remains were, unless you knew what you were looking at. He swiped the screen again, then again, held it up, his eyes narrowing on Fincher.

'Who's this?'

Fincher gave the photograph a quick glance.

'My brother's daughter.'

'And this?'

'Same. She's with her friend.'

'You don't say.' Watts paused. 'I'm hanging on to your phone for now,' Fincher looked enraged, 'because of the photographs you took at the scene.' He gave Fincher a direct look.

'I've heard what you said about why you took the photos at the scene, yet you're also saying that since then you've not approached anybody to try and sell them. That's not making any sense to me. So, I'm still wondering why else you might have taken pictures of a crime scene.'

'That's a public place. I didn't know it was a crime scene, I don't know what you're hinting at, but I need my phone!'

'So do we, Mr Fincher. It's potential evidence. Once we've downloaded the photos and looked at anything else that's of interest, you'll get it back.'

Watts let him go, Fincher looking ill-tempered. After a brief detour to forensics to drop off the phone, Judd pushed open the door of Watts' office, looking back at him.

'He took pictures of a *crime* scene!'

'A crime scene that wasn't taped off when he was there, so we can't have him for that.'

'I would,' Judd huffed. 'Not only is he a wife-beater with shots of the location of the remains at the site, he's also got photos of two teenage females whose identities we don't know. When Adam's printed them off, I'm following that up. Find out who they are—'

'You do that and you're the one breaking the law.' It was at times like this that Judd's wilfulness bothered him. 'The photos at the scene are evidence. The others are *his* property. You know the rules as well as I do.'

'So much for focusing on the detail! You're ruling him out of this investigation?'

'What I'm not thinking right now is that he's been moving between Manchester and the West Midlands over the last three years, abducting young women.'

Judd dropped the papers she was carrying on the table, selected one.

'According to the information we have on him, he's thirty-seven, which fits Julian's age estimate for the killer and to me there's no big difference between him and the CCTV image we've got.'

Watts frowned across at her.

'What about Traynor's prediction of IQ? Fincher doesn't strike me as particularly smart, just mouthy.'

She tapped the sheet.

'Think again, Sarge. According to this, he went to grammar school, got four A levels, then went onto university.'

'And?'

She shrugged.

'He dropped out halfway through his first year.'

Watts was giving some thought to this. It didn't prove anything but neither did it rule out Fincher. He gathered together the papers spread on the table, slid them into a file and took it to one of the filing cabinets.

'We know where to find him and you've already got plenty to keep you busy.'

Same day. 5.55 p.m.

Tired as she was, the simple act of coming into her own house caused Judd's spirits to rise. Closing the door, she leant against it and listened to silence. Pushing herself away, she dropped a book of fabric samples from a high street shop inside the sitting room and headed for the kitchen, lugging a plastic bag of shopping.

Some hours later, she was cross-legged on the sitting-room rug, a plate of pizza remnants to one side. She had gone over Fincher's interview in her head until she had reluctantly come to the conclusion that Sarge was probably right. Fincher fitted some of what they knew about the case, but so probably would a lot of males.

Yawning, blinking, she reached for the fabric samples and began looking through them, pausing at one of the patterns which had caught her eye in the shop. She looked up at the large bay window. The colours were exactly what she had in mind. The woman in the shop had said that she could have them fitted within four days of placing her order. Judd looked at the reverse side of the sample: Code A. Very expensive. She shook her head. What she needed was something affordable, maybe around a Code Z—

Head up, shoulders and the backs of her arms prickling, she listened. Nothing. Shaking her head, she got up and headed for the kitchen in search of a caffeine fix. Halfway along the hall, she stopped, listened. A car door slam? A gate? She stood, uncertain. Whatever it was, it had come from the back of the house.

She stepped cautiously, reached the closed kitchen door and stood, her breathing shallow. *This is ridiculous*, she told herself. *You're dead lucky to be here, on your own, a whole house to yourself and what do you do? You get spooked*— She jumped as the sound came again, her heart thudding her chest.

Reaching for the handle of the kitchen door, she grasped it and paused. Annoyed with herself, she pushed it down and threw open the door. It swung wide, hit the inside wall. The kitchen was in darkness. She flicked on the nearby light switch, walked inside.

'See? *Nothing*. It was probably the people in the house on the other side you haven't met yet.'

She made instant coffee, took the mug back to the sitting room, telling herself to get a grip. This was her home now. She had to get used to being entirely alone here. Which was good.

'What I'll do is get a burglar alarm fitted . . . and stop talking to myself.'

She sat on the floor, took a mouthful of coffee, a sudden pounding at her front door causing the mug to jerk and spill.

'What the *hell*!'

Dennis was standing on the other side of the bay window. She went into the hall and on to the front door, thinking of something else she needed: a spyhole. She opened the door.

'Dennis. Were you in your back garden just now?'

'What?' He looked tired for somebody with no work, who seemed to be home much of the time.

'Doesn't matter.'

'Have you caught the news today?' he asked.

'No.' She waited. 'What news?'

'I know you're a southerner by your accent, but are you familiar with the Brampton area just over the city boundary?' She wasn't about to tell him anything.

'No.'

He looked pleased.

'There's police crawling all over it!'

'How do you know?'

'It was on the television.' He jabbed a thumb over his shoulder. 'It'll be that lot from police headquarters. A dead woman's been found there.'

Judd saw something that looked like excitement on his usually bland face. He looked past her into the hall. She made a counter-move sideways.

'I expect the police are keeping it hush-hush. I'm just going out but I thought I'd knock on your door as a concerned neighbour to tell you about it. Make sure you're all right. Tell you to keep your doors locked. It's a few miles away, but if some lunatic is on the loose, you can't be too careful, a young woman like you, on her own and,' his eyes drifted to her and away, 'on the small side.'

It crossed Judd's mind to ask if he thought that a knock on her door at almost nine thirty p.m. with this kind of news, plus his personal observations, would be reassuring to most lone women, small or otherwise. She reminded herself that she wasn't 'most women'. She had several karate moves which could render him or any other man into a senseless heap on the brick path on which he was standing. Possibly.

'That's nice of you, Dennis. I'm fine. I can take care of myself.' She relented. 'But knowing that you're just the other side of the wall is . . . something.' He nodded, pushing back his lank hair.

'You can count on me.'

Before she could respond, he was off. She watched his odd, gangly walk as he went down the short path, walked past his car and headed across the road towards a waiting taxi. Why was he so interested in goings-on at Brampton? And where was he off to?

Closing the door, she headed for the sitting room, stopped, went back and clicked the lock.

ELEVEN

Friday, 12 April. 4.50 a.m.

Watts surfaced, dispersing images of an infinite number of keys and mismatched locks. Before he was fully conscious, he was on his feet, staring at Chong who was on her phone.

'Have forensics been alerted? And SOCOs? I'll be there in half an hour. No need. I'll inform him.' She ended the call, and to Watts who was already pulling on clothes.

'That was Igor. One of the officers you posted to secure the site overnight has made an arrest. Actually, that's the least of your worries.'

Thirty minutes later they left the BMW and walked onto the site, Chong diverting to a group of white-suited SOCOs, Watts to the two officers he had sent to guard the site now standing either side of a scruffy-looking male. Closing in on them, seeing the remains of a small fire nearby, he quietly swore. One of the officers came to Watts, spoke into his ear.

'When I challenged him for being here and starting a fire, he got bolshie. Threw a couple of punches at me. He's also the one that found it.' Watts glanced at the man who looked back at him. The worn face registered surprise as Watts approached.

'Mr Watts! What are you doing here—?'

'This is no social chat, Artie. Tell me what you've been up to.' Getting no response, he said, 'OK, I'll tell *you*. You've trespassed on a crime scene.'

'He also brought alcohol with him, Sarge,' whispered the officer. Artie looked outraged.

'I didn't know it was a crime scene! How was I supposed to know?'

'Shut up and come over here.' Watts took him by the arm, led him a few steps, turned to face him. Realizing that Judd wasn't here, he gestured to the arresting officer. 'Get ready to take some notes. OK, Artie. I don't want any of your buggering about. Let's hear it.'

'Mr Watts—'

'That's Detective Chief Inspector Watts to *you*,' snapped the officer.

'All right, keep your hair on!' Artie looked up at Watts. 'You know *me*, yeah?'

'Unfortunately.' Watts looked at the reddened eyes, the whiskered face. 'Last I heard, you were off it.'

'I *am* . . . but it was bloody hot at my place, what with all this global warming, and I just fancied a cold beer—'

'How'd you get here?'

'I parked way over in that direction then walked.'

Artie, true to form. Not a planner of anything, including his conversations with law enforcement. Watts turned to the officer. 'Breathalyse him.'

'*Yes*, Sarge!' The officer shot Artie a triumphant look.

'Oh, come on!' Artie was looking put-upon. 'It was only—'

Watts held up his hand, stopping the flow of words. The officer was back with the breathalyser kit. A couple of minutes later, he was holding it towards Watts.

'It's nudging, Sarge,' he whispered. 'If we hang on a bit—'

'I want to look at what he found.'

'It's over there.' They started walking, Watts pointing at Artie who was also on the move.

'You! Stay put.'

'Where am *I* going? He's got my bloody keys!'

With a warning look, Watts got out his phone, waited, spoke a few terse words into it, then followed the officer to where Chong and specialist workers were grouped around a small area. Reaching them, he crouched, his eyes moving over several large stones, similar to those he had seen around Artie's fire. He still almost missed it.

One of the SOCOs activated a hand-held light. Lowering his face, Watts followed the twisting, snagging loops through flourishing undergrowth and between stones. Hair. Long. Dark. He looked up to see a couple of SOCOs heading in his direction with cameras.

'This could take a while,' said Chong quietly. She spoke to the SOCOs.

'Synchronized record-and-recover is what's needed so let's get started.'

Watts took out his notebook, walked back to where Artie was waiting.

'I want all of it.'

Artie's eyes slide away from him.

'I don't know nothing.'

Watts reddened.

'In which case, I'm glad to hear you know *something*. Tell me what you *saw* and everything you *did*. Now!' Artie shifted from foot to foot, glancing to where the action now was.

'I've left a half a bottle of beer where they're standing and there's no law says I can't be here. It was getting a bit nippy earlier, so I decided to get a fire going. Just a small one.' He pointed. 'I could see some stones down there where the ground slopes away so I went and fetched a couple.' Watts looked at Artie's now-defunct fire, counted seven stones. His eyes moving to Artie's skinny frame.

'That took you two journeys at least.' Artie glanced upwards, eyes drifting over fir trees looming to one side of them.

'I did it, quick-like, no lingering. There's something about this place after dark. I wanted some warmth, some light, so I just took the stones and brought 'em up here where it's a bit flat. All this unseasonal weather we've been having, I didn't want to start no wildfire, did I?'

'Very public spirited. Get to what you saw down there.' Alerted by movement some way off, Watts glanced in its direction. Judd had arrived.

'It was nothing,' said Artie. 'Just some stuff, like. I couldn't see very well in the dark.'

'Did you touch it?' Artie looked back to where SOCOs were working, his mouth twisting in disgust.

'. . . My hand just skimmed it. It felt soft. Like fur but cold. That's when I got my lighter out. Had a look.'

'What did that tell you?'

'Nothing. I've got better things to do with my time—'

'Than *thinking* apparently!' Watts' eyes were fixed on his. 'What *you* did was expose human remains.'

Artie's face rearranged itself into a look of revulsion.

'But you never mentioned it to the two officers on guard here. When did your single-digit brain cells tell you it was something you'd better keep to *yourself*?' Judd was nearby, she'd taken over notetaking. With a glance at her, Watts stepped closer to Artie who was now looking jumpy.

'Tell me what else you saw.' Artie violently shook his head, a puppet on speed.

'I never saw nothing, honest. I never said I saw anything. Did I say I—'

'Shut *up*!' Watts fixed his eyes on him. 'I say you did— and *don't* start shaking your head. I've been in this job long enough to know when somebody's stringing me along, which in your case is every time you open your bloody mouth!'

Artie clamped his lips together.

'Try it again. What did you *see*?'

'Just some bloke.'

'What bloke? Doing what?'

'I dunno! What d'you think I am, a mind-reader?'

Watts closed in, towering over him, index finger raised to Artie's face.

'If you were, you'd know that you're one minute away from being arrested and on your way to headquarters. Tell me what you saw!'

'*All right* . . . all right. It was nothing.' He pointed to higher ground. 'Just somebody moving about up there.'

'And?'

'And what?'

'You're *really* starting to get on my nerves. What did he *look* like? What was he *doing*?'

'He wasn't doing nothing, just walking up to them trees there—'

'*Description.*'

'It was just a bloke—'

'Hair colour?'

'So, now I'm a bloody hairdresser?' He flinched as Watts' face came closer.

'Wearing?'

'It was too dark to see! He might have had something dark covering his head. A hoodie or something. When I first saw him, I wondered what he was up to and I decided to get off home, which is when that stroppy bastard came from nowhere—'

'One of my officers.'

'All the "big-I-am"!' Artie straightened, pulling together shreds of dignity. 'I told him about the stuff I'd seen over there by the other stones.'

'To deflect attention from your drinking. You didn't tell him you'd seen somebody here.'

'That bloke had cleared off by then. I was trying to be helpful.'

'Course you were.' Watts studied the worn face. 'What else?' Artie's eyes darted in the direction of the dense trees above them.

'I didn't see nothing else.'

Watts was weighing the benefits of taking a statement from him now, or waiting until the alcohol had dispersed and he was clear-headed. Artie and clear-headed didn't coincide often. He pointed at him.

'When you've told PC Judd here all you know, and I mean *all* of it, you can clear off.' Watts headed away, Artie's voice following.

'Tell that stroppy bastard to give me my keys!'

Watts turned, his temper rising.

'You're probably over the bloody limit now so you're not driving anywhere! Unless you want to be arrested again!'

'How am I going to get home then?'

Watts did a count of ten.

'That's your problem. Get that layabout son of yours to come and pick you up. He's never had a job, so he'll have nothing pressing on.' Giving a nod to Judd, he turned away, seeing Artie's face change to a mix of umbrage and pride.

'That's where you're wrong. He's on the council now.'

Watts stopped, looked back at him.

'Your Dwayne? On the council? He's never had any interest in politics. Or, anything else so far as I recall.'

'. . . Politics?' Artie was slow-processing Watts' words. 'What's politics got to do with it? Our Dwayne's on the *council*. He works on the *bins*.'

Watts' head dropped forward. He rubbed his face.

'Jesus wept.'

Artie's voice trailed after him on the still night air as Judd began questioning him.

Watts headed to where activity was building, powerful lights now up, illuminating the ground. Among the stones and thick vegetation, the tangled swatch of dark hair was easily visible, still secured within the earth. He recalled the photographs of the missing women. There was only one victim with hair that long, that dark. He watched the careful process of freeing it get underway. About twenty minutes later, Judd arrived at his side.

'Get anything from him?'

'Only what he'd already said.' She glanced back to Artie. 'Want me to check him out?'

'You'll find nothing but alcohol-related, plus a couple of fights over the years, both times coming off worst. After a few beers, he thinks he's Charles Atlas.'

'. . . Charles Who?'

Watts' eyes were moving over the extensive site, preoccupied by the small number of officers he had available to guard it. Recalling the brief upward glance Artie had sent to the mass of trees, he looked towards them, now seeing the first hints of sunrise.

'Stay here.'

Leaving Judd observing the recovery of the hair by forensic officers, he started up the steep hill towards the trees, covering the distance in long strides. Reaching what looked like a solid wall of bark and branches, he took a Maglite from an inside pocket, switched it on. The single beam drilled the dimness, moved over thick trunks and low branches as he made his way into them. Artie had seen something up here.

Ducking his head, pushing aside one branch then another, the close proximity of so many trees claustrophobic, limiting his vision despite the Maglite, he moved slowly forward, the slim beam bobbing ahead of him. A low rustling somewhere to his left brought him to a stop. He turned at another rustle on his other side, breathed, moved forward, reached a small clearing, the beam drilling tall ferns and brackens, feeling snags on his sleeves. Pressed by nature on all sides, he tensed at a sudden, rhythmic sound some distance ahead. Something, somebody was moving. Fast.

'Stop! *Police!*'

He followed the sound, his heart banging his chest. After several yards of whipping branches and pine needles hitting his face, he stopped, listened. Probably some animal or other he'd rather not know about. Gone, now. Retracing his steps to the small clearing, he slowed at the tiny pinpoints of light coming back at him. Reaching them, the slim torch clamped between his teeth, he got latex gloves from his pocket, put them on, reached down among the bracken and ferns and gently lifted it free.

Same day. 7.45 a.m.

Julian glanced up as Watts came into his office followed by Judd, a double-take bringing him to his feet.

'What's *happened*?' He pointed at his own face. 'You've got some blood just here and around here—' Judd shrugged off her jacket.

'He thinks he's Somebody Atlas—'

'Coffee, Judd.' Watts sat down. She sent him an irritable look. 'I'm always making it.'

'I'll do it,' said Julian.

'Easy, lad.' And to Judd, 'Three sugars, fat milk, and whatever Julian wants.' He rubbed his face, winced, gently ran his fingers over his forehead.

'I was called to the scene early this morning. An idiot I happen to know had decided to spend some dark downtime there with a campfire and some booze. He got more than he bargained for.' Julian stared at him, waiting. 'We've located more remains.'

'No!'

'I think he saw something, but he's a waste of time as a witness.' Judd set down two mugs of black coffee between them, looked at Julian.

'He hasn't yet told you why he's looking like Freddy Kruger—'

'*Fat* milk!'

She fetched the plastic container, dumped it next to him. Julian was still staring at him.

'Come on, Bernard. What happened?'

Watts poured milk, took a mouthful of coffee, swallowed, reached inside his jacket, pulled out a plastic bag and laid it on the table. Julian looked down at it then up at Watts.

'What is it?'

'A scarf,' said Judd. 'He heard movement among trees above the scene and went to have a look, which is why he's such a mess.' Julian looked to Watts.

'Did you stop whoever—?'

'No, he didn't.' Judd pulled the plastic bag taut.

'But he did get this. See? It's got small gold stars all over it. He's hoping that it might be connected to one of the victims but there's no reference to a scarf in the data we've got so far.' Watts took the plastic bag from her.

'Now you know why I keep Judd here: she knows every thought I have, every move I make and, best of all, she explains it all so I don't have to.'

'Oh, tee *hee*.'

'A lengthy of human hair has been found at the site. I'm waiting for a call from Dr Chong about it.'

Hearing the formality, Judd glanced across at Julian, wondering if he was aware of the relationship between Watts and the pathologist, an open secret at headquarters. The phone rang. She watched him reach for it, absorbing the details of the one-sided conversation with Ray Boulter, SIO of the Manchester investigation, heard Watts' request for all of the information available relating to Amy Peters, plus the other victims.

'Ray, was there ever a reference to a pale-coloured scarf covered in gold stars? Or any scarf, for that matter.' After five more minutes, he replaced the phone.

'No scarf.' He looked at Julian. 'What's your view of Boulter as SIO?'

Julian gave it some thought.

'I didn't work on the Manchester investigation for that long but it seemed to me Boulter was probably out of his depth from day one.'

'And what you ended up with was an investigation which took months to realize that all of these five victims had been abducted.'

Julian frowned.

'I wouldn't put it that strongly, Bernard. Each of them was followed up. It was more the time it took to establish what had probably happened to them, that they *had* probably been abducted. There were no witnesses—'

'None that Manchester ever found,' snapped Watts.

'You're right about a general lack of focus, but that's easy for somebody like me to say because I didn't have Boulter's level of responsibility. I think he, that whole team, was overwhelmed once it was evident that all five had disappeared. From that point on, it never got any better.'

'I'm hoping you'll be as generous about me, as and when this investigation plays itself out.' Julian stood.

'I'm going to the incident room to see if anything's come in since yesterday.' Judd was on her feet.

'Anything you need me to do, Sarge?' He slid the plastic bag towards her.

'Check the scarf in with forensics. Fill in the when-where-what form while you're there.'

It was just after five when Traynor arrived and the call finally came from the pathology suite. Igor let them in. Amid the steady hum of extractor fans, they joined Chong at the examination table.

'Got an ID confirmation for us?' asked Watts. Chong nodded.

'So far, I've conducted only a superficial examination, but yes. It's Erica Trent.'

They stood either side of the earth-stained bones, Traynor his arms folded, his eyes methodically taking in the remains, Julian gazing down, his facial expression remote. Judd was lost in thought. They already had the remains of Amy Peters, the first of the Manchester victims. Now, they had those of the fifth. Which had to mean that victims two, three and four were located somewhere at that site. Which meant the whole case was now theirs.

Watts rolled his shoulders, trying to shift knots of tension, his eyes fixed on the bones. He had to have more officers. Not just to guard the whole godforsaken site but to search every single mound, dip, slope and gully to find what else it was holding onto. His eyes moved over the skeleton. There was a lot more to see than there had been for Amy Peters. Chong was pointing out various aspects of what was lying in front of them and he focused on what she was saying.

'Erica Trent's disappearance was comparatively recent: November 2018. That, plus the fact that her killer provided her with a semblance of a burial has given us more to work with. Note the very limited areas of remaining flesh here, here and . . . here.' She pointed, and moved to the head of the examination table. They followed. She lifted the skull with both hands, carefully rotated it.

'See? It's intact. No damage. I'll do all possible to establish a cause of death but it's not going to be easy.'

Watts glanced at the luxuriant swatch of dark hair lying nearby, thinking of the Trent family which had raised a clever daughter, seen her off to university, no doubt with pride similar to that which Watts and his wife had felt, years before when their daughter went to Oxford. He closed his eyes against the waste of it all. Chong's voice came again.

'My full report won't be available until sometime tomorrow at the earliest. What do you know about her, Julian?' He blinked at her.

'Sorry, this is just awful to see . . .' He flipped pages of a hardcover notebook, became neutral once more. 'I requested an investigative update from Manchester two days ago and got confirmation by phone late yesterday that there's been nothing new to report since the time Erica disappeared,' he turned more pages, 'but I have the notes I made from when I was still involved, which merely confirm what we already know. Erica had a tutorial on the evening of Monday, 12 November. It lasted approximately forty-five minutes. She left at around seven p.m. According to the tutor, Erica wasn't explicit about any plans she had for that evening, but her impression was that she intended to return to her bedsit on the edge of the campus.' His eyes roved over the page.

'No one at the shared house recalled seeing Erica during that evening and there were no sightings of her during the following two days. Her parents were contacted by the student welfare service at the university. They confirmed that Erica wasn't with them and that they hadn't seen or heard from her. They described their daughter as a very reliable person,' he looked up, 'which confirmed the faculty's views of her. They knew of no plans she might have had or where she might have gone. The tutor I mentioned earlier described Erica's mood as consistent with her usual presentation.' He closed the notebook. 'As I say, it merely confirms what we know.'

'Confirmation is good,' murmured Watts.

'Did the tutor provide the police with a description of Erica?' Judd asked.

Julian searched his notes.

'Erica Trent, five foot eight tall, slim build . . . here it is: wearing a heavy, dark blue jumper, black trousers or leggings, she wasn't sure which, possibly boots and a long black coat, oh, and a bookbag containing textbooks, notes and personal effects. No handbag.'

'She didn't mention anything else? A scarf?' He shook his head.

'No. No scarf.' He closed the notebook again.

'What were Boulter and his sidekicks doing in the days following the report that she was missing?' asked Watts. 'Did they release a description of Trent, bearing in mind that by this time they already knew there were four missing women?'

'They did. They widely distributed copies of the photo we have. I suggested a walk-through of the campus by a female officer dressed in similar clothes to those Erica was known to be wearing. It was done but produced nothing.'

Judd looked from Julian to Watts.

'Amy Peters was the first. Now we've got the last – as far as we know. Sarge, we need technical help for an in-depth search of that whole Forestry Commission site.' She watched him jab his phone.

'I'm already on it.'

'And I'll continue doing my thing,' Chong added, gazing down at the remains. 'I'll let you know if I find anything useful.'

TWELVE

Friday. Early evening.

Chong stepped away from the examination table and rotated her shoulders, added a few deep side-stretches.

'Nobody told me when I chose to specialize that forensic pathology is really tough on the back.' Igor glanced across at her.

'You're probably standing all wrong.' He raised both hands. 'Want one of my quick "magic-fingers" manipulations? Jed says it works wonders.'

'I dare say he does. I'm fine, but I appreciate the offer.'

She returned to the table, her attention on the remains taken from the refrigerated compartment for the second time that day. She reached for a sterile swab, gently applied it to one of the small areas of tissue still adhering to the skull's facial aspect, her eyes fixing on the swab's soiled surface. She reached for another, then another, repeating the process. Placing the three swabs on separate glass slides, she leant close, studied each of them in turn through a strong lens.

'Igor, remind me what we know of Erica Trent.' She heard pages being turned.

'Erica Trent, twenty years old, from Hampshire, . . . doing a combined science-maths degree . . . height, five-eight, slim build, dark hair worn long—'

'Do we have anything which indicates her general demeanour? Her physical presentation?' More pages turned.

'There are several repeats of what I just gave you, plus references to her as highly regarded by all of her tutors as extremely intelligent and committed to her studies . . . No details of her social life . . . Family members described her as serious-minded, driven to achieve.' He looked up at Chong. 'Any of that help?'

'No. Do you have a copy of her photograph there?'

'. . . Yep.' He brought it to her. 'Here you go.'

She took it from him, looked down at the young, open face, the direct grey eyes gazing back at her, the long, dark, no-nonsense hair worn straight and off the face. Her attention returned to the swabs.

'This is making no sense at all.' She turned to him. 'Question, Igor: would you describe Erica's presentation as that of a young woman who spent considerable time on her physical appearance?' He came and stood next to her, looked down at the photograph.

'You know I'm no expert on females in general, but I'd say she worked a neat, clean look, about covers it.'

He returned to his work station as Chong's attention went from the photograph to a further, close contemplation of Erica Trent's skull.

'Igor, have I told you that you are a star?'

'Not lately, no.'

'As of now,' she said quietly, 'that's exactly what you are.'

Returning to the swabs, she pulled down the strong light suspended above the table, looked at them again.

'What I'm seeing here is cosmetic in nature.'

'Sounds like Erica had a life beyond her studies, after all. Good for her.'

'Whatever that life was, her tutors weren't aware of it. According to what I have here, it involved some heavy-duty cosmetics.' She glanced across at Igor.

'There's no reference by family members to Erica participating in am-drams?'

'Nothing in what I have here.'

Chong frowned. 'I didn't think so. Following that last tutorial, there's no indication at all that Erica had a social commitment. Not even a plan for one.'

'Maybe she changed her mind? *Or*, she fancied the tutor? It happens.'

'The tutor was female, and don't give me that *Your point?* look. I haven't heard or read anything which raises those queries.' She contemplated the swabs some more.

'What I'm seeing just doesn't fit what we know.'

Igor glanced at his watch.

'And I'm getting a "late-work-evening" vibe. You want me to stay?' She grinned, shook her head.

'No. Go and have fun. I'll live vicariously through you while you're out there clubbing or whatever else you have planned.'

'Meal for one and an early night. Jed's working.'

'The early night is enviable.'
'You're sure you don't want me to stay?'
'I am. See you in the morning.'

Same day. 8.45 p.m.

Igor was long gone. The large room was now in shadow beyond the lamp throwing its white light onto Chong's desk. Having microscopically examined the swabs, she now knew what was on one of them: traces of adhesive. Wanting the whole story, she tapped the computer keys, searched for possibilities, read the text of one in particular: *full coverage cream in stick form, favoured by make-up professionals.* Another tap and the screen filled with rectangles of colour. She gazed at each of them, returned to one, shook her head.

'Erica, even the little I know about you is telling me that *this* is not your style.'

Chin supported by her hand, she considered all of the information she had. A thought came into her head. More a picture than a thought.

'That's just crazy.'

She tapped more keys, selected an image, hit *Print*, returned to an earlier screen and studied it, hearing the door open.

'What happened to the early night?'

'Had we planned one?' She grinned, not looking up.

'I thought you were Igor.'

'I was on my way home when I saw light down here.' Watts came to her, placed his big hands lightly on her shoulders and looked down at the screen.

'What're you doing?'

'Familiarizing myself with the art of theatrical cosmetics.'

'I prefer you without.'

'Only because you're totally unaware of the vast skill and expense involved in appearing to be "without".' She pointed. 'Take a look at that lipstick colour.' He peered at the screen.

'I'm looking.'

'What does it suggest to you?'

'It's . . . bold.' She grinned again.

'*That* is Scorch-Kiss. A sort of theatre-grade cream rouge.'

He looked down at her.

'This isn't anything to do with the early night you mentioned?'
'It's already gone eleven. Follow me.' He sighed.
'As always.'

She crossed the big room to the wall of refrigerated compartments. Switching on an overhead light, she selected one of them. It slid smoothly out. Watts narrowed his eyes against the remains, responding as always by turning his face slightly to one side.

'Have to say, it hasn't improved since my earlier viewing.'

'You might be about to change your mind. First, I'll bring you up to speed on what I've found on the torso. See these small areas of flesh here?' She pointed to each, looked up at him. 'It isn't easy to see, but there's evidence of bruising which suggests that Erica Trent was beaten prior to death.' He looked down at them.

'I had a case like that years back, committed by some low-life who hated women.'

'You might want to hold onto that thought while I tell you what else I know. You'll need your glasses.' She pointed to the skull, her finger moving to a tiny area of flesh clinging to one side of the eye orbit.

'It's hard to see but there's a tiny white-ish line just around there, the merest trace of adhesive.' She moved to a second minuscule area of tissue on one side of the facial area, pointed again.

'See that?' On a quick intake of breath, he lowered his face.

'. . . You mean, this bit of bright red just here?'

'Yes. That is also Scorch-Kiss.'

'From what I've seen of photos of Trent she was your plain Jane type. Not an exhibitionist, which you'd have to be to wear that.' She looked up at him.

'You are so rewarding in all kinds of ways. Prior to the attack on her, Erica Trent was wearing Scorch-Kiss lipstick, plus,' she pointed at the tiny remains of flesh within the eye orbit itself, 'false eyelashes.'

He stared at her.

'That makes even less sense than the lipstick. Where are they, the eyelashes?'

'All I have are the remnants of adhesive but it's sufficient to indicate their presence at around the time she was killed.'

'Looks like she was going out somewhere dressed to kill.'

'An appropriate, if somewhat tasteless observation.' She looked down at the remains. 'I doubt that that lipstick and the eyelashes were applied by Erica herself.' She headed for the printer. He looked down at what remained of the young woman.

'What you just said has got my skin crawling.' She came back to him carrying a printout.

'It may be about to crawl some more. See the small area of flesh on the left side, close to the temple?' He took a closer look.

'This chalky-looking area?'

She nodded.

'I've got a suspicion as to what it is but I need to be sure before I say anything further.' She glanced at the wall clock. 'It's very late. Let's go home.'

Monday, 15 April. 7.30 a.m.

Watts was in his office when Judd arrived, looking tired. She took off her jacket, dropped it on the back of her chair, searched her bag for her phone.

'Don't say it. I'll get the coffee on.'

'How do you feel about the hours you keep here, Judd?'

She shrugged.

'Big investigation, big hours. I'll carry on reading the Manchester documents we've got and adding anything which looks relevant or useful to the victimologies. I want just *one* biographical link between Peters and the other victims while they were alive, I don't care how minimal it is, and we'll be motoring—'

She studied him—.

'No offence, but you look like you've seen the cat's breakfast a second time.'

He looked down at the information he had from Chong.

'You've done some first-class work here over the last couple of years, Judd. You've seen a lot of bad things that somebody your age shouldn't see.'

'I'm twenty-one. An adult.'

'The thing is, in police work there's always going to be more of that. More bad stuff, that a young woman like you—' They looked up as the door swung open and Traynor came inside. He stopped, his eyes on them.

'You're looking serious. Has something happened?' Judd shook her head.

'Sarge is mansplaining something and I'm waiting for him to get to the point.'

Watts reached for the information he had from Chong. 'I'll get straight to it. We know that what happened to these young women was bad, but it could be a whole lot worse than we thought.'

The door swung open and Julian appeared.

'Come on, Jules. You need to hear this. Late last night, Dr Chong's examined Erica Trent's remains.' He tracked the words on the A4 in front of him. 'She's saying that Trent was beaten prior to death, but there's something else. There's evidence of high-grade, theatrical-type make-up, including thick cream rouge lipstick and adhesive from false eyelashes on small remnants of facial tissue.'

Judd's brows shot up.

'That doesn't sound like the Erica Trent I've read about. Nor does it fit the photograph we've got. She looked to me like a soap "n" water girl.'

'Dr Chong's view is that both lipstick and eyelashes were applied to Trent's face by somebody other than Trent.' Judd and Julian looked back at him, stunned. Julian was the first to speak.

'If you're saying that her killer put that stuff on her face, that's a highly deviant action.'

'He might have been trying to re-create something,' said Watts, placing a photograph on the table. 'Take a look.'

This time it was Judd who broke the silence.

'What's a Chinese woman with a white face got to do with Erica Trent?'

'Japanese,' said Traynor.

'So? I still don't get it.'

'It's geisha.' He reached for the photograph. 'Historically, women like this were entertainers, dancers. That style of physical presentation is still followed by some young Japanese women even now.'

Watts looked at him.

'One of these days, Traynor, I'll get hold of evidence that silences even you.'

'Wouldn't bank on it,' said Judd. She looked back to Traynor. 'You're saying that before whoever killed Erica Trent, he made her look like *this*?'

He reached for it, thinking of his daughter and how much he

protected her from what he did professionally. Judd was more or less the same age. He studied the geisha print. What he was seeing suggested that this killer was a voyeur, a heavy user of pornography. What Chong had found on the remains was a clear indication that he had eroticized Erica Trent's appearance, created his personal version of whatever pornographic images were fixed inside his head. Traynor chose his words.

'*This* is our killer's "ideal". A female who, according to his understanding of geisha, is utterly compliant and accepting of any and all male sexual behaviour, as no living, breathing woman could or ever would be.'

'How do you know that?' asked Julian.

'From how the remains of Erica Trent and Amy Peters were left by him. Erica's were fairly accessible, Amy Peters very much so.' He looked at each of them in turn, seeing no indication that their thinking was aligning with his, although he had anticipated that Julian's might. He had to be explicit.

'The accessibility of both women was intentional. Purposeful. As I said, he required these young women to be totally acquiescent. Which they would have been whenever he returned to that site. He visited them in death. Until their condition made it impossible, even for him.' He waited for a response. Watts and Julian looked stunned. It came from Judd.

'That's . . . *grotesque*.' She looked up at Julian. 'You know about stuff like that?'

'Not really. This is the first time I've encountered it directly.' He looked at Traynor. 'She would have been terrified when he tried to do that to her face. Surely, she would have fought him?'

Julian's few words told Traynor that despite laying out clearly what he believed happened to Erica Trent, Julian was still operating at some level of psychological self-protection. More than two decades before, during his own studies of aberrant sexual behaviour, Traynor had experienced a similar resistance. He tried again.

'This is an extremely grim area of criminal sexual psychopathology.' He looked at each of them in turn. 'He brought each victim to that site, alive. He made them walk to the place where he killed them. The cosmetics and whatever else was done to them was all post-mortem.'

Julian reached for the picture.

'And this geisha business exactly fits into his thinking?' Traynor shook his head.

'No. Whoever he is, he has a fairly common misunderstanding of the true meaning of geisha. He made the error of assuming that such women are subservient to men. They aren't. They're skilful, highly trained entertainers.' Julian let his pen fall to the table.

'I'm trying to fit together all you're saying, Will, but—' He raked his hand through his hair. 'I just don't know where this case is going. It feels like everything I thought I knew or understood is slipping away from me. I'm starting to feel like I did in Manchester—'

'Take it easy. We all know that feeling.'

Watts glanced at Judd who seemed to be in shock, then at Julian whose face was paper-white.

'Nobody expects you to have the experience Will has.' Watts looked to Traynor.

'And you're going to tell me that you think this killer is sane.'

'Yes. Very much so. And also personable, or he couldn't obtain his victims so smoothly.'

Judd gave Traynor a direct look.

'He's presentable, yet he does – *this*, because he only wants women who'll never diss him? Because they *can't*? Because they're *dead*?'

'Exactly.'

'I've never come across anything like it.' Julian looked up. 'You've actually met this level of deviance in your work, Will?'

'Yes. Two long-ago cases I won't forget.' And to Judd, 'I regret having to tell you such ugly things.'

'Your students are my age. They hear them.'

'They do, but they sign up for the courses I teach. They're already familiar with aberrant psychology. They know what to expect.'

'And I have a job here, Will, so I need to know these things.'

'I see that. I still regret that it's me that has to say them.' Watts was on his feet.

'Will, I want you with me for a meeting I've got with Brophy in five minutes. He needs to hear what you've just said.' He glanced at Julian and Judd. 'On second thoughts, I want both of you there as well. Brophy is a bean-counter with a CV so light on murder investigation it was non-existent until he came here. He has to know what we're dealing with here. Other than the cosmetic traces we've got, how likely is it that there's forensic evidence of this killer spending time post-death with his victims?'

'He's much too forensically aware to risk leaving traces of himself.'

Reynolds came into the room, waving an A4.

'For you, Sarge.'

Watts took the email from him, looked at the sender's name, Sergeant R. Jacques, then at the date and time of arrival.

'Wait!' Reynolds stopped, turned. 'Where's *this* been?'

'Don't know, Sarge. I just found it tucked behind the waste paper bin. It's got your name on it.'

'Most things have around here.'

Same day. 11 a.m.

The early sun had disappeared, leaving Brophy's office in deep shadow. To Watts' eye, he looked like he'd aged a decade during the time it had taken Traynor to deliver the same detail he had given to them almost an hour previously. Brophy looked at Traynor.

'Could you be mistaken?'

'No. It fits with my professional knowledge and experience.' Watts leant forward, ready to move Brophy to practicalities, wanting him focused.

'Sir, it's only a matter of time until the media is onto the fifth Manchester victim being found at the Brampton site. You know the impact of that. It'll be all over the Midlands and then the UK. They'll be there in droves. I need more officers right now just to secure that site. What Will has said is telling me that the other three victims are there. That means an in-depth search of that whole area—'

'Your focus is that first victim.'

'Not any longer, sir. We need technical support. Routine search methods won't work there. Too many trees, undulations, steep rises—'

He took a breath, waited for Brophy to respond. He didn't. He went with his second line of argument without reference to the two young sisters accosted on the road on which they lived. Brophy was already agitated. Any more stress and he'd be as much use as a chicken searching for its own head. He still had to know the score.

'Whoever murdered these young women is a massive risk to

females in Manchester *and* Birmingham. God forbid that he abducts anybody down here, but in light of what Will has just told you, you can surely see that we need technical support as well as more officers on the ground.' Brophy's head came up.

'Technical support?'

'Yes. For the in-depth search. I've already got an idea where to get that, sir. I'll be onto it as soon as we finish here—'

Brophy rallied, 'If I agree to these demands and flood that area with more officers, the media will know about it and go into a frenzy anyway.'

'We still need it. Think of the outcry if we delay a thorough search and it emerges that all five missing women are there and have been from the start of the investigation.' Brophy looked across to Traynor.

'What if this woman, this last victim – whatshername—'

'Erica Trent.'

'What if, prior to abduction, she was dressed up to go to some party? Or one of those raves I'm always hearing about? Have you considered that?'

Traynor regarded him.

'No. As I said earlier, those cosmetics were applied post-mortem. People who knew Erica, and the photograph we have of her, consistently describe a serious-minded young woman who did not make time for such self-embellishment.'

Brophy leant back in his chair.

'I've never come across anything even remotely like what I've just heard. What kind of world are we living in?'

Traynor gazed at him.

'It's a sexual aberration. It isn't unique—'

'It is to me! It's *monstrous*.' Watts eyed Brophy, saw him sag, a glove puppet missing its operating hand. 'I'm assuming he's some kind of madman?'

'No. He's a sexual deviant. His deadliness lies in his presentation of normality. That is, until he allows that aspect of himself to be seen. He's supremely confident in his ability to take and maintain control of his victims. He knows the Midlands. As DCI Watts has indicated, the very least the Brampton site requires is more security. Dr Devenish is in agreement about the need for more search officers.' Julian straightened at the use of his name. Brophy stared at his desk, then up at them.

'Why did he bring these women down here? Why didn't he do what he did to them up there in Manchester?' Watts heard the nimbyism. He had been looking for an indication that Brophy was fully aware of all the implications of the case and was now abandoning the hope. Traynor spoke.

'I believe he transported the victims to that particular site because it has some kind of personal resonance for him.'

Brophy waited.

'*Well?* What kind of "resonance"?'

'I don't know.' Brophy's colour climbed. He looked across at Julian.

'I want another media address, but none of Dr Traynor's theory is to feature, is that clear? All that's been said stays inside these four walls until I say otherwise.' Julian nodded. 'When you talk to the media, I want an emphasis on the problem common to *all* university campuses: that they're "porous", people coming and going at all hours, *plus* the students themselves lacking parental oversight.' Brophy nodded. 'Yes, that's how we'll play it for now. Be subtle, but make sure the message is clear: the responsibility for what has or might happen belongs to the students and the university.' Julian stared at him thunderstruck, glanced at Watts for support. Brophy pointed at him.

'You emphasize that West Midlands Police understands the anxiety generated by what's happened and is doing all it can etc, etc.'

Judd gazed at Brophy from beneath half-lowered eyelids, wondering how he had ever risen to the rank he had. Traynor thought of his daughter and the sexual risk to all young women until this killer was caught. Watts spoke.

'What you just said about responsibility, sir. Claire Walsh wasn't a student. She was twenty-three, employed and living an independent life. Her abduction doesn't fit the others but it's an indication of this individual's level of confidence in his ability to engage with and abduct women. Any woman.' Brophy's index finger stabbed at the rosewood desk.

'I *know* what we've got here! This is now a damage limitation exercise. What I *don't* want from the media is how good *he* is and how *useless* we are! We know he has a vehicle. If he drove to the Manchester campus, why haven't we got him on CCTV?' He looked at Julian.

'Was that checked out?'

Julian rubbed his eyes.

'Sir, all campuses have a number of official entry points over-seen by university security. In addition to thousands of students, many of whom have their own vehicles, there's staff, technical support workers, ancillary staff, visitors. The numbers run into the thousands. It's not likely, given this guy's purpose, that he would present himself at a security gate and there's no campus I know of that has a fence around it.'

'It's vital we operate on the basis of what these abductions are telling us,' Traynor added. 'The individual who abducted and murdered these women presents as confident yet non-threatening when approaching his victims with well-developed social skills to persuade them to go with him. I don't know what else to say to convey the potential risk he poses.'

Picking up annoyance in Traynor's tone, Watts swiftly added, 'He knows the West Midlands, sir. We have to consider the possibility of similar abductions occurring down here.'

Watts saw that coin slowly drop as Brophy pulled copy-statements from his in-tray and waved them at him.

'If you're thinking that you can get whatever you want on this investigation by extending its remit, think again! You don't have to concern yourself with budgets. I've read the statements from that woman and her daughters about some man approaching them in a car. It's nothing like the same situation!'

'It's geographically very close,' said Traynor. 'We can't rule out it being the same individual.' Brophy gave him a look.

'I can't run major investigations on potential instances! I still can't see why a Manchester-based repeat killer would choose to bring his victims to the Midlands, *and*,' he looked at Watts, jabbing the statements in front of him, 'according to you, after he's done that and escaped detection for years until now, he's now decided to try his luck with another abduction in the same area where he must know we're investigating the murders he's already committed barely a mile away!' Brophy paused for breath. '*Why* would he do that? It's senseless!'

'Confidence,' said Traynor. 'Mobility. He does what he does, not only because it's his obsession, but because he *can*. He's free to come and go as he pleases. He likes driving long distances. He believes he's invincible.'

'Ha!' barked Brophy, glaring at them. 'That's *your* job: to show him he isn't!'

'I agree with what Will just said about this offender's confidence,' said Julian. Brophy's eyes moved from him back to Traynor.

'Have you considered that you might have this case all wrong?'

'No. All I've said is based in recognized psychological and criminological theory. It also fits my direct, professional experience of repeat murder cases with motivations similar to what we have here.'

Watts was picking up a subtle change in Traynor's tone. Urbane and agreeable as he was, Traynor did not suffer fools. He watched Brophy make more trouble for himself.

'So where exactly has all of that got us right now?' Traynor stood, looked down at him.

'To the realization that you want quick results. I wish you luck in finding somebody who can provide them.'

Brophy's mouth fell open as Traynor reached for his notes, went to the door and out. He turned to Watts, enraged, 'He can't walk out on an investigation, just like that! I'll report him to his professional body—'

'Leave it with me.' Watts stood, Judd and Julian did the same. 'What I said earlier, about the additional personnel. We need it *now*. I'll follow up the technical search angle.'

They left Brophy and went downstairs without speaking, until they were inside Watts' office.

'He's an idiot,' said Judd. Watts shook his head.

'If you were expecting higher-order thinking from Brophy, that's your mistake.'

'Talk to Will, Sarge. We can't lose him just as he's making investigative sense of it all.' She glanced at Julian. 'What do you think about Will's theory?'

'Pretty sound. Except for what he said a few days ago about the killer being free to move around, particularly if the age range he suggested is accurate. How many males in their twenties or thirties have that much freedom from work? From relationships? I know I don't. Neither do you, Bernard, and neither does Will himself.'

Watts thought about it.

'I'm back to wondering if we're actually looking for a loner with mental health issues from here to forever . . . But that doesn't fit with the confidence he's obviously got around his would-be victims.' He shook his head. 'Forget Brophy. When he's calmed down and sees he's got no choice, he'll probably give us all I've requested. I'll smooth things with Will.'

Judd reached across the table for her bag, a large envelope bearing the police logo and followed Julian, already on his way to the door.

'I'll spend what's left of Monday getting to grips with this stuff that's come from Manchester. See if there's anything in it worth adding to the victimologies.'

Reaching headquarters entrance, getting a brief wave from Julian as he got into his car, she wondered about the restrictions he had on his freedom in Manchester.

Alone in his office, Watts reached for the email Reynolds had delivered earlier, read it again. He picked up the phone, rang the number, waited, drumming his fingers on the table. If there was one thing he didn't like, it was being handed information he was clueless about—

'This is DCI Bernard Watts, headquarters. Put me through to Sergeant Robert Jacques.'

'He's not here. He's got a day's leave.' Watts' irritation surged.

'Lucky *him*. He emailed headquarters a few days ago in reference to an abduction of a young woman which occurred close to the city centre. The complainant's name is Carly Driscoll. Who else is there who knows about it?' He waited, monitoring his own breathing, listening to papers being scrabbled through. The voice came back.

'Sergeant Jacques and a colleague dealt with that, but he's not here either.' There was a brief silence. 'This is a small station. It's due for closure in a few weeks. There's just me here today and I finish in half an hour. I don't know anything about what you've said.' Watts rubbed his eyes, wondering if asking who 'me' was would increase his frustration. Probably.

'When is Sergeant Jacques next on duty?'

'Tomorrow morning.'

'*Time?*'

'. . . Nine thirty.'

He put down the phone, looked at the message again. It contained no details, only a suggestion that DCI Watts might ring Jacques. He looked again at the heading: *Attempted Abduction by Adult Male Posing as Police Officer.* He wasn't rushing to knit up any theory that it had anything to do with the current investigation. As a ruse, it wasn't unknown. He still wanted to talk to Jacques as a matter of urgency.

THIRTEEN

Tuesday, 16 April. 5.15 a.m.

Watts drove along the dual carriageway, something having woken him over an hour before. Traynor's theory about this killer's preference for non-responsive females. He had unfinished business and he was on his way to sort it. He had passed Brampton three or four miles back when he finally turned off the carriageway and onto a side road, which became a muddy track, eventually widening into a yard surrounded by trees.

Stopping, he looked out at large areas of soft mud and started unlacing his suede shoes. Reaching for the rubber boots Chong had bought him a while back which he'd never worn, he slid his feet into them, tucked his trousers inside. Somewhere a rooster started up and now a dog was barking. He looked across at the farmhouse, more a cottage, seeing lights go on. Somebody was dragging open the front door. Watts stepped out of the BMW.

Fincher was at the open door, backlit, a shotgun at his side. He came outside and stood. Watts left his vehicle and headed for him, stopped a few feet away. He nodded at the shotgun.

'Got a certificate for that, Mr Fincher?'

Fincher gazed at him then turned and went back inside. Watts followed.

The state of the kitchen floor told Watts that Fincher didn't expect visitors to remove their footwear. The place was untidy, plates and cups piled in the sink. Fincher was coming towards him, still holding the shotgun and something else out to Watts. He took it. A shotgun certificate. He handed it back.

'I want a chat with you.' Leaving the shotgun on the other side of the kitchen, Fincher sat down at a table, supporting more dirty plates and cups. Watts sat, uninvited. Fincher eyed him.

'We've already had one and I've got nothing else to say.'

Watts' eyes moved around the kitchen.

'Cleaner's day off?'

'Do I look as though I can afford a bloody cleaner?'

'How about a girlfriend?' Fincher didn't respond. 'Have you got one?'

'No, have you?' Fincher looked away. 'I prefer being without.'

'How's that?' asked Watts.

'It's quiet. If there's no woman about the place, I don't have to listen to demands and complaints. I like things quiet.'

Watts slow-nodded.

'Got any family around here?'

Fincher looked at him.

'Two brothers, both a waste of space.'

'What do they do?'

'Bugger all, apart from putting our mother into an early grave.' Seeing Watts' eyes fixed on him, he shrugged.

'Figure of speech. I'm saying they did nothing for her when she was alive.'

'How about you? Did you help her?'

'When I could, money-wise.' He nodded to a photograph, sitting in a muddle of items on a dresser. Watts looked at it, seeing cracked glass, a haggard-looking face behind it. Fincher lit a cigarette, blew smoke.

'They never came near her when she was ill. I had her here, and a nurse came in to help. She was all right, the nurse. Not a talker, but then, neither am I. She just got on with it.' He paused. 'A few weeks later, Mom died in the night. I helped the nurse lay her out.'

Watts eyed him.

'Tough job.'

'No, it wasn't. She was my mother and she never hurt me when she was alive. Me and the nurse made her look nice. Combed her hair and that.' He looked up at Watts. 'When you do my sort of work, you can't be sentimental or squeamish.'

Watts reached inside his jacket, took out Fincher's statement.

'You've admitted taking photographs of human remains at the Brampton site.'

'Yeah? So?'

'I might be more ready to believe that you thought they were an earner except for the fact that you did nothing to capitalize on what you'd got by offering them to the press.'

'I thought you'd be pleased I didn't.' He sighed. 'I told you, I didn't have a clue how to go about it. I thought of offering them to one or two of the reporters hanging about there later, but I wasn't sure what they'd do. Rip me off? Report me to the police?'

'Going back to the day you took those photos, what did you see?' Fincher stared at him.

'You're in charge of that investigation, so you must know what I saw!' He shook his head. 'Whoever did that can't be right in the head.'

'How do you find life here, Mr Fincher?'

Watts listened to Fincher's voice, his attention on his face as he talked. He had had to come here and check him out. He had already done the same for the allegations of domestic violence against him which were thoroughly investigated and indicated no physical evidence in support of them. Fincher's own statement had indicated that the woman who made the allegation believed he had money and demanded some prior to going to the police. Watts had investigated enough such allegations to know how complex they could be. The man sitting across from him was happiest in his own company. He looked around the kitchen. It might not suit anybody else, but it suited Fincher.

Declining an offer of tea, Watts left.

Back at headquarters, Watts still wasn't done. He got out Carl Fincher's record. None of it was sex-related. He reached for the phone, had a quick conversation with one of Fincher's 'waste-of-space' brothers, a chartered surveyor who confirmed much of what was in Watts' notes, describing his brother as hopeless with personal relationships.

'He's always been the same. He dropped out of university because he couldn't get on with anybody there. That broke our mother's heart. He's better on his own. The job he's got suits him. He doesn't want the bother of pleasing anybody, but he's very generous towards the kids.'

Asked what he meant, he said that Fincher always remembered their birthdays, although he had little direct involvement with them.

'My eldest daughter saw him out and about one day when she was with a friend and asked him to take a couple of photos of them. He sent them to me to give to her. It's like he doesn't want to reach out to us. We invite him over but he doesn't come. He's happy with how things are. He had a woman living with him and he couldn't cope with it.'

Watts went for what he really wanted.

'I have to ask you this but has there ever been anything about your brother which concerned you,' he paused, 'sexually, I mean.'

There was a brief silence.

'That's so wide of the mark where Carl's concerned, it would be funny if it wasn't, well, tragic. He got mumps when he was about thirteen or so and our mother always traced his difficulties back to that. He's got no interest, if you understand what I'm saying, and on the very rare occasions when there has been a woman in his life, it caused a lot of bad feeling between them.'

Watts thanked him and put down the phone. It looked like Fincher really did have the kind of life that best suited him.

FOURTEEN

Tuesday, 7.50 a.m.

A sudden need for caffeine sent Judd to the corner of the office where she got out the coffee.

'Want one, Julian? He looked up at her and smiled.

'That would be nice.'

The smile squeezed her heart. She turned from him, reached for a third mug, not needing to ask Sarge if he wanted one.

'We can forget Fincher as a person of interest,' he said.

Watts described the phone conversation he had had with Fincher's brother, took the mug of milky coffee Judd was handing him.

'Thanks.' The door opened and Traynor came in.

'Morning, Will.'

They watched Traynor place copies of the five victims' photographs on the table.

'Every officer on this investigation knows that the families of two of these young women are now in a living hell because their daughters are never coming home and the families of the other three are worried sick.'

Watts searched for a positive response. He began, 'In my experience of the job, knowing what happened can give some kind of peace—'

'You're welcome to tell yourself that if it helps, Bernard.' Traynor went back to the photographs, lowered his voice. 'What I'm seeing are five young women who look like my daughter.'

Watts felt his tension climb. What he needed right now was Traynor cool and rational, not the exhausted, driven shell he'd been months ago. He glanced at Julian who had stopped what he was doing at the computer, his attention fixed on the criminologist. If anybody else had said those words, Watts would have responded along the lines of '*Come on, mate. Don't let it get to you.*' He couldn't give that line to Traynor. Because Traynor had experienced first-hand a similar heartbreak. He kept his voice low, his tone measured.

'It's part of the reason you're here, Will. Along with your professional know-how, nobody knows the impact of these murders on families better than you. We need you to help stop him making other people's daughters into victims—'

'Right now, we're nowhere near that,' said Traynor. 'Because we're seeing only the end-product of his psychopathology. We're very late arrivals to his homicidal behaviour.' Julian looked from him to Watts, his face tense.

'I did all I could in Manchester, applying psychological theory, sharing my ideas, my theories.' Julian shook his head. 'It wasn't enough. I couldn't come up with an answer.'

Watts looked at him, still seeing the skinny eighteen/nineteen-year-old, working alongside him on cold case investigations right here in this room.

'Listen to what I'm saying, son. *Never* take what does or doesn't happen on an investigation to heart. This is years of experience talking. Stuff comes at you, including pressure from the brass and everything you thought you knew turns out to be wrong, so you start again.' Watts shot upright, coffee spilling.

'I've just remembered something you said, Traynor. About him crossing lines, changing his modus, moving from stalking women to hands-on attacks. You said you thought he might have made a mistake.' He turned to Judd who was pulling on her jacket.

'We need a Manchester-Birmingham data search of offences going way back prior to Peters' abduction. Starting say fifteen years ago, search window-peepers, stalkers, hands-on sexual assaulters. Find every single offender who was nailed young as a result of an early mistake.'

'There could be a lot,' Judd said, pocketing her phone.

'Best get started, then. When you've got the data, we'll look at the nature of the mistakes made— He looked at her, her jacket half-on. 'Where are you off to?

'You said you wanted to go over to the site this morning. Or, shall I stay and start the data search?'

'I'll do that,' said Julian. 'I'll start it right now.' He hit a key on his keyboard, banishing the screen saver, smiled. 'See? I've started.'

Watts lifted his jacket from the back of his chair, then looked thoughtfully at Julian.

'While you were part of the Manchester investigation, was a search ever done against the names of known sex offenders with mental health problems?'

Julian shook his head, his eyes on the screen in front of him.

'I raised it as a possible line of enquiry with Boulter. Twice, in fact.'

'What happened?' Julian looked up.

'Nothing is what happened, oh, apart from him telling me that I was an academic, that his team was at the sharp end and wasn't about to waste valuable time chasing ideas that would probably produce nothing. That's when I realized that I wasn't achieving anything up there and that that whole investigation was on a losing course.' Watts looked to Traynor.

'What do you think, Will? Is it worth a check of mental health records for the Greater Manchester area, and the same for down here?' Traynor shook his head.

'You'll be inundated with hits. Think of the apparent ease with which this killer was able to persuade five intelligent women to go with him. He doesn't have those kinds of presentational problems.' Watts frowned.

'Just so you know, I'm not picturing him as a *Rocky Horror Show*, foaming-at-the-mouth type—'

'I *know* that.' Traynor gave him a steady look. 'But the kind of search you've just described is likely to net a huge number of complaints from women about men they considered odd in some way and whose behaviour ranged from unpleasant looks and gestures to verbal harassment to hands-on offences. I've seen zero indication of any specific reports made by women living on or near the Manchester campus which indicate those kinds of experiences. On the contrary, whoever he is, this offender is able to move quietly, methodically around a campus, a city, without attracting any attention whatsoever.'

'Got any angles you'd like to pursue?' Before Traynor could reply, Watts' phone rang. He answered it, ended the call and turned to Julian. 'Brophy wants you doing the media release early tomorrow morning.'

'In that case, I'll make a start on it before I do the search. He'll want to see it and give it his seal of approval before he lets me loose with it.'

The door swung open. Miller leant inside with a wide smile for Traynor.

'Sarge, I've got Manchester's chief admin officer requesting a date and time that suits you for the video conference call.'

'Any response from Boulter about the investigative documentation I requested days ago?'

'Not so far.'

Watts felt a quick surge of frustration.

'Tell them I want that conference call as soon as possible. *And* the data.'

'Will do.'

Sending Traynor a second eyes-and-teeth smile, she withdrew. Watts glanced at Traynor, but it appears he had missed it or wasn't interested. Thinking of a call he needed to make, he reached for the phone, replacing it within a minute. Sergeant Jacques was unavailable.

'Come on, Judd. This is no time for hanging about. I want to see what's happening at the site.'

She rolled her eyes, pulling her jacket fully on. Traynor also stood

'I'm coming with you. I'll drive.'

'I'll see you there,' said Judd.

Within thirty minutes, Traynor had parked the Aston Martin within the line of multiple headquarters vehicles on the road now closed to general traffic. Neither Watts nor Traynor had spoken during the journey but Traynor's words about the victims resembling his daughter were still inside Watts' head. Back when they

first worked together, Traynor's mental health had been a real
issue. With sheer grit, he had got himself together to where he
now was, clear-sighted and focused on whatever case he was part
of. He also had a woman in his life. Chong was right. Don't
manufacture problems. He already had enough. He got out of the
Aston Martin, a sudden, cold wind hitting his face. He looked up
at grey-to-black clouds.

'All I need now is bloody *rain*.'

He followed Traynor up the steep slope, seeing again the extent
of the whole site, the dense tree cover, the undulations, the deep
gullies filled with undergrowth, all of it needing meticulous
searching. He pulled out his phone, located a number and left a
brief message for someone he thought might provide the necessary
expertise.

Then, he continued up the steep rise to the two retrieval sites
and looked down at the site stretching before him. From this
vantage point he could see SOCOs moving around, a few of them
looking up to where he was standing. Their demeanour said it all.
Zero progress. If there was more evidence here, they wouldn't find
it without some real help. He watched a line of officers in shirtsleeves despite the coolness, probing the ground with long sticks,
lifting the soiled ends to their faces. Watts shook his head. It was
a macabre twist on the scratch-and-sniff books his daughter had
loved as a two year old. He walked on to where Judd was standing,
arms folded, her attention fixed on the activity. She turned as he
approached.

'We need that technical support, like, yesterday.'

'I always know where to come when I want yet more pressure.
I've made the call and now I'm waiting.' A stiff wind hit them,
ruffling Watts' hair. Judd's quiff stayed put.

'Brophy is moronic.' He sent her a sharp look.

'No, just totally lacking in investigative experience, having
managed to get where he is by keeping his pens and paperclips neat
and tidy. Since he came here from Thames, he's learnt about homicide investigations, but nothing on this scale. And he's got people
above him with sharp eyes on costs.' Judd was unimpressed.

'He needs to man up. Make the decisions, no matter what.' Her
eyes moved slowly over the site.

'Do you know how many people are reported missing in the
UK each year, Sarge?'

'Not offhand, but it sounds like you're about to tell me.'

'I've seen a figure of two hundred thousand. And of those, around two thousand are still missing after twelve months.'

'Not all of them are female. Most aren't deceased.'

'You know what I'm saying.'

He did. He had worked too many missing persons cases over the years where there was no definitive answer, whose families he'd had to go and see to offer words of regret for the 'lack of closure' people are always going on about, having worked all hours and failing to give it to them. It was the job. It was why he wanted out. Sad stories. Too many. His eyes moved over the site below them. This was the other part. The part where you got yourself and your team together to meet the challenge with determination, occasionally optimism which slowly faded, no matter how many hours you put in, leaving you ground down by your own failure to get a solid lead, let alone a conviction— His phone buzzed. He answered it. His face cleared.

'Dr Petrie! Thanks for getting back to me. Look, I'm guessing you're busy but we've got a situation— I won't say too much on the phone but it's just over the city boundary on Forestry Commission land— Yes, that's the place. A manual search is underway but it's a difficult set up and we're getting nothing.' He listened to the words flowing into his ear, feeling Judd's eyes on him.

'From what we know so far, if what we're looking for is here, we're probably talking "not wrapped".' More seconds of silence, then, 'Any chance you can pop into headquarters soon?' Another pause, a nod. 'I appreciate it. See you then.' He ended the call, glanced at Judd. 'That was Dr Jake Petrie, geoscientist, University of Birmingham. You probably remember him.'

'No.'

'A bit before your time, then. He advised us on a case around three years back. He's coming into headquarters tomorrow afternoon to talk about the help he might offer us.'

'What was the bit about not being wrapped?'

'Petrie says it's easier to locate remains if they're clothed or wrapped in something. Amy Peters was left unclothed in undergrowth, a similar story for Erica Trent. If Brewster, Walsh and Ricci are here, I'm anticipating the same applies to them.' His phone rang again.

'Yeah? What time tomorrow? Tell him, yes.' He ended the call. 'Miller's contacted Ray Boulter, SIO in Manchester. He's citing "pressure of work" and wants the conference call at seven a.m. It looks to me like the investigation up there is now running him, which is never good, Judd.'

'According to Julian, and I'm paraphrasing, he's a bit of a twa—'

'Rein it in!' He frowned. 'I've just remembered. Jules will be doing his media address inside the reception area at around the same time as that conference call. I don't want any journos getting wind of it, so be at headquarters no later than six in the morning. I'll contact Boulter to suggest we make the conference call earlier.'

He moved away, checked the time on his phone, tapped a number and waited. 'This is DCI Bernard Watts. I want to speak to Sergeant Robert Jacques.'

Jacques came on the phone and within six minutes Watts had the whole story.

'You went to the street where she said it happened?'

'I sent a colleague there. He found her shoes. Haven't you got them yet?'

'Yeah. How's she bearing up?' He listened, nodded, his eyes on Judd, who was now in conversation with Adam. 'Do you think she's up to talking to me and a female officer at headquarters?' He nodded again. 'As she's still off work, I'll get a female colleague to phone her and arrange to pick her up from home this afternoon. In the meantime, email me any notes you took at the time ASAP.'

Call ended, Watts gave the proposed interview more thought. Traynor was lecturing later and, anyway, it was a big ask to have the young woman talk to three of them. On the other hand, he wanted a psychological take on her and whatever she might tell them. Julian was closer to Judd's age and he would be able to provide that kind of insight. He made another call.

'Jules, how are you fixed this afternoon to be part of an interview with a young woman who was attacked off Broad Street two, three nights ago? She's coming into headquarters later this afternoon—'

'Sorry, Bernard, I can't. I've got the media conference early tomorrow, I'm back on the data search and, to be honest, I'm feeling lousy.'

'No problem. I know you've got a lot on. Don't work too late.'

Ending the call, he walked to where Judd was standing with

Traynor and Adam. They looked up as he neared, Adam already shaking his head.

'Sorry, Bernard. Nothing to report, yet.'

'Things might be looking up,' said Watts. 'I'm anticipating additional officers and I'm already onto some technical search support.' He turned to Traynor. 'You staying here for a while?'

'For the next half hour, till I leave for the university. I want to see the scene photographs of this whole place, its contours, everything.'

Watts read the text that had just arrived on his phone from Manchester. The conference call next morning was now rescheduled for six fifteen. He told them, then, 'Come on Judd.'

'Where?'

He rolled his eyes at her usual default response as they walked down to her car.

'Ruling out Paris and New York, my guess is headquarters. This afternoon, we're talking to a young woman who was attacked close to the city centre a couple of days back.' He squeezed himself into Judd's small vehicle.

'Go easy on the accelerator.'

FIFTEEN

Same day. 2.15 p.m.

Judd was driving cautiously with intermittent glances at Carly Driscoll in the passenger seat, handbag clutched on her lap, a large plastic bag on the floor at her feet. She had a good idea as to how this young woman was probably feeling. During a case a while back, Judd herself had been sexually threatened. She still remembered it like it was yesterday. She went over what she and Watts had agreed for the interview. The focus would be on engaging Driscoll to obtain her best account. The interview would be a standalone with no indication that it might be linked to a larger investigation. She glanced at her.

'It'll be just me and my DCI – sorry, detective chief inspector.' Seeing her look away, Judd wondered if she should say it. She went for it anyway. 'He's really nice with witnesses. Gentle. Patient. He knows his job.'

It got no response. To Judd's eyes she looked tired, no colour to her cheeks. Her mother had been upbeat, encouraging, but Judd had seen the anxiety flicker across her face as they left. Judd guided the car into headquarters' rear entrance to avoid loitering media and parked. Five minutes later she led the way into Watts' office and introduced Driscoll.

'And this is Detective Chief Inspector Watts.' Aware that his height could be seen as intimidating, Watts stayed seated.

'Thank you for coming in, Miss Driscoll. We really appreciate it.' He paused. 'Remember I said that you could have a parent with you—'

'I don't want them hearing any of it.'

Judd indicated one of three comfortable chairs that Sarge had fetched from somewhere. Driscoll sat down, placing her handbag and the plastic bag on the floor beside her. Judd also sat as Watts explained in basic terms the purpose of the meeting and its process. She sent quick glances to Driscoll as he got that process under way. Driscoll was now looking relatively at ease, some colour returning to her face.

'I'd rather you called me Carly.'

'No problem, Carly. We understand something happened to you recently. We'd like you to tell us about it. Whatever you do tell us will be at your speed. Chloe is going to listen, write and ask some questions. She's first-class at all three. Let's start with your full name, address and date of birth.'

'My name is Carly Driscoll and I live at . . .' Judd wrote details, pausing at the birth date. Eighteen. 'I really wanted to go back to work today but I . . . couldn't.' Judd smiled encouragement.

'I'm guessing that, like me, you enjoy your job.'

Driscoll nodded.

'I do. I work for the city as a junior clerical officer.'

'We understand that this whole situation is difficult,' said Watts. 'What we would like is for you to take us through the main facts of what happened.' Driscoll shifted on her chair, folded her hands together.

'I'm a bit worried in case I get it wrong. Say things in the wrong order.'

'Don't worry about that,' said Judd. 'Just tell us all you remember, as it comes.'

'. . . OK. I'd met some friends to go to a concert at Symphony Hall. I drove there, parked in a road off Broad Street. I've parked there before and never had a problem.'

'We understand that you don't know the name of that road?'

'Actually, I do now. I checked it online. It's Sheep Street. I parked my car there at about seven p.m. and I think it was around eleven, eleven fifteen when I went back to it.'

A nice, relaxed start, thought Watts. Judd wrote quickly, looked up at the young woman.

'Carly, as you left Symphony Hall to return to your car, did you particularly notice anybody as you were walking along?'

'No. There were a few people in Broad Street but it was raining hard and they were rushing along. I was doing the same. When I reached Sheep Street itself, it was deserted but I wasn't at all worried.' She was more comfortable now, looking at each of them in turn as she spoke, Judd moved the interview on.

'Carly, we need you to describe all that happened in that street, everything you can recall, from the time you reached it. If you want to change anything you say, that's fine, no problem.' She looked at Judd, her words coming quickly.

'As I said, there was no one there. I just walked along— I don't know whether you know that street but it slopes down so I could see ahead. I heard his voice before I saw him. I was about halfway along, starting to cross over to my car and it came from somewhere behind me. I stopped, sort of turned and – he was there. He told me he was a police officer and that he worked in terrorism. He used the word "assigned" when he told me that. He said that something was happening in the street.' She paused, took a breath, her hands gripped tight.

'I don't remember his exact words but he pointed in the direction I'd come from and said that his colleagues were now closing off the road. He said that they already had somebody in custody, somebody who was seen tampering with my car.' She looked from Judd to Watts.

'I never saw anyone else, but I just believed what he was saying to me.'

'What happened next, Carly?'

'He told me I had to go with him to a police station nearby to make a witness statement, that I wasn't allowed to drive my car until it had been tested, or something, and that someone would collect it and bring it to the station.' She looked at each of them, her eyes wide. 'I told him I hadn't seen anything but he just, sort of, dismissed it. That's when I first got an odd feeling about the whole thing. I could see why they might want to examine my car but not why *I* needed to go anywhere. I told him again that I hadn't seen anything and that's when he got a bit official with me, saying that I had to cooperate, that he and his men were in a serious situation there, protecting the city.' She looked down at her hands. 'I've seen things on the news. About bombs and . . . it was all so . . . believable. I did ask to see some identification which he showed me but I didn't get a good look at it.'

'Did he give you a name?'

'Yes. I think it was Huntley or Hunter, something like that. I don't remember him saying a first name.'

'Did he say anything else about why he wanted you to go to this police station?'

'Yes. He said something about being shown photographs, to see if I could identify whoever had tampered with my car.' She looked up at them. 'When he said that, I told him again that I hadn't seen anyone but he was suddenly hurrying me to his car . . .' Reaching into her coat pocket she brought out a tissue, pressed it against her nose. Judd said quietly.

'You're doing fine, Carly. What happened next?' Driscoll straightened, blinked several times.

'He opened the door for me and . . . I got in. He got in. Started driving.' She looked at Watts then Judd, her words coming quickly.

'My parents have always told me that you should do what the police say . . . but as soon as I was inside that car with him, I could smell alcohol. Up until then, he was sort of official, but quite talkative, but as we drove along, he got really quiet, not saying anything. I was getting uneasy but I knew the road we were going along. I'd driven along it loads of times and I'd seen the police station he said we were going to. It wasn't far. At that hour the area was pretty much deserted. Hardly any traffic.' She pressed the tissue to her eyes.

'. . . Sorry. Suddenly, he pulled over and stopped. I looked around. We were close to the entrance to some place that was in darkness, like a small factory or warehouse or something.' She pushed her hair from her face, her hand shaking.

'There were one or two street lights, but the whole area looked dark, deserted. That's when I started to get frightened. I asked him why he'd stopped, that the police station was just a bit further along the road. That's when everything changed, his face, *everything*.' Her tears were flowing now.

'He just became a completely different person.' She sobbed. 'He lunged at me, grabbed hold of both my arms. He had this – this *thing* with loops that he was trying to get onto my wrists.' Judd wrote, not looking at Watts, but taking quick glances at Driscoll, her face a testament to what she was saying. She was back inside that car.

'You're safe now, Carly.'

She looked up at Judd, tears unchecked, whispered, 'That's when I knew I was in the worst trouble of my whole life. That I had to *do* something. Had to fight. I pulled my hands away, started hitting him.' She looked from Judd to Watts and back.

'I'd never done anything like that before. Never hit anybody. I tried kicking him but I couldn't, there wasn't enough room, so I just kept hitting him with my hands, my fists. He tried to put his hands on my neck but I kept fighting and fighting and . . . he threw me against the passenger door and it just opened and—' She stopped, breathless.

'I fell out of the car onto some grass . . . I heard his door open, heard him get out, heard him coming around the car! That's when I saw lights further along the road. I got up and ran towards them. It was two cyclists. I was crying, screaming, just, like, out of my *mind* . . . and they stopped.' She bowed her head, the thick curtain of dark hair obscuring her face.

'What about the man?' asked Judd. 'What happened to him?' Driscoll pushed back her hair.

'I don't . . . I'm not sure. I heard a car start up, but by then I was hysterical. I reached the cyclists and just sort of collapsed. I couldn't walk without help. The cyclists took me to the police station.' She looked up. 'It wasn't until we got to the police station that I realized I had no shoes on.'

'What happened when you arrived there, Carly?'

'. . . I calmed down a bit, told the officers there what happened, about Hunter or whatever his name was. They'd never heard of him. I made a statement and that was it. One of the officers rang my dad and he and my mother came and picked me up.'

'You weren't seen by anyone? A doctor, for example?'

'No. I wasn't hurt. I felt sick at the station and the officers there let me use the bathroom. Once I'd washed my face and hands, I felt a bit better.' Judd avoided eye contact with Watts. 'I wasn't really hurt,' she insisted. 'Just a couple of broken nails.'

'Can you describe the car that this man was driving?'

'Yes. It was a Mini.'

'Can you recall any features, such as its colour, its registration, even just part of it?' She frowned, shook her head.

'Not the registration, no. The streetlights there aren't that good but I think it was a kind of red-brownish colour. Something like that.' She fell silent, dabbing mascara.

'That's it. That's all I remember.'

'Carly. Can you describe this man "Hunter"?' They waited while she calmed.

'. . . Tall. I'd say about six feet, like my dad. Dark hair. Slim but not thin, you know? I don't remember what he was wearing but he looked neat and he smelled clean. I mentioned the alcohol, didn't I?' Judd nodded.

'Was his hair long or short?'

'Short.' She looked from Judd to Watts. 'I know it sounds stupid, the way I just went along with what he said but . . . the way he stood, the way he moved and spoke to me, I never for a minute doubted that he *was* a police officer. There was just something about him that made me believe he was, even when I thought the whole situation was a bit weird.' She frowned at her hands, looked up at Judd.

'He wasn't rough in the way he spoke. He sounded, I don't know, professional, very polite to begin with, just . . . normal. Before he changed.' She fell silent, then, 'That's it.'

'We appreciate you doing this, Carly,' said Judd. 'It can't have been easy.'

'That's OK. What happens now?'

'We'll give you a few minutes to go through your statement and if the details are correct, you can sign it before you leave. If you think of something else to tell us—' Driscoll's head came up.

'He had a moustache. A small one. I remember thinking that it made him look older than he was.' She frowned. 'Which is stupid because I don't know how old he was.'

'How old would you guess?'

She thought about it, shook her head. 'Not more than early thirties. He was nice-looking, intelligent-sounding. Like my boss.'

Judd smiled.

'What does your boss do?'

'He's an urban planner, but this man didn't look anything like him. My boss is nice but he's pretty old. Late forties, early fifties.' She stared ahead. '*Why* would he do what he did to me? To anybody?' She looked down at the plastic bag near her feet, reached for it.

'I've just remembered, I've brought in the clothes I was wearing that night. I've noticed that there are marks on the jacket. I won't *ever* wear any of them again— Sorry, that's my phone.' She took it out, looked at its screen. 'It's my dad. He's outside waiting for me.'

Carly Driscoll had left. Watts took the bag of clothes to forensics. Adam took the bag from him, peered inside.

'The victim-witness has told us there are marks on the jacket,' said Watts.

Adam nodded. 'We'll see what we can do.'

Watts used the phone there to request urgent CCTV footage of Sheep Street and the route Driscoll had described her abductor taking. He went back to his office where Judd was clearly fuming.

'Immediate observations?'

'Only that she should have been taken from that police station straight to hospital for DNA testing. What do they do? They let her wash her *hands*!'

'She's given us a reasonable description of her attacker. He had it all planned out, what he was going to say, matching it to the way he presented, which makes him crafty as well as smart. What's your view of the car she described?'

'I'm guessing the same as yours,' Judd said, looking at him, 'it sounds very like the one driven by the man who attempted to abduct Olivia and Mia Fielding. If it was him both times, he's out there doing what the hell he likes. He's every woman's nightmare.'

Watts reached for Driscoll's signed statement, his eyes moving quickly over it.

'*If* it is him, he's blatant and a massive risk. Yet Driscoll's description of him as calm and believable doesn't fit with the mental health theory.' Judd waited.

'So, where does it leave us?'

'We carry on as if the attack on Carly Driscoll and the attempted abduction of the two schoolgirls are connected and that there could be a connection to Peters, Trent and the other three women,' Watts said. 'Which means we're extending an investigation that we're already struggling to get a handle on.

'By extending it, it's possible we'll get more avenues to follow up. We have a Mini identified in two locations. Metallic brown and red aren't that different, particularly under street light. I wanted to avoid putting any pressure onto Driscoll but now that she's been here and talked about it, I'll phone her tomorrow, see how she is and ask her to come back and help construct an E-FIT.' Watts stood. 'I'll also have a word with Jacques about collecting DNA from *all* females alleging assault.'

'He needs reporting, Sarge.'

'Would that get us this "Hunter's" DNA?'

'It might get Jacques to do his job properly.'

'As will the conversation I'm planning to have with him.' He waited as she made copies of Carly Driscoll's statement. 'Judd, if you get to a position where you have some responsibility for other staff—'

'Make that "when".'

'—you might want to think over things that have happened to you since you joined the force. Things you got wrong or that you could have done better.'

'I get it. When Carly Driscoll comes to do the E-FIT, I want to be part of it.' Judd slid a copy statement towards him. She gave him a couple of fleeting glances, decided to go for it. 'Remember what she said? About him acting as well as looking the part of a cop?'

'Yeah. And?'

'He knows how cops behave.'

SIXTEEN

T raynor was inside his office at the university, the vast building gradually quietening around him over the last couple of hours. Two of his students had left folders on his desk following his request that they track down cases of attacks on women which had involved instances of asphyxia. He read the pre-court psychological evaluations relating to the convicted males. In every case there was an indication of antisocial personality. None of the victims had been subdued to the point of death. What he was not finding in those evaluations was a developmental explanation for such behaviour. What he really wanted to see were indications of escalation from time-limited asphyxia to where it became an intentional cause of death. Not finding what he wanted, he closed the folders, reached for one he had tracked down himself.

It contained notes on a case three decades old. That of a middle-aged taxi driver who had persuaded lone female fares to accept an alcoholic drink. Many did so, regaining consciousness several hours later, bruised and disoriented, with little awareness of what had happened to them. If those assaults had continued, it seemed highly likely to Traynor that that offender's behaviour would over time have escalated to murder. Development. Escalation.

Traynor stared ahead. Something was niggling at him. What if the problematic sexual behaviour in this case had begun to show itself at an early age? Say, around puberty? In such a situation the escalation could surely be regarded as a truly developmental issue.

Responding to a faint yet persistent tapping inside his head, he reached out and pulled open a low filing cabinet drawer containing old files. He read the labels on each, continued three-quarters of the way along and stopped. It was here. Removing the slim file, he opened it. He hadn't looked at it in over two decades. Not since he was a student. He looked down at one of his tutor's 'Find-the-killer' assignments, each of them a real case but anonymized. It was an exercise which required Traynor and his fellow students to firstly evaluate the given details of biographical history, personality indicators, adolescent and adult offence characteristics. A second challenge followed: to identify that anonymized offender, link him to his known crimes, whether historical, contemporary, UK-based or otherwise.

His tutor's long-ago voice resonated in Traynor's head:

'Come on, Will. Look at the homicides in this case. Really look at them. How do we know a killer? We know him by his developmental pathway, his strengths and weaknesses which lead eventually to what he did. Are you seeing him yet, Will? Do you "know" him, yet? My office this time tomorrow to tell me who he was and all that he did.'

Traynor had done exactly that. Now, he turned over copies of old police reports, stared down at a photograph of a good-looking, thirty-something male whom he had identified to his tutor as the killer. He had done so by absorbing the attributes of this man's personality, his early biographical experiences, his modus operandi and his homicidal actions beginning in the sixties and which had cut a swathe through several states of America and led eventually to his execution in Florida.

This was the case which had been tugging at Traynor's thinking since he had become aware of the significance of cosmetics, the post-mortem engagement with the remains of Amy Peters and Erica Trent. He turned over another page of information and stopped. He was here. The archetypal necrophile, repeat killer. A prototype of the individual Traynor and his colleagues were looking for, who had brought two, probably five, young women to their deaths at the Brampton site. The years-ago case was one Traynor knew to the smallest detail. It would now be his guide, his psychological blueprint for whoever had committed the Brampton homicides. He thought of the two men Bernard had told him about, the dog walker and the man who had built a fire and found Erica Trent's hair. No way did they fit and Bernard knew it. But there was someone else to consider.

Traynor had not felt the need for this kind of thinking since his university days. Most of the cases he was invited to work on provided him with much more than this current investigation. It was late now. He needed to be home with Jess, but he had had to be here. Had needed to confirm to himself that his thinking was taking him somewhere. To someone. He gazed down at the face of the long-ago killer, at the smile in his eyes beneath the well-defined dark brows, the mouth curving slightly upwards.

Reaching for a piece of paper he placed it on the photograph, covered the mouth and looked into those dark eyes. There was no smile there, only a cold, implacable intensity.

Jess was in the sitting room reading when he got home. She looked up.

'I was beginning to think you'd lost your way home.' He leant down and kissed her.

'Never. I'm sorry, I should have phoned.' And to the dog now circling his legs, '*Hey*, Boy.' He stroked and patted him, conscious of Jess's eyes on him.

'Tell me you're not wearing yourself out on this case, Will.'

'Don't worry about me. It's a tough one but I'm beginning to see where I'm going.'

She knew that he was driven in his work. She also knew that there were times when he found it a useful buffer for keeping emotions at a distance. The difference now was that it wasn't denial or raw grief that drove him. He had accepted that his wife was dead. It was his commitment to doing the best he could for those left behind after a homicide which kept him working long hours, with such determination. No one knew better how it felt to be left. She felt his eyes on her. She smiled up at him.

'Boy hasn't had a real walk since lunchtime.'

'I'll take him now.'

She watched him reach the door and take down the dog's lead.

'I love you, Will.' He paused.

'I . . . won't be long.'

They walked along the wide avenue, Boy straining at his leash as Traynor pulled up his jacket collar. The temperature had dropped in the last hour or so. They turned into extensive, well-lit parkland where Traynor knelt, released Boy and watched him race away from him. He grinned, as he reappeared, front paws pounding, tongue lolling, eyes fixed on Traynor, then bounded away again.

'On my way, buddy.'

He followed after the dog. The face he had seen earlier in the file was back inside his head. A man widely regarded as intelligent, personable, and likeable, qualities which many had accepted as truth for years, even after he was incarcerated. A man who had had a life, a relationship, seemingly stable mood and behaviour.

Destined to go places. Which he had. To wooded areas off the main highways around the city where he lived, bringing with him young women who accepted without question the person they believed him to be and where he gave free rein to those aspects of his personality he hid behind the façade.

Catching up with the dog, he patted him then watched him dash ahead. It was the earlier phone call from Watts with the news that Carly Driscoll had been duped by a man posing as a police officer that had started Traynor thinking about this infamous killer. He had used a similar ploy, one of many at his disposal, supported by his own easy authority and well-developed intellect behind which lay a childhood of petty thefts, teenage use of violent pornography, those negative behaviours gradually assuming dominance. Watching women had reduced his stress, rewarded him with a sense of his own power. Of being in control. Until mere watching was no longer enough. He wanted complete control in life and in death. He morphed into a power-control killer. No one suspected because he was outwardly successful. In reality he was an abject failure. Whenever his stress and negativity soared, he had to exercise that power, that sense of control. And somewhere a young woman died. Thirty, it was believed. Possibly more.

The rush of detail brought Traynor to a halt, eyes fixed straight ahead. As a killer he would come out of the shadows, able to maintain a false face. This was what they were looking for.

Boy's *hey-come-and-get-me* barks brought Traynor back. He headed for him, ran with him, chased him, then called him to come. He came, a shiny black rocket, to his side. He put his arms around the panting dog, felt the soft fur.

'Time to go home,' he whispered.

Arriving there, he went straight to Jess, threw his arms around her. After a few seconds she looked up at him. 'Tell me you're OK.'

He gazed down at her. 'I am and I love you, Jess. I just couldn't tell you before because . . . it felt disloyal to Claire.'

Later, lying next to Jess, listening to her quiet breathing, his hand resting on her waist, Traynor was thinking about the investigation. The few items of evidence they had, one of them still missing. If he was wrong in his thinking, if there were no significant developments, they could be facing failure and the murders of five young women would eventually slide into the morass of cold cases. He stared into darkness. He knew first-hand how that felt for those who were left behind.

He had to examine his own observations, test them to the point where he finally knew their truth.

SEVENTEEN

Wednesday, 17 April. 7.10 a.m.

DCI Ray Boulter looked out from the wide screen as he described the pressure that he, his team and the Manchester force was continuing to experience. His reddened eyes and downturned mouth were testimony to what he was saying, his tone a clear indication to Watts, as if he needed it, that things weren't about to get any easier in terms of collaboration between their two forces. Watts had prewarned Judd to monitor her facial expression during the video call. Right now, her face was eerily void of anything. If that didn't prod Boulter out of his despondency, nothing would.

'I hear you, Ray and believe me I know the feeling, but there's still information we need from you which is way too slow arriving. When it does, it's in dribs and drabs. There are copies of some statements but not others. We need *all* of them, including the families' statements, their views of their daughters, any CCTV footage which we haven't yet seen, the victims' phones, which I understand you've got—'

'Whoa, hang on!' Boulter's face darkened. 'This liaison with Birmingham is about you focusing solely on Amy Peters.'

Watts shook his head.

'No, Ray. My chief has told you that's all changed. Erica Trent is *here*. Which victims' phones do you have?' He watched Boulter and his colleagues exchange glances.

'Only Peters and Walsh's phones. Both processed. Nothing useful or relevant on either of them. The Italian girl's family already told us that she lost hers a couple of days before she went missing. No signals from it and it's never been located. I'll send you anything relating to the Peters' abduction which you haven't had, but I'll be talking to my boss before I release anything else.'

'That won't change the fact that we've got Erica Trent, Ray.'

Boulter and his colleagues were clearly unhappy. Watts understood. This had been their investigation for months. Birmingham was a late arrival and, on that basis alone, not about to be welcomed. Or willingly assisted. Watts wasn't impressed by what they'd achieved but the Manchester team had slogged away at it. He had been in similar situations himself during his career. But this time, the remains of two of the victims discovered a mere five miles from where Watts was sitting meant things had to change.

'Ray, I want copies of everything you've got on all five women. *This* is where their killer chose to leave his first and fifth victim. It makes sense that the other three victims are here. There's a pattern: abduct up north, dispose in the Midlands. We've got extra personnel all over the area where we found the remains. I need everything you've got and soon.' He waited. Boulter knew he had no choice. Which didn't mean he would jump to it.

'We appreciate the pressure you and your lads are under, Ray,' Watts added, 'but as of now we're investigating all five homicides, which can only assist your investigation because we'll share whatever we get.' Boulter was evidently not happy.

'I'll send it but you're in for a big disappointment. We've been over all of it. The best, make that the *only* lead, is the CCTV footage you've already got of a male following Walsh. Our problem was always the time lag between the dates they were first reported as non-contactable and the time it was established that they'd probably been abducted. By then, any potential witnesses we might have had struggled to recall the detail of what they'd seen and when.' Watts listened impatiently to a few seconds more of Boulter's woes. He had problems of his own.

'I hear what you're saying, Ray—'

'You've got Peters and Trent. All I can say is good luck if you find the other three. I won't organize any celebration until I hear from you.'

Watts knew Boulter had gone down the road to being overwhelmed by the enormity of his investigation and was now well into drift mode. He glanced across at Traynor, knowing that Traynor was thinking much the same.

'When do we get that info, Ray?' he pressed. They waited, eyes on Boulter.

'I'll get it pulled together and delivered to you in three days.' He sighed.

'We'd appreciate it in two, max. As a matter of interest, did you do any checks of local mental health facilities, halfway houses, drop-in centres, talk to staff there about problematic patients—?'

'No. Devenish, the psychologist we had working with us, suggested it but, between you and me, he lacked the experience and commitment for an investigation of this size and complexity. Half his time was taken up with his university work while we were working twelve-hour days. By the time Walsh went missing, I was hardly going home. There was no indication, no reason for us to do the sort of checking you've described and we had our work cut out just tracing these girls' movements, following up leads that turned to nothing and being inundated with tips that went nowhere.'

Watts was more than ready to bring the conference to a close, yet there was something he wanted to straighten out.

'Dr Devenish is down here working with us. You know that Dr Will Traynor, the criminologist, is also on board. I'm surprised to hear what you say about Dr Devenish's commitment. I've worked with him in the past and my experience is very different.' He and Traynor watched Boulter's face and that of his second-in-command grow weary.

'No offence, Bernard, but my faith in psychologists in general has declined. I've never used a criminologist, but it sounds the same to me.'

Seeing Judd's colour rise, Watts said, 'They're both providing valuable psychological theories of repeat homicide—'

'Want some advice, Bernard? Forget the theorizing. I'll tell you what you need. *Evidence*. How's the media treating you?'

'Nothing to complain about.' Boulter gave a harsh laugh.

'Wait till they find out you're investigating all five cases!'

'Have you got any photographs of Claire Walsh's workplace, this television company?'

'There weren't any. Why would there be. She wasn't killed there.'

Watts chose his words. 'Her colleagues there were talked to?'

'Give us some credit! Nothing we got from them led anywhere.

Most of the people she worked with were short-contract graduates
in their early twenties, all mad keen to work in the "*meedja*".'
Watts watched him hook index fingers. 'And in case you're
wondering, yes, we talked to friends and associates of the other
four. We got nothing, and *that's* the problem—'

'What about Melody Brewster?' said Traynor. 'We understand
she had a boyfriend.'

A quick conflab between the Manchester officers was followed
by Boulter saying, 'No, she didn't. No boyfriend.'

'Our information indicates that she did.' Watts eyed Boulter.
'What information?'

'Last week, one of my team phoned one of yours who said,'
he looked down, 'and I quote, "She," meaning Brewster, "had a
boyfriend, sort of." Asked what "sort of" meant, the reply was,
"None of her family nor friends knew anything about him", that
he was a shadowy figure and that your investigation decided not
to pursue the issue further.'

'I don't know where you got that from—'

'I just told you, Ray. One of your team.'

'Look, our experience of looking for the killer is that there's
no evidence that he knew any of these girls, or they him. Like I
said, good luck with it. You'll need it. I hope your officers have
got understanding wives.'

'Send us the information in the next two days, Ray.' The screen
went black. Judd stared at it.

'Clueless, sexist git! What's *his* problem?'

'Knackered and demotivated, at a guess.'

'He needs to do his job, part of which is to support us in our
investigation.'

'I'll be surprised if we get what I've just requested in the next
four days. But if it isn't here in three, I'll get Brophy onto it. He
values paperwork above everything.'

'Good idea, Sarge.' He sent her a weary glance.

'No, Judd, it isn't. Because it'll involve the brass up there and
likely cause added friction, which isn't going to do much for
force-to-force co-operation.'

'As and when that data does arrive, it may help us, my friend.'
Traynor stood, laying his hand on Watts' shoulder. Watts looked
up at him.

'Thanks for your notes on this murderous individual. I've

circulated them to the team. At least we've got a sense of the type we're looking for. I just hope we lay eyes on him soon.'

Leaving the incident room, they walked the corridor, pausing at the sound of Julian's voice addressing the media in the ground-floor reception area. It sounded like it was going well, journalists and television representatives asking questions by turn, Julian responding with agreed-upon details in straightforward terms. Where he was reluctant or unable to offer more, he indicated it. Judd sent Sarge a quick glance, seeing what Jonesy called his 'my boy' face. Watts turned to Traynor, keeping his voice low.

'Manchester never had a clue about the value they had in him. If they'd listened to him, they might have done better – and he's way ahead of me where the media is concerned. To me it's a red rag.'

'What's on the agenda now, Sarge?' asked Judd.

'Brophy's confirmed that more officers have been drafted to the Brampton site from other parts of the city. I want to see how that's progressing.'

Same day, 12.30 p.m.

They stood in a cool wind, looking down at the increased numbers of officers moving in a steady wave between trees and over undulating land, using long poles to thrash and prod the dense undergrowth. Within a few minutes of their arrival, there was a changeover, the freed-up officers walking down to a refreshment wagon, faces ruddy. Jones and Kumar were among them, Kumar limping. They helped themselves to drinks, Jones' voice drifting on the breeze.

'Did you catch him on the morning news? Posh Boy spouting Will's ideas, turning his best side to the camera, the self-satisfied *twat*—'

'Watch it,' hissed another officer, seeing Watts approaching.

'How's it going, lads?' he called.

'Hot work, Sarge,' said Jones. 'I've volunteered to do some overnight guard duty.'

'Thanks.' Watts looked down at Kumar sitting on the grass. 'What's up with you?'

'He's walking wounded.' Jones grinned. 'Got his foot wedged under some tree roots,' he winked at Judd, 'or, so he reckons.' Watts surveyed the whole site.

'Nothing to report, so far?'

'Nothing, Sarge.'

Watts turned away, checked his watch, thinking of the specific search support he still needed. He glanced back at Kumar.

'It's no good you limping about here. Come with us.' Jones' face fell as Kumar hobbled away with them.

'You jammy *git!*'

Same day. 3.40 p.m.

Watts handed the young officer on reception a transcript of his conference call with Manchester's SIO.

'See that Superintendent Brophy gets that.' He started walking away.

'Sarge, wait! There's somebody here to see you.'

Watts checked his watch, then moved his eyes over the individuals in the reception waiting area, settling on a tall, thinnish, late-twenties male with short brown hair and metal-framed glasses, a crammed satchel at his feet. Watts went quickly to him.

'Dr Petrie!' He seized Petrie's hand, shook it. 'Thanks for coming in. I wasn't expecting you for another hour.'

'I've only just arrived. I finished early so I thought I'd drop in on the off-chance—'

'No problem. Come on through. It's been a while since you were last here, yeah?'

'Three years, I think,' said Petrie, lugging the satchel.

'*That* long?' They came into Watts' office.

'This is Dr Petrie from the University of Birmingham,' Watts introduced him to Judd and Traynor. 'He's here to advise us on our best chance for searching the site.'

'Hi, I'm Jake.' He raised his hand to the young woman with striking hair and the man he recognized, standing before him.

'This is Police Constable Chloe Judd and Dr Will Traynor, criminologist, from Central University.' Traynor and Petrie smiled, nodded.

'Dr Traynor and I have met before,' said Petrie.

'I guessed you might have. Our other colleague Julian Devenish is a forensic psychologist. Right now, he's busy in the incident room. You might remember him from that cold case investigation you assisted us with.'

'Probably, if I saw him again.'

'Grab a chair.' Watts sat facing him. 'I'll get straight to it, Jake. We really need your help. I've also got a superintendent who's rattled about costs.'

'No worries. The way I work hasn't changed. Any assistance I provide is gratis because I'll get a research paper out of it eventually, which is all I need.'

'We'd really appreciate any help you're able to give us. I briefly mentioned the case on the phone and you've probably seen media reports. Five females – four students and a recent graduate – disappeared from Manchester over the last three years. Now it's our problem because the remains of two of them have been found close to a place called Brampton, just west of the Birmingham border.' Petrie nodded.

'Forestry Commission land. I know it. I sometimes take my mountain bike up into that general area.'

'Much of the location where the remains were found is densely wooded. What we've got so far are incomplete remains left in thick undergrowth or shallow-buried, both unclothed. Our current thinking is that the three other victims are also there, possibly better concealed. You introduced us to the use of drones when you helped us on a previous case. We've got our own drone now, but we're not getting the results from it that we need. The problem is the heavy tree cover, plus there's the undergrowth: thick roots, bracken, ferns, you name it. I'm hoping you might come up with an idea for searching that whole area to establish that the remains of those three missing women are there.' He paused, giving Petrie a chance to consider all he had said.

'In my experience of working on police investigations, it isn't that unusual for bodies to be left with little to no groundcover, as opposed to being buried. In fact, wooded areas like you've described are relatively common dumping sites. It sounds like whoever chose Brampton was confident that the remains would gradually become covered by vegetation and overlooked, except by insects and animals, and would quickly decompose.' He looked at each of them. 'The likelihood of there being remains still to be found is high. Having said that, if there is anything still concealed there, technically speaking, woods can be *really* tricky for a drone search.' Watts nodded.

'We know, from what happened to our drone. If there are more remains out there, what are the chances of locating them?'

'My research over the last three years has included the application of thermal imaging to detect near-surface remains,' said Petrie,
delving into his satchel, and bringing out a clutch of papers. 'Did
you know that the specific heating capacity of a body is quite
different to soil?' They eyed him in silence. 'It heats up and cools
down depending on time of day. If you do thermal imaging, say
at dawn, the results will be relatively low and the same for the
late afternoon. Which means that the optimal time for identifying
concealed remains is after midday. I'm talking here about remains
with sufficient flesh.' He sifted through his papers.

'What you said about one of the remains being skeletonized
– they wouldn't emit such temperature fluctuations. For remains
retaining some flesh, all I can say is that there's a chance of locating
them. What proportion of flesh would you guess might still be
present, based on what you know of the second set of remains?'
Watts hesitated.

'I won't mislead you by suggesting that there'll be a lot to work
with.' Petrie looked dubious.

'It's a case of the more the better because ideally we want fleshy
remains which are likely to host a large maggot mass. That's what
contributes to the high heat signal I mentioned.'

Traynor nodded. Judd's eyes were fixed on Petrie. Watts felt a
wave-like movement in his mid-section.

'Right. Got any more ideas that might help us, Jake?'

'Like I said, burials in woods are really tricky. One option is
ground penetrating radar which reaches down a couple of metres
but it also picks up a host of anomalies you wouldn't be interested
in: tree roots, large stones and the like, which can waste valuable
search time. I sometimes use an electromagnetic conductivity
meter, which works well on bodies, particularly if there are metallic
objects with it, such as belts, jewellery and implants.' He looked
at each of them. 'What you said about the age of the individuals
you're looking for suggests that replacement joints are very
unlikely.' Seconds of silence slid by before Petrie spoke again. 'I
don't want to build false hopes here but what I do have is a UAV
fitted with a hyperspectral camera which I think might help.'

'UAV?' He turned to Judd.

'Unmanned aerial vehicle, another name for a drone, but it's
the camera on this one that's the business for your kind of situation. It uses a very narrow bandwidth of non-visible wavelength

values—' He stopped, looked at each of them. 'What I'm saying is that in those ranges it's possible to pick up changes in plant cellular tissue such as roots.' He paused again. 'Changes caused by decomposition fluids, to be exact. They can make some plants pretty sick. Changes in those roots compared to others nearby show up in hyperspectral data as spectral signatures.' The wall clock ticked on.

Watts glanced at his colleagues then back to Petrie.

'Any chance you can come with us to the site today, now, while there's still some light, just to have a look at it?' Petrie glanced down at the satchel at his feet. Watts pressed on. 'That way, you can tell us if this UAV and its camera is a real possibility or a non-starter. What do you say, Jake?'

They waited.

Petrie grinned.

'Let's go and have a quick look.'

Thirty or so minutes later, they walked onto the site and up the densely wooded slope, getting tired glances from officers searching nearby. Prior to this investigation, it wasn't a place Watts was familiar with. It was no beauty spot offering Birmingham's residents a welcome break from noise and traffic. Right now, with the sun lowering and the shadows cast by the trees lengthening, the word for it was bleak. Another was depressing. Unwelcoming. It felt to Watts like the place itself knew what had been done here and was happy to hold on to whatever it had. His eyes drifted over thick masses of ferns, a band of tension wrapping itself around his head.

'I heard that both of the victims were abducted from Manchester. Is that right?' Petrie said to Traynor.

'Yes.'

'That's unusual.' The two words grabbed Watts' attention.

'Why do you say that?'

'What I know of homicide cases, the transportation of abducted persons or bodies is a high-risk undertaking. Consequently, the dumpsites are usually within at most a few miles of the place of abduction – particularly if the killer has plans to engage in sexual activity with a victim.'

Traynor expressed agreement and Watts' already positive view of Petrie swiftly climbed. This wasn't just some amiable young academic with expertise around the impact of burial on human remains. He had obviously added to his knowledge of criminal activity from collaborating with police forces. Petrie was speaking again, his attention on Judd.

'Apologies for saying that – about the victims.'

'No apology necessary. I'm not new to homicide cases.' Petrie grinned down at her.

'That has to be one of the coolest responses I've heard in a while.' Watts reached out and took his arm. He lowered his voice.

'Jake, on a scale of one to ten, how optimistic are you that this hypersensitive camera of yours can help us locate anything here?'

'I see there's two choices,' Petrie said. His gaze moved over the burgeoning groundcover as he spoke. 'We try it, or you spend weeks searching it on foot, which is expensive in terms of time and labour, plus you risk having to bring in cadaver dogs and you probably don't need me to tell you about the variations in training and success rate associated with those.' He waited. 'It's your call.'

Same day. 7 p.m.

Petrie was gone with one of the officers to retrieve his car from headquarters, with an assurance to Watts that he would check his current availability. Watts had emphasized that they needed what he was offering as of yesterday. Since then, two more hours of searching by officers on foot had produced nothing, despite the addition of lights holding back fast-encroaching shadows. He moved to where Judd and Traynor were standing, midway between the two body recovery sites. Judd glanced up at him.

'It sounds to me like Jake's UAV camera is the business, Sarge. If it locates anything, that whole Manchester case is ours.'

'Lucky us.' He looked to Traynor.

'Manchester has to have areas like this. My question is *still* why drive eighty miles to this one?'

'This area must have a particular meaning for him.'

'Like, what?'

'That's something only he knows.'

Traynor walked away, to a place on the hillside which afforded a view of the surrounding countryside. They followed, Watts shielding his eyes against a low sun.

'Your theory, Traynor, about what he does to victims and why. I don't want the media knowing about it.' Judd looked at him.

'It might open up a few lines of inquiry if we release it to psychiatrists, mental health workers who might link it to a patient,' she suggested.

'Yes, but once the media has it, this whole city will go from disgust to fear to making links to people in their area who they see as dodgy because of how they do or don't put their bins out and they'll all be phoning *us*. We've got enough to do.' He looked down at Judd's young face.

'None of this fazes you, does it, Judd?'

'Not enough to keep me from thinking. Whoever he is, he's not my idea of a fun date, but we know he's got this paraphilia.' She glanced at Traynor. 'Even among sexual deviants, that'd be unusual? Getting aroused by – what's the word – *atypical* objects or fantasies?'

'It's relatively uncommon.'

'Sarge, we have to capitalize on it, get the word out to professionals who might link it to a name.'

'You've got those kinds of professional contacts, Will,' said Watts. 'How about making some subtle inquiries?'

'I can do that, but it's not an interest that individuals in treatment are likely to rush to acknowledge. Officer Miller has checked the data on unsolved homicides and found no indication in any of them that this particular paraphilia was a feature.' Watts sighed.

'This is a bloody nightmare. Miller has got some years of service behind her but I don't like Judd knowing about it.'

'Don't talk about me like I'm not here!' Judd snapped. 'I *don't* need looking after. I *don't* need special treatment. I hate all of that.'

A sharp wind had sprung up, followed by a gust, strong enough to cause the branches of nearby firs to creak, dip and wave, like beckoning fingers. Chilled, Watts pushed his hands deeper into his pockets, his thinking occupied by an otherwise anonymous dark-haired male whom they now suspected of leaving two dead women, probably more, right here. The same man who had approached two young sisters as they walked along a road almost visible from here, eating ice cream? The same man who abducted Carly Driscoll? If the answer was yes, to both, this was an ultra-confident killer, prepared to take massive risks. He wasn't going to stop. They had to stop him.

'This is some view.' Judd was looking into the far horizon,

shielding her eyes. She pointed. 'Look at that long line of low cloud way over there. More rain?'

Traynor came and stood next to her.

'Not clouds, Chloe. That's the Malvern Hills.'

They turned away and walked back to Watts' vehicle. He started the engine.

'I've had a sudden thought. It's not a good one.' He edged out of the line of vehicles. 'Whoever he is, he's playing games with us.'

They came into headquarters car park. Watts reached for a large envelope on the dashboard, looked at Judd via his mirror.

'Julian's working at his place. Can you drop this into him on your way home?'

'Won't it keep till tomorrow?' said Traynor. 'Chloe has done enough today.'

'You heard her, Traynor.' He passed the envelope back to her. 'She doesn't need any looking after.'

EIGHTEEN

Same day. 4.30 p.m.

Reynolds raised a quick hand to Watts as he came inside.
'You're wanted, Sarge.'

'You don't say.'

'Kumar says for you to go straight to the incident room ASAP.'

Watts went upstairs to find Kumar wearing a pair of old tennis shoes, one without a lace. He was looking jittery.

'There's something here you need to see, Sarge.'

Watts went to where he was sitting at a screen filled with the jerky movements of a CCTV recording. Watts leant forward as Kumar restarted it, looked at the date at the bottom of the screen.

'This is a couple of weeks ago, Sarge. It starts off close to the Brampton site but I've managed to track it.'

He pointed to a dark vehicle moving at night time, making a slow turn to join another road. Kumar pointed to the rear of the vehicle and a yellow-and-black plate now visible.

'See that?'

'Private hire vehicle.'

'Fake, Sarge, and there's more.' Kumar hit keys. The scene changed to one better lit. He pointed to the same vehicle now heading through an urban landscape. 'Here he is again, forty minutes later.' Watts pointed at the screen.

'I recognize where this is.'

'Guessed you would. He's heading into the city and —' Another series of key hits.

'Bloody hell,' murmured Watts.

'He's about to join the M6 heading north.' Kumar reached for some A4s. 'I haven't managed to track him further, but I searched prosecutions for displaying false private hire plates. This is what I got.'

Watts took the sheets from him, looked at the name highlighted in red. *Oliver Roth.*

'How sure are you that this is him?'

'He's been done twice for using the same plate information. He's local.'

'I want him in here.' He read the details again. 'Wellington Road. That's no more than a half hour's drive from here.' Watts turned to two officers who hadn't long returned from the site. 'I need you two on this—'

'There's more, Sarge,' said Kumar. 'Like I said, I checked his record. Have a look.'

'Any of it connected to this specific vehicle?' Watts asked, skimming the on-screen details.

'This data doesn't say.'

Watts reached for a phone, pointed to the two officers. 'I want you at this Wellington Road address. Get yourselves sorted while I fix something up.' He spoke into the phone then cut the call. 'Two SOCOs will meet you there. I want that vehicle.'

'What if Roth isn't there?'

'You wait. Keep me informed.'

Same day. 5.45 p.m.

Watts was in his office absorbing detailed information on the life and times of Oliver Roth. His eyes slid over several convictions for theft from female shoppers' handbags in 2015 and on to when

Roth posed as a cab driver and used his vehicle to pick up a woman in the inner city. He drove her a short distance, stopped and demanded sex. Her screams alerted a group of young males on a night out who managed to gain access to the inside of the vehicle and drag her out before Roth drove off at speed. The charge against him of abduction was dropped, he denied allegations of a sexually motivated attack, pleading guilty to demanding money by threat. Given a fifteen-month sentence, he served barely eight. Watts read on. In late 2017, Roth was arrested again, this time for following a woman, not a known sex worker, in his vehicle. She declined his offers of transportation after which he attempted to force her inside it. Again, members of the public, alerted by her calls for help, came to her assistance. Roth immediately left the scene. She later identified him and his vehicle and he was arrested, but the case was not proceeded with. Watts dropped the A4s on the table and sat, his eyes fixed straight ahead.

The phone rang. He reached for it. It was Kumar.

'They got him, Sarge. He's here.'

'Tell them to take him to Interview Room One. Stay with him. I'm on my way.'

Moments later, Watts entered the interview room where Oliver Roth was waiting. Watts sat opposite him, nodded at Kumar, who left his post at the door and joined him. By some miracle, Roth hadn't yet demanded a lawyer. Watts introduced himself and Kumar.

Roth interested Watts, partly because of the nature of his offences but also because of his biographical details which Watts had brought with him. Roth was not from the familiar mould of offender. He was an arts graduate. Watts recalled Marella Ricci, who disappeared on 2 March 2018, had been following an arts degree course. Watts switched his attention to the man himself and his dark good looks. Thirty-five years old, casually dressed, hair on the long side but well-kempt. Five foot eight inches tall. Two years ago, Roth had been arrested for posing as a potential customer at an art shop, from which he attempted to remove two drawings purported to be by a well-known artist, but which were later revealed to be fakes. The management at the shop declined to pursue the matter further. Watts looked up at Roth, who seemed to have the luck of the devil, to put it mildly. Sensing Watts' attention, Roth met his gaze and grinned amiably.

'I haven't been informed as to why I've been brought here, why my car has been seized. Where is it?'

In no rush to respond, Watts regarded him across the table, seeing the hint of arrogance in the way he was sitting. Yes, Roth interested Watts very much.

'What's up north that interests you, Mr Roth?'

'Excuse me?'

'CCTV indicates that you drive the M6 quite often, so, I'll ask you again. What's up there that's worth the effort.'

'I have family near Manchester.'

'A big area, that.'

Roth sighed, looking bored.

'My mother lives in Altrincham.' Watts nodded.

'Nice part of the world. Close to her, are you? Enough to make regular trips to visit?'

'Look, I don't know what this is about—' Roth was starting to fret.

'It's about your run-ins with the law which involved women.' Watching Roth's face, Watts saw something unexpected. Relief.

'I was wrongly accused by a woman who got into my taxi—'

'Illegal private hire vehicle.' Roth grinned.

'We all have to make a living, D.C.I. Watts, and most people would agree that there's too much red tape.'

'The woman you picked up alleged that you demanded sex and when she wouldn't comply you started hitting her.' Roth yawned, blinked.

'That's her story.'

'You got a custodial.'

'For the illegal hire and throwing her out of my vehicle, not for sex.' He shrugged. 'You'll know how seriously it was taken by the fact that I only did a few months.' He smirked. Watts had a sudden urge to hit him.

'What about the kerb-crawling?'

'I do *not* "kerb-crawl". I had engine problems at the time and was driving very slowly. That was a different woman. There's a lot of anti-male sentiment around these days.'

There was a knock at the door. Kumar went to it, had a low, brief conversation, closed it and returned to the table, placing an A4 in front of Watts. He reached for it. Read it. Roth's vehicle had been examined for prints and DNA which might be found to match those of their five victims at some point. They had found something else of interest in the boot. A fine powder over the whole surface where the spare wheel was housed. Test result indicated cocaine.

'When you play happy families with your mother and any other relatives in Manchester, does it involve the use of illegal substances?'

'That's too ridiculous for me to make a response. You may be unaware of this, but my father is a cardiac surgeon—'

'And you must be the disappointment of his life. Oliver Roth, I'm arresting you for possession and transportation of a Class A drug with intent to—' As Watts finished charging him, Roth responded by taking out his phone.

'I'm saying nothing further, until my solicitor gets here.'

Watts was now in the incident room where Kumar was complaining at length.

'I was hoping the sex angle would stitch him up for Peters and Trent.'

'Roth doesn't fit Will Traynor's profile, plus he was in prison when Claire Walsh went missing, but,' Watts got to his feet, 'according to Will, we're looking for somebody not a million miles from Roth but more subtle. Don't get downcast, lad. You did some first-class work today.'

He left the room and headed downstairs. He was as disappointed as Kumar at the outcome with Roth, but that's how it went sometimes. You were onto a potential winner and ten minutes later you weren't. He came into his office, thinking about a possibility for the Brampton murders which had occurred to him a few days before. He hadn't liked it then, liked it even less now, but it needed further consideration.

NINETEEN

Same day. 6 p.m.

Swooping into a parking space outside her house, Judd got out of her car. Dennis looked up from prodding his small front garden with a fork as she hurried up the path.

'Hi, how's it going?'

'Sorry, Dennis, I can't stop.'

She pushed her key into the door, opened it and quickly closed it after her. Dropping her bag by the stairs she went up to the bathroom, gave her reflection in the mirror above the washbasin a quick once-over, prodded her hair, cleaned her teeth, rinsed, added mouthwash, spat and looked at herself, teeth bared. She had considered a quick change of clothes but decided against it. It might look obvious. Over-keen. A quick blast of perfume and she was downstairs and out of the house, feeling Dennis's eyes on her even though he was nowhere in evidence.

She felt relaxed until she drove through the entrance to the apartment complex. Parking in a space near the main entrance, she looked up at the building. Her heartrate spiked. The whole place whispered money. It wasn't the first time she had seen it. She had been here months before, again to deliver something to Julian. Reaching for the envelope Sarge had given her, she got out of the car and fetched her handbag from the boot.

Coming inside the spacious entrance, seeing no one around, she headed for the chrome-and-glass lift. It delivered her silently to the second floor. She found apartment 2B, pressed the bell and waited, eyeing the exotic-looking plant arrangements nearby. The door opened.

Julian was standing there, looking surprised.

'Chloe!' He grinned down at her. 'Come on in.'

She stepped inside and followed him into the vast sitting room which looked to be not far off the entire ground floor of her house. Her eyes drifted over the expensive furniture, then on to Julian. He was wearing a pale blue sweater, jeans and flipflops. There were printed sheets spread on the floor in front of the vast, cream-coloured sofa. She waved the envelope.

'Sarge asked me to drop this in to you.'

'Great. I'll be needing that soon.' He took it from her. 'Actually, I need a break. What would you like? Coffee, tea?' He looked at his watch. 'Or, shall we hit the hard stuff?' He grinned at her sudden change of facial expression, inclined his head towards her.

'That was a joke. Come on. I'll make us something to eat—'

'*No*, I can't—'

She followed him, again overwhelmed by the place, the way he lived. She would leave as soon as she could.

'I'll just have a quick coffee and—' He held his index finger to his lips.

'Sit. Relax.'

'Actually, I'm not hungry,' she began, sitting carefully on a pale leather swivel stool, one of four around the kitchen island.

'According to what I've heard Bernard say, plus my own very casual observations, I think that's very unlikely to be true.'

She watched him move to the tall fridge freezer, open its double doors and reach inside.

'How about I slap some topping on a pizza base?'

'. . . That sounds good, but I can't stay long.'

'Any allergies, personal dislikes, loathings of a serious nature?' Hands full, he elbowed the fridge closed.

She looked down at large, perfect tomatoes, a hefty chunk of pale-yellow cheese, a bunch of dark green leaves and a small bowl of lemon slices. She felt her tension slowly ebb.

'None, from what I can see. All of it looks yummy.' She sounded like an idiot.

'That's what I like to hear!' Julian grinned at her. 'A woman who enjoys good food.'

He opened a cupboard, brought out olive oil, dark-coloured vinegar, a bottle of something clear. She watched him pour from it, add tonic. He held out a large glass to her.

'Time for a drink! One G and T, ice "n" slice and, in case you fancy another, I've made it weak so don't worry about driving later.'

She took it from him, sipped. He was right. Not strong. Nice.

An hour later, they were sitting either side of the dining table, the pizza and salad gone, as were the strawberries which had followed. Judd was listening to the soft music that was playing.

'What is it?'

'Elgar's cello concerto in E minor, Opus-Not-a-Clue.' He grinned, stood. 'I'll make coffee. No, stay there. Relax.'

'I've done nothing else since I got here.'

'Where's the problem with that? You could use some downtime.' He picked up the plates and dishes. She frowned after him.

'What do you mean?'

'It wasn't an observation of just you, Chloe. We're all tired.' He put the plates down on the island, then came back to her, lightly took her hand.

'Come on.'

He led her to the massive sofa, began gathering up the printed sheets lying on and around it.

'We *all* need downtime, no matter how much we enjoy the way we earn a living. Let's just talk, *not* about work.' He sat down, not too close to her.

'Talk to me, Chloe,' he said softly.

'. . . I've got nothing much to say.' Her eyes drifted away from him.

'I can hear Bernard quibbling about that, too. If you'd rather talk about work, tell me about this woman I've heard about who claims she was abducted in the city centre.'

'She was. She's made a statement. Sarge thinks it could be a breakthrough for the Brampton investigation.'

'I don't know what the connection is, but let's hope so. Has she given a description?'

'Tall, dark haired.'

'Mm, that fits a lot of males.'

'There's more. He told her he was a police officer.' He shook his head.

'Not the most creative line he could have come up with. Was she hurt?'

'A bit bruised. Terrified out of her wits.'

'Poor girl. OK, no more work talk. Tell me about yourself.' Seeing her hesitate, he said, 'OK, I'll start.'

She listened to him, absorbing every word about his family, his parents' divorce when he was twelve years old, going to boarding school.

'That must have been tough.' She watched him run his hand through his short blond hair, saw it ripple neatly back into place.

'You're right. It was. Being away from home didn't help, although the people at my school were really understanding. There were a lot of other pupils in a similar situation.' He shrugged. 'I'm not saying it wasn't a problem for me. It did have an impact, but I adjusted. My dad took me on a few of his business trips during vacations.' He smiled. 'I saw a *lot* of very nice hotel rooms and pools. I went to university, though *not* Oxbridge which he wanted. I chose Exeter. During the summer, he'd rent property for the two of us: quality Dad/me-time.'

'Did you miss your mother?'

'By that stage, she had married somebody else, but she was there during some of those vacations. My dad's a good guy and he did his best to fill the space when she wasn't, but he's very traditional, my dad. He doesn't *talk*.' He grinned at Judd. 'My mom is the talker.'

Judd wanted to hear more about his family but knowing how much she resented those kinds of questions she wouldn't ask.

'I suppose Exeter would have been as far as you could get from them.' Hearing him laugh, realizing how her words sounded, she flushed. 'Sorry. I didn't mean that the way it came out . . . that was a really clumsy thing to say.'

He laughed again.

'No harm done, Chloe. My parents don't live in the UK. My dad's main place is in Vancouver and my mother lives with her husband in California.' He smiled at her.

'Your turn.'

'There's nothing much to say.' Panic bloomed. She felt her face heat up again. 'It's a bit complicated.' She couldn't think of a way out. She had to say something. 'I – actually, I grew up in care.'

She watched the smile leave his face.

'Sorry, Chloe. I didn't mean to pry. I had no idea.' He reached for her hand. Seeing the sympathy in his eyes, she pulled it away.

'It wasn't some big tragedy, just that things got . . . actually, my mother was taken ill, which is the reason . . . and then . . . she soon got better and she came and . . . took me home.' Flustered, she bent to slip her shoes on.

'Sorry, I have to go. I've got things to do and so have you.' He put a hand on her arm to stop her.

'It's just you and me, Chloe, two friends talking to each other.' He smiled. 'Change of subject: how do you find Bernard as a boss?'

'He's great. I've learnt such a lot from him. He finds me annoying.' Seeing him throw back his head, hearing his laugh, she laughed too.

'Bernard is a great guy. I was still at uni here when I got to know him through one of my lecturers.'

'Not Exeter?'

'I got thrown out of there after six months.'

'Why?'

'Cannabis use. I haven't done any of that in a long time.'

A phone rang somewhere in the apartment. He went to answer it. She listened to the sound of his voice drifting from a nearby room. Within five minutes he was back, carrying a guitar. He sat on the edge of the sofa, his arm around it. She couldn't recall ever seeing a guitar up close before. Her eyes moved slowly over it, taking in its curves, the richness of the browns and golds.

'That's beautiful,' she whispered.

'It is, isn't it. It's a Gibson L5.'

She watched him bow his head, his fingers settling on its strings, listened to the soft sounds, feeling suddenly awkward to have somebody played something just for her. Watching his fingers, she started to relax again, aware of his low humming. There was something familiar about the tune. Closing her mind on Jonesy and his likely mockery if he could see her right now, she lost herself. After a few minutes, Julian stopped playing. She looked across at him.

'That was really lovely.' Feeling awkward again, she looked at her watch, leapt to her feet.

'It's half past nine! I really have to go.'

He stood, put down the guitar.

'Next time you come, I'll make you the best meal you've ever had.'

She hesitated, feeling silly and presumptuous. It still needed saying.

'You've got someone in Manchester.' He nodded.

'Yes. That was her on the phone. We get on fine. We both know it's not going anywhere, but there's a child.' Seeing shock arrive on her face, he clarified, 'No, no, she's not *mine*, but I've been around for most of her life so I can't just leave the situation. We're both trying to find the best way to end it without her being upset.' He gave her a direct look. 'Chloe. I'd like to get to know you better.'

She looked up at him, wishing she could be more comfortable with people when things got personal. It wasn't all people. With Jonesy, for example, whenever he started in on such things, she told him to sod off. Jonesy. Julian. Two men. Different planets. She reached for her jacket and bag. He came down in the lift with her, walked her to her car, watched as she drove away, his hand raised.

TWENTY

Thursday, 18 April. 7.15 a.m.

Watts came into the kitchen, running an electric razor over his chin. Chong placed a cup of coffee in front of him. 'I was beginning to wonder if you were nurturing something permanent there. It suited you.'

'Too busy to get rid and it's itchy.' She glanced at him.

'Have you recovered from the Oliver Roth thing?'

'Yeah. It's one of the first things you learn in the job: what looks like a real lead—'

Catching movement on the small television screen, he silenced the razor, stared at a news reporter, microphone in hand, standing on a familiar narrow lane.

'That's the Brampton site!' Chong reached out, increased the volume.

'*—at what has been a scene of intense police activity here for several days, following the recovery of yet more human remains from the area behind and directly above me. West Midlands Police are remaining tight-lipped but a spokesperson has now confirmed it. Detective Chief Inspector Watts who is leading the investigation has not yet spoken directly to the media . . .*'

'And that's how it's staying.' He snapped.

An hour later, they walked into headquarters together, Chong going to the lower floor, Watts to reception.

Taking post from an officer on duty, he paused at one of the early newspapers, read its banner headline: *MORE HUMAN REMAINS AT CONSERVATION AREA.*

There was also a photograph of officers searching the site taken from somewhere within it.

Walking into his office he found Judd surrounded by documents.

'Morning, Sarge. Look what's arrived from Manchester! Statements. Lists of clothing and other effects of the five victims. Biographical information from the missing women's families. Now I can really move on the victimologies—'

She looked down at the newspaper which had landed on the table in front of her, read the headline, looked up at him.

'How did they manage it? We had that road completely sealed off.'

'Apparently, not.' He looked through the window to the car park then to the wall clock which was showing eight thirty-five.

'She's an early bird. I said nine.'

'Who?'

'Carly Driscoll.'

Judd came to the window, watched Driscoll aim her fob at a small car, then walk towards the main entrance. She was within a few feet of it when several officers came out of the building, moving in her direction. She came to a sudden stop, the officers going past her, one of them giving her an appraising glance. Judd tutted. Jonesy. True to form. Always on the look-out where females were concerned.

Watts went to the phone as Reynolds appeared at the office door.

'Sarge, the woman who was abducted near Broad Street is here. She says she's come to put together an E-FIT of her attacker. She's not due here until—'

'I'll be there in a couple of minutes.' As Reynolds left, he spoke into the phone. 'Gavin? Carly Driscoll has arrived.' He listened, nodded. 'I thought we'd do it down here in my office, if that's OK with you. She's already familiar with it and it's not as formal as an interview room. What do you think? OK.' He ended the call, turned to Judd.

'I'll go and fetch her.'

As Watts left, Judd quickly gathered all of the Manchester documents and photographs together, took them to one of the filing cabinets and placed them inside. The office door swung open and Gavin, headquarters' resident E-FIT expert, appeared carrying a laptop. Judd cast a quick glance over the whole room as the door opened again and Watts came in with Driscoll, who was looking pale.

'You remember PC Judd?' Watts said.

'Yes. I hope it's OK that I'm early but I said I'd go into work, just for a couple of hours. My parents think it's too soon, but I need to do it.'

Watts thought her parents might be right. She looked rocky.

The construction of an E-FIT demanded focus, concentration. They had one shot at it.

'You're sure you're feeling up to this? We can wait another day—'

'No, I'm fine, honestly, it's just— When I arrived a big group of men were coming out, most of them tall and . . . I don't know, I got nervous, seeing them walking towards me.'

'That's understandable.' He rubbed his big hands together. 'How about some posh coffee before we start? Gavin here likes his coffee, don't you, Gav?'

Nonplussed because he routinely brought a thermos of tea into work, Gavin nodded.

Judd headed to the makings, listening to Sarge chat to Driscoll about nothing in particular, hearing her respond with one or two brief laughs, her voice steady now. Sarge had an ability to relate to people, including those he didn't know well. Judd knew that her own 'default setting', as he called it, was to find people vaguely annoying on first meeting. It worked for her. It felt safe. She took a mug of coffee and a glass of water to the table, set both down beside Driscoll, then fetched the rest of the coffee. They drank, Watts still in chat-mode. After a couple of minutes, he looked at Driscoll.

'How do you feel about making a start on putting the E-FIT together?'

'I'm ready.' She nodded. She did look much better than when she arrived.

'Gavin's going to talk you through the process.' Getting a nod from Watts, Gavin tapped keys, his eyes on the screen.

'Carly, there's a process we have to follow to generate an E-FIT. Your job is to guide me by giving a description of the individual from what you recall of him.' She nodded that she understood. 'You'll see the results of what you tell me on this screen as we proceed. If at any point what you see doesn't fit with what you've said to me, if it doesn't fit with what you remember, or you consider it in any way inaccurate, you can request changes. You can make as many changes as you want until you're satisfied with the result. You are the only person who can make changes. If you're unsure of anything I've said so far, I can repeat it. It's not a problem.'

'I understand. I'm in control of what's produced and I'm the only one who can tell you to change it.'

'Exactly. Let's give it a go, shall we? Start by slowly describing all you recall of this individual.'

They listened as she did so, starting with the hair, seeing a face slowly emerge on-screen. Watts and Judd were silent, unobtrusive as Driscoll described the man who had abducted her, unaware that that same man might be responsible for another attempted abduction, plus the murders of five young women who looked much like herself. After a while her words slowed then stopped, her eyes fixed on what she and the software programme had produced.

'. . . The hair . . . The eyes . . . It's . . . *him.*'

She reached for her glass, her hand shaking. Gavin printed off the image, passed it to Watts.

'What will you do with it?' she asked.

'We'll release it to the media and hope that it identifies a potential suspect.' He slowly pushed a sheet across the table towards her.

'You did well, Carly. One final thing: you and Gavin need to sign this statement that you produced the image on the screen entirely from your memory and that you weren't persuaded or influenced in its creation by any other person.'

She looked down at the statement, glanced back at the screen, took a pen from Watts and signed.

Judd went with her to reception.

'Thank you for all you've done to help us, Carly.' Driscoll looked embarrassed.

'You must think I'm an idiot to get into that situation but – I'm a bit shy and I suppose I take people at face value.'

'How're you feeling now?'

'Coming here has made me see that, well, I saved my own life.'

'You won the fight of your life, Carly. You're stronger than you think.' Judd held out her hand to Driscoll, who shook it. She watched the younger woman leave, then went back to the office.

'How was she?' asked Watts.

'I think doing the E-FIT has helped.' She looked over Gavin's shoulder, frowned at the on-screen image.

'Let's hope it gets us somewhere.'

Gavin closed the laptop and went to the door.

'If you want more copies, let me know.'

Judd reached for the copy E-FIT. What she was seeing did not suggest a killer with a raging hatred of women. She put it down, eyes fixed on it, taking in the mild-looking face. Like Will had said, whoever this killer was, his real self was so well-hidden that no witness, no matter how observant, was likely to pick up on it.

Same day. 11.15 a.m.

Judd's attention had been on the detail contained in the Manchester documents as she pieced together the victimology for Amy Peters, followed by the same for Erica Trent. Alone in the office, she sat back. Despite her efforts at assembling the facts into a representation of both young women's lives, she knew there was nothing here that could be mistaken for a lead, not even a potential link between them. With no further information anticipated from Manchester, it looked like there was nothing more she could do that might take them nearer to the man who killed them both. She thought of Carly Driscoll's visit here early that morning. It seemed to Judd like they didn't have much on her abductor either.

Dispirited, eyes gritty, she stood, gathered papers together, slid them into their separate envelopes. Reaching for her bag, she carried them with her to the door. She was taking them home, where it was quiet, to check all of it again. Make sure she had missed nothing.

Same day. Noon.

Julian came into Watts' office holding up an A4.

'Bernard, you're going to love this.' He sat opposite Watts looking animated. 'Remember Fincher, the dog walker? I was data-searching and typed his name in.'

'I already checked and got his domestics.'

'I know. Under the name Colin Fincher. I did a general search of the surname and found this under "Norman Fincher".' He pushed the sheet across to Watts. 'It's the same guy, Bernard. Same age, same address, this time for theft around three years ago, but look at the employment section.'

Watts did. It brought him to his feet. He snatched up the phone, spoke into it, his voice terse.

'Is Jones up there? Right. Tell him to go to this address.'

Just over an hour later Colin aka Norman Fincher was shown

into the interview room where Watts was seated, arms folded. Jones pointed at Fincher to sit. He did, looking irritable. Watts stared across at him, and to Jones, 'Stay.'

He took the chair next to Watts whose eyes hadn't left Fincher's face. Fincher stared back, looked away.

'What's this about? I'm supposed to be working—'

'Tell us about the work you were doing in—' He looked at the details in front of him, 'March 2016.'

'I haven't got a clue what you're on about—' Fincher's eyes went from Watts to Jones.

'The Forestry Commission. You were employed by it back then, a small fact you never thought to mention!'

'For four months. What's the big deal?'

'Tell us about it. What the job was, the hours, all of it!'

They listened as Fincher described his brief stint as a Visitor Services Officer.

'I liked the being outdoors part of it, but I'm not much for being around people.' Watts stared at him.

'In that case, I'd have thought that the job title might have tipped you off that it wasn't your thing.' Fincher frowned.

'Look, I needed a job and I managed to blag my way into that one. It was all right. I was responsible for keeping the area tidy, free of litter, but the other part – the public can be very demanding, you know.'

'Really? Who'd have thought?'

Watts sat back, his interest spiking. The last time he had seen Fincher, talked to his brother about him, he had been more or less satisfied with what he knew and that Fincher had no connection with what had happened at Brampton. Now, he was busy rethinking that view. Fincher was a loner and he hadn't exactly put himself out to offer information.

'Exactly how long did you work at Brampton? I want *dates*.'

'Brampton?' Fincher's eyes widened. 'I didn't. I was based at a place about six miles away with a small visitor centre and—'

'During the course of that work you would have got to know about the Brampton site.'

'Yes, but you've got this all wrong—' Light dawned in Fincher's eyes. 'Come on! If you're saying I had anything to do with what's gone on there, you're out of your mind.'

Watts studied him. He looked at least in his mid-forties. He did a quick calculation. Fincher would have been in his early thirties when Amy Peters and Melody Brewster were abducted – it had clearly taken its toll on him.

'You would have had a vehicle to do the job you've just told us about.'

'Yeah. An old jeep. During the time I was working there, it broke down and this other worker give me a lift to and from—'

'That job would have also required job-related qualifications. Tell us about yours.'

Fincher glanced away.

'I did exams at school but dropped out of university. I told them at the interview. They said they weren't interested in formal education. They wanted somebody who had some interest in conservation, which I have.'

Watts looked at him steadily for several seconds, Traynor's words on the man they were looking for inside his head: Fincher had the intelligence. He didn't have the charm. Nor the self-presentational skills. The Commission must have been desperate when they interviewed him. If he changed his mind about Fincher, he knew where to find him.

'Drop him home, Jones.'

Same day. 1 p.m.

Traynor walked the site beneath gathering cloud, iPad in hand. Reaching the red markers designating the locations of the two victims' remains, he looked at their positions in relation to each other. He knew what he was seeing. Purposeful placement for a killer's convenience. He took a photograph, studied it. Whoever killed Amy Peters and Erica Trent had wanted them here, lying close together for when he returned. In Amy Peters' case, that was probably several times. He tapped the iPad, brought to the screen the white face, the mouth a small crimson bud within the whiteness. He studied it. He knew this killer's personality. Antisocial to a high degree. Zero empathy for others. Both characteristics which made homicide highly likely, particularly for a killer wanting an unresisting, non-rejecting sexual partner, incapable of refusing whatever he wished. The total ownership of another human being. A monstrous creation wrought from utter selfishness. It all fitted as a prototype, but not the individual he had in mind.

He turned and walked the steep rise, reached the flat area of land pressed around by more dense trees, his body temperature dropping as the trees closed around him. Hearing his name being called, he turned, saw Julian coming up from the direction of the road.

'We made today's front page!'

'So I saw.' He waited. 'It's best we keep our voices down.'

'You're right, Will, although from what I saw of the media as I arrived, they're reduced to interviewing each other.'

'You seem to get on well with them from what I hear.'

'Oh, you know. Needs must. They're not the kind of people I'd choose to spend time with.' Julian's eyes moved over the site. He looked back to Traynor. 'Have you heard from Bernard at all?'

'No.'

'Earlier today he thought he had this case cracked.' He grinned, shook his head. 'Remember the dog walker guy who found the first lot of remains?'

'Amy Peters, yes.'

'He failed to tell Bernard that he briefly worked for the Forestry Commission a few years back, but it seems to have come to nothing.' There was a brief silence, broken by Traynor.

'What brings you here, Julian?'

'I thought if I walked the whole site, it might get some more ideas flowing about this killer. How about you?' Traynor's gaze moved slowly over the dense firs.

'I have a very general impression of him.'

'Oh?' Julian waited. 'I'm still nowhere, with nothing but questions. To be honest, I've got questions about my questions.' He frowned as Traynor turned to him.

'What is it, Will?'

'Why here?'

'Sorry?'

'He *chose* this place. He has to have a connection to it. What is it?'

Julian looked around and shrugged.

'We'll probably never know.'

'We *have* to know. It has to be something so important to him that he was prepared to risk an eighty-mile drive to bring Amy Peters then Erica Trent here.' Julian's eyes drifted over the undulating land around them.

'Actually, hearing you say that, I did wonder if he's one of those environmental types. You know, a save-the-planet zealot, a loner, a total misogynistic conservationist with maybe a tenuous interest in what the Forestry Commission does, which might account for his knowing about this place. Like Fincher, in fact.'

'It's easy for anybody to know about conservation. Google makes it so.' Julian watched as Traynor tapped his iPad.

'Are you contacting the Forestry Commission?'

'No. I'm looking for parking places around this immediate area, other than the narrow lane we're all using. I'm not finding any.' He flipped the iPad closed. 'This place doesn't exactly welcome visitors, but whoever this killer is, he feels very much at home here.'

Julian gazed around, frowning.

'To me this whole site is a downer, really depressing, but each to his own.'

Traynor pointed towards lower ground.

'Look. Jake Petrie is here again. And there's Bernard. We might be about to get some answers.'

'I envy your optimism, Will. Not only am I totally out of ideas, right now I'm also low on anything resembling hope.'

TWENTY-ONE

Same day. 1.30 p.m.

All eyes were fixed on the drone as it hovered, dipped and buzzed high above them. Petrie manipulated the controls, tracking its movements, sometimes watching it with the others, mostly following its progress on his screen. Watts had been gazing up at it for the last several minutes, waiting for some kind of indication that what they were doing here might be paying off. So far, nothing. As the drone climbed again, Watts saw Traynor and Julian coming towards him. Traynor's face was unreadable. Was inscrutability a required characteristic of criminologists? He knew that Traynor's own preference was to divulge nothing of what he was thinking until he was ready.

Watts thought of the two calls he had had from Brophy in the last fifteen minutes, reminding him of escalating costs, asking after progress, cutting each call short on being told that there was nothing to report. He turned his attention to Julian walking along-side the criminologist. Another academic, but this one more your open-book type. As soon as he knew or knew he didn't know something, he told you.

Above them, the drone lost height then hovered. Watts moved quickly in its direction, calling, 'Got something, Jake?'

'A real possibility, plus two others a bit less certain.' Petrie pointed to his laptop balanced on his satchel. 'See, this anomaly right here?' He pointed to a mass of vague loops.

'Mmm . . .'

'It could be what you're looking for.'

Picking up the laptop, Petrie was off, moving at speed to the drone which was now sitting on grass just this side of the press of trees. Watts watched him go.

What is it with academic types? Sitting about for hours thinking, yet as soon as something gets their interest they're off. Traynor's the same—

He caught up with Petrie whose eyes were again fixed on his screen. Julian was already there, looking down at it, his face exhilarated. Petrie pointed at the ground.

'According to what I'm seeing, it's right *here*.'

'You can't give a hint as to what it is? Or, how deep?' Petrie looked up at Watts.

'The configuration is animal, in the very general sense. I'm estimating a depth of around two metres, possibly a little less.'

'Shovels! *Move* it!' Watts waved his hand, signalling to officers a short distance away.

Petrie pointed down at the ground on which he was standing as the officers arrived.

'Right *here*.'

'Who's got the spray?' Watts took the aerosol can from one of the officers, passed it to Petrie who created a white rectangle on the ground. 'OK, lads, start digging.' He turned back to Petrie. 'You said there were a couple more?'

'Yes.' He pointed. 'Both over there. I'll mark them out.'

With two more potential sites outlined, Watts signalled to more officers, one of them Jones. They set to work, a steady rain now falling. SOCOs brought lights up the steep rise to each of the search areas. Watts remained where he was, watching the progress. Waiting. Traynor came towards him and they stood and watched together.

'You think there's something here for us?'

'I bloody hope so.' Watts brushed rain from his face. 'I'm getting the feeling you don't have the same hopes.'

Traynor looked down at sodden grass.

'I'm guided by theory. I'm also a realist. Killers develop routines. They also change them. We know that he brought his first victim and his last victim here. Let's hope that the drone has identified three more potential burials. If not, those three young women could be just about anywhere. If you ever arrest him, he will never divulge their whereabouts. They'll remain a secret delight he will fantasize about and enjoy for years.' A silence formed between them. 'I heard about Oliver Roth.'

'I was pretty convinced Roth was the one,' said Watts.

'From what PC Kumar told me, I can see why.'

Watts scanned the land in front of them. It was more familiar to him right now than his own garden. Not to mention his untouched allotment. He watched Jones drive his shovel into the ground.

'There's something bothering me, Will. Has been for a couple of days or so and it's not going away. It's not a theory. More a hunch. I need your view on it sometime, but not here.'

Same day. 8.10 p.m.

Inside her house Judd was sitting cross-legged on the floor, a cushion supporting her notebook, her eyes moving slowly over the printed sheets spread around her. There was nothing haphazard in the spread. She had absorbed all the information relating to both Peters and Trent, had painstakingly sorted it into categories: family of origin, educational experience, friendships, personality indicators. The last one, relationships, had yielded nothing for either Peters or Trent. One non-serious boyfriend for Peters. No known relationships for Trent. A glance at the time told Judd it was time to stop.

She sighed, buried her face in her hands, beyond tired. After hours of examining all the data now available, she still had nothing. Not a single aspect of either victims' lives which linked them romantically to a third person. What had made Judd's task harder was that she had had to read all of the Manchester documentation before she was able to bring order to the chaos it presented. She reached for the single sheet she had separated out, because of the jumble of references it contained. She reread it, let it drop to the floor. Sarge would never tolerate such sloppiness.

She got up, went to the small table in a corner of the sitting room she used for a desk, came back with highlighters of different colours, using them one after the other on the printed lines. Thirty minutes later, having categorized all of the available facts, none of it was taking her any further.

Raking her fingers through her hair which now flopped into her eyes, out of energy just like she was, she left the room and headed to the kitchen. Kettle on, she got out a jar of drinking chocolate, tipped some into a mug, poured hot water and stirred. Locating a small packet of pink and white fluffy marshmallows, she dropped three onto the hot chocolate, paused, added a fourth.

Carrying the mug to the sitting room, she sat on the floor, methodically spooning the marshmallows into her mouth. Finishing the hot chocolate, she reached for the Trent victimology to give it a last, thorough read. After ten minutes or so, she gave up, moved to the armchair, rested her head against its softness and thought of Julian.

Same day. 9.15 p.m.

The whole Brampton site was now lit up, officers leaning on their shovels, their heads and faces wet with sweat and rain. Watts looked into the sizeable hole at tree roots twice the thickness of his own fingers, winding around and under a partially exposed dark mass. Watts got down onto damp grass for a closer look, picking up angles and spikes. Petrie's voice drifted down to him.

'. . . It's a deer . . . *Was* a deer.'

Weary, soaked, Watts got slowly to his feet. The other locations had been thoroughly excavated, both of them filled with sawn lengths of rotting tree limbs. He looked at the ten-plus officers who had done the excavating, their faces lined with exhaustion. Brophy was going to get a lot of mileage out of what he would regard as Watts' failure to locate anything relevant to the case, despite the extra officers made available. In the event that Brophy said as much, Watts was already planning to get him here to look at the spread of land and the difficulties it was causing. He knew he wouldn't. It was pointless. Brophy saw his job as holding people to account when they didn't deliver. Watts hadn't delivered.

'OK, lads. You're more than done here. I'll have other officers here tomorrow.' He turned to Petrie, crouched over his laptop, his eyes fixed on its screen.

'What's up?'

'You won't be needing them.' Petrie looked up at him. 'I've gone over all the available land which might lend itself to burial. There are no more anomalies.'

Watts stared at him. This lousy day had just got worse.

'How sure are you?'

'Nothing is one hundred percent, so I'll say 99.9.' He sent Watts a sympathetic look. 'I'm sorry we didn't get the results you wanted.'

Watts' tired gaze drifted over the whole site then back to him.

'You've done a thorough job here, Jake, and I'm grateful. It is what it is.'

Same day. 9.50 p.m.

Hearing rain hitting her windows, Judd was working, comparing yet again the personal characteristics she had for the two Manchester students whose remains had been located at the site. She spoke her thoughts, needing to hear the sense in them. If there was any.

'OK. Amy was much more outgoing than Erica. More up for stuff. Sorry, Erica, but I'd go as far as to describe you as a bit of a geek. Definitely an all-work-no-play kind of gal. Which is a real pity, if you ask me.'

Recalling what Dr Chong and Will had said had been done to Trent's face, she shook her head, reached forward, churning through the lists she had made, moving them this way and that until she found the highlighted passages she was looking for, made by Erica's tutor.

Erica is my most promising student by far, this academic year. Her grasp of mathematical theory is impressive, yet it concerns me that she appears to have few if any friends and in consequence, an extremely limited social life. I raised the need for life balance with her today.

Erica went some way to acknowledging that she'd been focusing

on her studies to the detriment of her social life. She also confided
to me that that might be about to change.

Judd reread the last few words. She was so tired that her eyes had slid over them the first time she had read them. She stared ahead.

'So . . . what do I make of that, if anything? Was Erica saying that to pacify the tutor? Or was she actually planning a change to her own behaviour?' Judd read it again, feeling her heart up-tempo. 'Is it possible that Erica had a specific person in mind? Someone she'd already seen around the campus, maybe even met?'

She read the tutor's comment yet again. If this investigation was going nowhere, it wouldn't be helped by Judd seeing meaning where it was never intended. She read it a third time, recalling one of her own teachers years ago describing her as a 'wordsmith'. Judd hadn't understood. She had had other things to think about back then. But since joining the force she had realized that that teacher was right. Words were like ripe fruit. You had to squeeze them to gain every bit of meaning. It had helped her understand the chaos of her own childhood. It was still helping her as an officer, but only if what it yielded was founded on something solid.

'Had Erica decided to extend her social life by involving herself in campus activities?' She shook her head. 'My money is on her having her eye on somebody in particular.'

She moved more papers, found the name of Erica's tutor and her contact number. She would phone her in the morning as soon as she got to headquarters.

Leaving her desk, switching off lights, she headed for the stairs.

Friday, 19 April. 1.30 a.m.

Judd sat up, her heart banging her chest. There it was again. She threw back the duvet, snatched up a heavy jumper, pulled it on and went quickly downstairs. It was coming from outside, behind her house. Phone clutched in one hand, she went quickly along the hall to the kitchen door, slowly opened it. The security light in Dennis's rear garden was blazing, making her kitchen window a bright rectangle of white. She went quickly to the window, saw trees at the end of her garden swaying in the wind. The rear gate was open! She watched it crash against its frame, wheeled at a sharp knock on the back door.

'Chloe, don't be scared. It's me.' Recognizing the voice, she went to the door, unlocked and opened it.

'*Julian!* What's—'

'I've been at the site and was driving home.' He stepped inside, closed the door, his hair and coat damp.

'As I passed your house, I saw someone going down the accessway on the other side of your neighbour's house, so I parked and came to check it out.'

'It was probably a neighbour who lives further along the road.'

'That's what I thought, but I wasn't happy to just leave it. I went down the accessway, walked along the alley beyond your rear fence and found your gate open.'

'There's a bolt at the top. It's always in place because I never leave that way.' She filled the hot water jug. He looked down at her.

'Were you expecting anybody?'

'Of course not.'

'I had to ask. In which case, I'm really concerned.'

'Why?'

'Look, it was pretty dark but the man I saw looked familiar.' She stared at him, waited.

'If it's somebody I know, tell me.'

'It looked like Adrian Jones. I caught a glimpse of his dark hair under the streetlight, the way he moves. It was him, but I wasn't sure if you and he are—'

'We're just mates.'

'I followed him, found your gate open, but he had gone. Disappeared.'

The hot water jug clicked off. She lifted it, poured water into a mug of instant coffee.

'Why would Jonesy be here in the middle of the night?' She saw Julian move to the back door, ready to leave.

'Wait! Have some coffee. I'll fetch a towel—'

'No, I just wanted to know that you're safe.' He had the door open. Judd felt a rush of quick anger towards Jones.

'When I see him tomorrow, I'll ask him what the *hell* he was doing here.'

Julian turned to her as he stepped outside.

'That's your call, Chloe. As I said, I only got a quick look.' He tapped the door. 'Lock this now. I'll secure the gate as I leave.'

She locked the kitchen door, watched him go, suddenly illuminated by Dennis's security light, saw him reach the gate, raise his hand, walk out of the garden, close the gate after him, reach over and slide the bolt.

Bloody Jonesy! What the hell was he playing at?

TWENTY-TWO

Friday, 19 April. 8 a.m.

Coming into a deserted office, Judd took her notebook from her bag, dragged the desk phone closer. The door swung open. Jones peered inside.

'Hey, Chlo—'

'I'm busy,' she snapped, not looking at him.

'I'm in Stockport over the weekend, so I just wanted to—'

'I don't care what you want. Get lost.' He frowned at her.

'What's got your pants in a knot!' Watts appeared behind him.

'Aye-up! Out the way, Jones.' He came into the office. 'What's with the shouting?'

'Nothing,' Judd said sharply.

After staring at her for several seconds, Jones turned and left. Watts sat opposite her. She reached for the phone, dialled the Manchester number, got the engaged signal.

'Damn!'

Banging down the phone, she looked up as the door opened. It was Julian. He smiled, brows and thumb raised. She nodded and the door closed on him. Watts eyed her.

'Doors opening, doors closing, voices raised. It's like a bloody West End farce in here. If I hadn't been up half the night, I might ask what's going on. Instead, was that a Manchester number you just dialled?'

'Yes, one of Erica Trent's tutors. I'm following up a possibility. If it comes to anything, I'll tell you.' He reached for a copy of the E-FIT and stood.

'Before I release this to the media, I'm going to check if it's a reasonable likeness to anybody already in the system.' As he left, she reached for the phone again and dialled. Her call was picked up.

'Department of Mathematics, University of Manchester. How can I help?'

'Yes, hi! I'd like to speak to Helena Jamison who—'

'I'm sorry, Dr Jamison no longer works here.' Judd bowed her head, took a breath.

'This is West Midlands Police. It's very important that I contact Dr Jamison as soon as possible.'

'I believe she's now at the University of Warwick—'

'Thank you.'

Judd replaced the receiver, thinking that that was good news. Warwick was close. She googled the phone number, tapped it into the phone, waited.

'Helena Jamison.' Judd gripped the phone.

'Dr Jamison, my name is Chloe Judd. I'm a police officer calling on behalf of West Midlands Police.'

'Is this about Erica Trent? I read somewhere that the case was being investigated down here.'

'Yes, it is. Dr Jamison, I really need your help. I've spent several hours looking through statements made to the Manchester police investigation. One of them has an attachment: notes of your last tutorial with Erica Trent.'

There was silence, then, '. . . I'm not too happy to discuss this on the phone with someone I don't know.'

'Dr Jamison, I meant it when I said I need your help. How about I give you my headquarters' number and you can ring me back?' Judd waited out another silence.

'Tell me what it is that you want.' Relieved, Judd grabbed the tutorial notes in front of her.

'When you talked to the Manchester police, following Erica's disappearance, you said that you'd formed an impression directly from Erica that she had an extremely limited social life.'

'That's correct. During tutorials she rarely referred to spending time with other students. Erica came across as very mature for her age, very self-contained and I did wonder if she found other students somewhat juvenile. I was a little concerned that her apparent lack of a social life might impact on her studies over time and I mentioned that to her.' Jamison paused. 'Perhaps

I should make it clear that I was not suggesting that Erica had mental health problems. Quite the contrary. She was an extremely able and confident student who participated fully in lectures. She was also very ambitious. During that last tutorial she talked to me a little about her life in Manchester. I was pleased she did because she was extremely gifted and I wanted her to reach her full potential in all areas of her life.' Judd made swift notes.

'What did she tell you?'

'She said she was aware of the lack of balance in her life and had decided to do something about it. I got the impression that she had met someone.' Judd's pen stopped.

'Did she identify that person?'

'When I say "met", I got the sense that this was someone she had seen around campus. She said he was attractive and that she tended to look out for him.'

'You don't have any idea as to whether her contact with this person might have progressed at all?'

'I'm sorry, I don't.' Judd's head was racing.

'At the time she said all of this to you, did you get *any* idea at all as to who it might be?'

'I suppose I assumed he was another student.' There was a brief silence. 'She lived off-campus in a student house, so it's possible he lived there.'

Judd doubted it. She shared Sarge's low opinion of the efforts made during the Manchester investigation, but having read the data now available she knew that officers had gone to Erica Trent's accommodation and interviewed her fellow students: all female except for two who were new to the university and a couple of years younger than Erica. Whoever this man was, Judd doubted that he was a housemate.

'I'm really grateful for your time, Dr Jamison—'

'I feel somewhat guilty for not telling the police more about it but the tutor-student relationship is built on trust and there was no real detail in what she said to me.'

'You've been a great help now, so thank you.'

Ending the call, Judd sat back, staring straight ahead. One of the main messages from the investigation so far was that this man, whoever he was, abducted his victims without attracting attention. No cries. No struggle. Amy and Erica just – went. How did he manage that, particularly with Erica? By the time of her abduction, she and probably everyone else on that campus was aware of danger there. He still took her silently away.

Judd's eyes moved over her notes, one name claiming her attention. Carly Driscoll. Her abductor had presented himself as a police officer. It had been considered a likely ruse by Sarge, Jonesy and several others. What if it wasn't? What if he *was* an officer? An officer in the Manchester force. But Driscoll lived here. OK, so he drove down and abducted her. She recalled the black tape found at the scene. It had been here in this building and now it was missing. Sarge was playing it down but she knew he was worried about it. Since Judd had started work at headquarters, she couldn't recall a single item of evidence disappearing. She thought about it. Somebody was messing around? Having a laugh? Jonesy was a joker but surely, even he wouldn't mess with evidence?

Was somebody in this building causing problems for this investigation? Jones was back in her head.

He was also in my garden late last night and I don't know why.

Same day. 4.30 p.m.

Traynor left his students packing away and went into his office. Closing the door, he went directly to the shelves of textbooks lining one wall, his hand moving slowly along them. Selecting five, he carried them to the desk, turned to the indexes of each to underline several items in pencil. He knew well the detail of most of these books. He should. He had contributed chapters to three of them. What he was now seeking was confirmation.

Forty minutes later, he read through the notes he had made. There was creativity in what he did to assist the police, but there had to be more. He looked down at his written profile, wanting to be certain that it was firmly locked into known theory:

Presents as socially adept, self-assured. Good level of intelligence. An easy confidence with females. Perceived deficits: insincerity, avoidance of commitment. Indifferent to other people's thinking, feelings and opinions, but has sufficient social intelligence to exhibit positive qualities as required. Possibly a braggart.

Save for these small, incidental indicators, his is a 'hidden self', grossly divided and distanced from his outward presentation. That hidden self emerges only when he allows it free rein. He read the last few words a second time.

'And at least five young women witnessed him do exactly that.'
He added a summation:

*A cold, relentless primary psychopath who selects his victims
with care, uses superficial appeal and glibness to disarm. If he
was acquainted with any of the victims, it indicates an ability to
maintain a façade until such time he is ready to show his true nature.*

'And God help anyone who sees it.'

He had what he needed. First, a prototype, second, a profile
firmly embedded in theory, each supporting the other, a description
of a man to whom words came easily. Because words meant
absolutely nothing to him.

Traynor walked slowly to the window, gazed down at the inner
city far below. He turned away, exhausted, with a desperate need
to be home with Jess. He switched off lights, left his office and
walked to the lifts, waited for one to arrive.

How do we mark life events we consider worthy? We commemor-
ate them with flowers, cards, gifts. Had this killer done similar,
each time he killed? Left some sort of gift? More likely, he took
something away with him. Something only *he* knew was a marker
for what he had done. The scarf Bernard had recovered from the
scene. If it was commemorative, why *hadn't* he taken it with him?
Had he concealed it there, only for animals to dig it up?

Traynor thought of all the theory, the detail, he had gathered
together about this killer. How long did he dare hold on to his
suspicion?

The lift arrived. He stepped inside, got out at the secure underground car park, went to his car, dropped his backpack in the boot,
silently repeating the mantra *Home*. A place which for much of
the last decade had evoked unimaginable grief and terror and now
meant love and peace because of Jess.

After an uneventful drive, he came into his house and headed
for the kitchen, picking up Jess's voice and that of his daughter,
both of them laughing. He smiled as he came inside.

'You two sound happy.' He took the glass of wine from Jess,
giving her arm a gentle squeeze. His daughter grinned up at him.

'Jess has lent me this cool top which I've decided to wear as
a dress.' She stood, moved away from the table, did a twirl.

'Ta-*dah*. What do you think, Dad?' A soft, persistent roar
started up somewhere inside Traynor's head.

'What else are you wearing with it?'

'What?' She looked at Jess then back to him. 'Come on, Dad. It's not that short—'

'Yes, it is.'

Jess laid her hand on his arm, whispered, 'She looks lovely and she's right. It isn't that short.'

'I disagree.' He pointed at his daughter. 'You're not going out wearing that—'

'*What?*' She stared at him. 'You're *unbelievable*. Get real! I'm an adult, Dad. I make my own choices and I'm *going*.'

He watched her reach for the small handbag on the table, slip its strap onto her shoulder. Jess was right. She looked lovely. Too lovely. The roar inside his head now pounding, he saw Jess glance at him, then follow her to the door, heard her say, 'You've got money, your phone? Have a great evening!'

He looked out on the dark garden, hearing the door close, the sound of a car starting, driving away, fading to nothing. Jess's voice drifted to him.

'Where did all of that come from, Will?'

He had told her little of the police investigation, although he was sure that she was following media reports. He poured more wine, walked away from her. Yes, his daughter was beautiful, and yes, she had a right to make her own choices.

He thought of her and of the profile he had created and realized that he didn't dare keep his suspicions to himself. He had to act.

TWENTY-THREE

Same day. 7.12 p.m.

Tired, preoccupied by thoughts still bothering her, Judd opened the fridge and peered inside. Taking out a pasta dish for one and some floppy salad leaves, she straightened, listened. Somebody was at the front door. She dropped both items back inside the fridge. If it was Dennis— She opened the door and stared up at Julian.

'Tell me you haven't eaten,' he said.

'I haven't eaten.' He grinned at her.

'Take this as an observation from a friend, but I saw you leaving headquarters and, well, you looked a bit down.'

She looked at the red, flowering pot plant clasped in his hand, down at the carrier bag he was holding, bearing the name of the best Chinese restaurant in the area.

'I felt a little responsible because I brought you unwelcome news last night, so I thought I'd bring us both dinner this evening.' He nodded at the plant. 'This is for the house. I thought a bouquet might be a bit much.' He waited. 'Can I come in?'

She nodded, stood back as he came inside.

'Go through to the kitchen.'

He walked ahead of her and she realized for the first time how tall he was. As tall as Sarge and Will. At scarcely five-three, everyone was tall. Reaching the kitchen, he turned to her.

'Warm plates or eat right now?'

'Eat now, and . . .' She went to the fridge, reached inside, brought out a bottle. 'Yes?' He grinned, nodded.

'I've had better days so, yes please.'

The cartons of food opened, wine glasses located, they sat opposite each other at the small kitchen table. Judd took a mouthful of food, closed her eyes.

'Mm . . . *fantastic*.' She looked at him. 'Thank you for rescuing me from a ready-made pasta dish.' He mock-saluted.

'Had to be done.'

They ate in easy silence, topping up their glasses, Judd feeling her tension fade, her mood lightening. After a minute or so, she said, 'I didn't say anything to Ade Jones about being in my garden. I was really annoyed with him but when I thought about it later, he was probably just checking on me and on the house. He's like that.' No way, would she divulge to anyone her earlier thoughts on Jones. Julian forked chow mein.

'It's your choice, Chloe. If you're happy, so am I.'

After another half hour of sipping and eating, plus small exchanges of talk interspersed with easy silences, she sat back, one hand on her stomach, her eyes on the near-empty cartons between them.

'*That* was delicious, Julian. Thank you.'

'We both had to eat, right?' He pointed to the plant. 'Don't eat that. Just water it every couple of days, but not too much— oh, and it doesn't like cold air.'

'I'll take care of it.'

She gathered the food containers together, went to a drawer, got out a large plastic bag, brought it to the table and dropped them inside it. Julian took the empty wine bottle to the sink, placed it on the window sill and looked out at the dark garden. She ran hot water, put their plates to soak. He followed her to the sitting room.

Walking into it, she was acutely conscious of her lack of furniture. What there was, was low-budget. She hesitated close to the one armchair, watched as he crossed the room and sat on the floor, next to her desk-table, his back against the wall. She sat in the armchair.

'I rang Erica Trent's tutor earlier—' He raised his hand.

'*That* is "shop". How about we just gossip?' She grinned.

'Anyone particular in mind?' He leant his head against the wall, long legs crossed at the ankle. She saw the red stripe running the length of each sole of his trainers. Expensive.

'Let's see . . . How about Bernard and Dr Chong?'

'Not gossip-worthy. Just two people getting on with life, making each other happy.'

'I got that same vibe. I'm glad for Bernard. He was alone when I first worked with him. Will isn't married, is he?' She hesitated, wondering how much he knew, guessing that it wasn't much because Will's situation wasn't talked about. At least, not around her.

'No. He isn't.' She saw him nod.

'Now I get it.'

'Get what?'

'He has somebody. Josie is *really* into him and getting nowhere.' She laughed.

'Josie is into most men.'

'Not me, she isn't. Which is fine, by the way.'

'What was it like working with Sarge when you were still at uni?'

'It was a great time. He and my tutor were a good team, but like most things it ended.' He looked at his watch. 'Like this evening.'

'What time is it?' she asked.

'Ten past midnight.' Judd felt the air tauten between them.

'. . . You don't have to go . . . and . . . I'd like you to stay.' He gazed at her, then slowly stood.

'I want to, Chloe, but I think it's best I go back to my place.' He shrugged his way into his jacket, came and lowered his face close to hers.

'How about we think of that as a work in progress? No, stay there.' He leant closer, gently kissed her cheek. 'I'll see myself out.'

Her fingers on her cheek, she listened to the front door close, his car engine start then fade quietly away.

Much later, she was in bed, still awake, eyes fixed on the ceiling. She had liked Julian from the moment she first met him. He was nothing like the officers she worked with. Most of them were taken, anyway. Jones wasn't. She knew how this evening would have panned out if he had been here for dinner. He would have been pushing all evening to stay over. She would have ended up having to chuck him out. There was no chemistry there. Just a nagging suspicion which was back again.

Helped by the wine and food she was asleep within ten minutes.

Saturday, 20 April. 3.40 a.m.

Traynor came up raging, tearing at his daughter's killer with his bare hands—

'*Will! Stop*. Stop! It's *all right*!'

On her knees, Jess put her arms around him, held him, listened to the harsh, dry sobs. The bedroom door drifted open. Boy came inside whining, his nails clicking on the wooden floor. She got out of bed.

'Ssshhhh, Boy . . . come with me, come on.'

She led the reluctant dog out of the room, waited as he went to his bed at the top of the stairs. With a staying motion, she came back into the room, to Traynor's side of the bed and sat close to him. She took his hands in hers, held them.

'Bad dream?' He looked at her, still lost.

'. . . She's gone.'

'No. She's home, Will. Safe in her room, asleep.' He stared at her. She put her arms around him.

After a minute or so, he said, 'I'm sorry . . . Just the thought that something was happening to her, that I was losing her too . . .'

'I know.'

She did. About three years before, a case he was working with the police had brought him to her newspaper office. She had seen his stress, the still-raw pain of his wife's murder. In the last twelve months or so, he had really got himself together. She knew how strong, how loving he was from their life here, knew of his commitment to his work. To see even an occasional glimpse of what he had been was heart-breaking.

'Emelia has to be free to live her life, Will.' He lay down, turned to her, his arms going around her.

'Do you think I upset her earlier?' She smiled, stroked his face.

'Annoyed is my guess, which she's probably forgotten about.' She looked up as the bedroom door drifted open. Boy was there, looking from her to Traynor and back.

'You can come inside on the strict understanding that this is a treat, yes?' She watched him head for Traynor, then lie down on the floor close by.

'I'm sorry, Jess.'

'Everyone has bad dreams, Will. Yours have a cause. We both know that.'

'Maybe I'll arrange to have a couple of therapy sessions. It's probably the demands of this case. We're all tired.'

One hand supporting her head, she looked at him. It needed saying. 'Might it be to do with the actual nature of the case itself? A repeat murder case, like your wife's?'

He was silent, then, 'What if I can't cope with the reality of this work?' She ran her hand gently over his hair, his face.

'It looks to me like that dream was a one-off. Don't let it undermine you.' He touched her face.

'You make it all sound – fine.'

'That's what it is, Will.'

After a few seconds, he reached for her.

TWENTY-FOUR

Saturday, 20 April. 7.15 a.m.

Traynor drove into the headquarters car park. Having spent much of the previous day thinking about the investigation, the decision he had come to was giving him real pause. Bernard had to know about it. He wasn't going to like it. Watts looked up as he came into the office.

'You look like a man with a lot on his mind, Will.'

'We need to talk. Starting with the missing tape.'

'You read minds? That tape's bothering me, and not because Brophy would blow a gasket if he knew about it. I'm thinking there could be more to it being missing than carelessness. How about somebody on this investigation is playing games?'

'I'm thinking much the same,' said Traynor. 'This killer knows Birmingham as well as he knows Manchester.'

'And?'

'I think he lives here.'

'Based on?'

'He knows his way around this city, Bernard. He really knows that site. He's at ease there. He felt entirely comfortable accosting two teenage girls close to it.' Watts reached for a file, his eyes on Traynor. Opening it, he flicked pages, ran his index finger along a printed line.

'Playing devil's advocate, according to Carly Driscoll, her abductor was well-spoken, with *no* regional accent—' Traynor shook his head.

'That's not an argument against what I just said. It merely indicates his awareness that he has to hide his geographical origins. She also told us that he was a police officer. That she followed what he said because she was convinced that that's exactly what he was.'

Watts' face reddened. He pulled at his tie, took it off, dropped it on the table, undid his collar.

'I don't like where we're going with this, Traynor. This case is a bloody horror show for me and, if I'm getting your drift, you're saying you think there's an officer on my team who is responsible for what we've seen at that site— I can't get my head around what you're suggesting. I *know* the lads on my team. This was always a Manchester case for me: victims abducted from there, their killer local to it.' He paused. 'But I admit it's that missing tape which has got me thinking otherwise. In my experience, it's rare for a key item of evidence in a murder investigation to go missing. In my years on the force, I can't recall it happening more than a couple of times.' He sighed, ran his hand over his hair.

'I went with what seemed the obvious explanation, the Evidence Room door left unlocked, somebody removing the tape in error, too afraid to admit it because of the high-profile nature of the

investigation. It was the likeliest explanation. I didn't think further.'
He looked up at Traynor.

'I didn't want to think further. Now I have. I've been through
who was at the site the day the tape was located: I was there, you,
Judd, Julian, Connie, Igor, Jones—' The last name hung in the air.

'Jones is from the north,' said Traynor. 'I've been considering
him.'

'I see.' Watts looked across at him, his face conflicted. 'He's
been on my team for a couple of years, possibly more. Never a
problem with him. OK, a bit of a Jack the Lad, but lately I've
heard one or two comments about his attitude to women. He and
Judd are good mates. If he was like that with her, she'd soon show
him what for. His appearance fits the CCTV footage.' He shook
his head.

'I can hardly believe I'm saying any of this.' He took a breath.
'He also fits the description we've got from Carly Driscoll. She
said her attacker presented himself to her as a police officer. It
makes no sense to me that if he is an officer, he would say that.'

'It does if he was assuming that she would be in no position
to tell anyone.'

'It's only what he said, just words, and it's a known ruse.'

'Carly Driscoll was convinced by her attacker's manner, his air
of authority. It's one thing to introduce yourself in a specific role.
To carry it off successfully takes more than words. It takes awareness, plus direct experience, of the actual authority figure—'

'You're saying you suspect Jones?' Traynor was not ready to
confirm his actual thinking until he had more information.

'At this stage, it's wise to consider all possibilities. He has
family in the north. Southport?' Watts gave a weary nod. 'And he
has first-hand experience of how the police work.' Aware of Traynor
studying him, waiting, he did not respond for several seconds. He
was thinking of a recent event which was now taking on a whole
new significance.

'Carly Driscoll has been here. Twice. Once to make a statement.
The second time to construct the E-FIT.' He reached for a file,
turned pages. 'When she arrived here that first day, a group of
officers was coming out of headquarters. She was as white as a
sheet when she came into this office. I put it down to what had
happened to her and the stress of coming here to talk about it.
Now I'm wondering, was Jones part of that group of officers?'

'Did you see him?'

'I can't remember. Judd might have. She never forgets anything.'

'Be discreet when you ask her.' Watts' face changed.

'I know how to play this,' he snapped. 'I'm not rushing into anything.' As the door swung open and Julian came inside, he said, 'He's popular with his colleagues, hardworking—'

'Aw, thanks guys, but that's enough about me.' Losing the grin, Julian stopped, looked at them in turn, shut the door behind him.

'What's happened? What's going on?' Watts hesitated. Like Traynor, Julian wasn't an officer. He needed to know.

'This is confidential, but we're considering Adrian Jones as having possible involvement in the Manchester abductions.' Traynor was waiting for Julian's response. It took some seconds.

'Oh.' Watts stared at him.

'Is that it? "Oh". If you've got something to say, let's hear it.' Julian looked from him to Traynor.

'You probably know that Jones and I don't get on, but you're asking, so I'll say it. His attitude to females is often dismissive. He talks about them a lot, uses sexist expression like "asking for it".' He shrugged. 'That's it.'

Julian waited out the silence, then went to the door, saying, 'Will? I need to ask you about the collaboration you've suggested, but I'll catch up with you later—'

'What you've just heard in this room is confidential, Jules!' Julian looked at Watts.

'Don't you think I *know* that?'

The door swung closed on him.

'What collaboration?'

'I've asked for Julian's assistance. If anything comes of it, I'll let you know.'

Watts went to the filing cabinets, took out a file, brought it back to the table, began leafing through it.

'I'm checking to see if I can knock this idea about Jones as a potential person of interest on the head.' He pointed to details. 'He arrived here during the summer of 2017. A year prior to that he was based in Stockport, his home town.' Watts' finger moved down a list. 'He took no leave until 2018, and then only odd days. Later that same year, he took eighteen days' leave, all of it well after Ricci disappeared but before Erica Trent went. I know. It means nothing, given the distance from Manchester but there's no dates here which specifically tie him to any of these abductions.' He showed the file to Traynor who looked at it and gave it back, shook his head.

'Jones being a northerner is the only biographical fact we've got. On that basis, we might just as well be considering Judd's oddball neighbour, who, according to Judd, is highly interested in police work, has transport, hours of time on his hands and nothing to fill it.' Watts sat back, his thick forearms crossed, his eyes still fixed on the file.

'As a possible person of interest, he makes about as much sense as Jones. Judd's no stranger to dealing with dodgy males. Like I said, she and Jones are mates. If she had seen anything, picked up on anything sexually weird about him, she would have said so, mate or not.' Traynor looked at him.

'The key point, Bernard, is that no one would *see* it. Not Chloe or Julian, you, me or anyone else. Those young women in Manchester didn't see it. Until it was too late. He has another self. One diametrically opposed to that which he presents in his daily life.'

'You're saying he's psychotic. Schizophrenic.'

'No. This killer is as rational as you and me. All we know of him comes from what he *does*. That's one reason I'm going to Manchester. I want to meet Boulter and his key officers. Ask them about any males who came to their attention, no matter how incidental, during the course of their investigation. I want to know about those they dismissed on direct meeting because they saw nothing to either raise or confirm suspicions.'

'That won't take long. They've had next to no leads throughout.' Watts let the silence between them grow.

'OK. We consider Jones a potential person of interest— I can't believe I just said it. We don't have a shred of real evidence.' Watts rubbed his eyes. 'My head's splitting.'

'I have an idea, Bernard. Let's call it an hypothesis.' Watts sighed.

'I'd rather stick with "idea".'

'I've said that we know this killer by what he's done. I want to evaluate every single known fact or reasonable inference arising out of his known actions. Julian and I share theoretical knowledge. He doesn't have my years of criminological experience, but his forensic training is much more recent than mine. I want us to try it. See what we get.'

'In that case, make it soon.'

'I've already raised it briefly with him and I'm planning for us to make a start later today.'

'If Jones' name comes up during that discussion, bear in mind that there's no love lost between them. On second thoughts, I think that as SIO I should be there. Judd's phoned in sick, so I'll do some notetaking as well. We need anything and everything that psychology and criminology is able to throw at this bloody mess.'

TWENTY-FIVE

Same day. 8.10 a.m.

Judd was curled up in her armchair, the sleeves of her sweater pulled down over her hands, her eyes fixed on the table she had been working at since six a.m. She reached for the remote, aimed it at the television, ready to lose herself in early morning chat. Two minutes in, she got up, switched it off, dropped the remote on the chair, went back to the table.

Her eyes moved to the copy E-FIT produced by Carly Driscoll. She reached for it, looked at it for what seemed like the hundredth time. E-FIT was regarded by many officers as a silver bullet. This one looked to Judd to be a fairly typical example: a bland, pulled-together representation of everyman. She had said as much to Sarge. He'd gone on about cases he'd worked, where E-FITs had helped nail the offenders. Helped. Not identified. She let this one fall back to the table, gazed out of the window then at the E-FIT again, drawn to it. The face gazed back at her. She reached for her phone, tapped a number, waited.

'Forensics. Adam speaking.'

'Hi, Adam. It's Chloe Judd.'

'Hello, Chloe Judd.'

'I was wondering if you had any results for the marks on the jacket belonging to Carly Driscoll which I dropped off?'

'We do. I was just about to send them to your boss.'

'Can you read them out to me?' She waited, pen poised.

'They're pretty straightforward. We found DNA which doesn't belong to her.'

'*Really?*'

'Yes, but we've checked. No matches on the system.'

'Oh. Anything else?'

'Analysis of the marks on the jacket indicated an innocuous basis: benign, non-toxic molecules and organic pigment, about covers it – literally, as it happens.' She made swift notes.

'. . . So, what is it? What caused the marks?' She heard his laugh.

'Sorry, didn't I say? It's hair dye. We'll need to know from Driscoll the actual product she uses. It could be useful as and when we get a suspect and examine his clothing. But, having said that, those marks could have come from any number of people, such as friends.'

'I'll ring her. Thanks Adam.'

She sat, chin resting on her folded arms. DNA. The twenty-first century's magic bullet. But with no match. Judd was a fan of Locard's Exchange Principle, which she had learnt about during her training. It said that whenever two persons have contact, whether incidental or intimate, all kinds of stuff got transferred, from one to the other. It was never a one-way street. Something left. Something taken away. She searched papers for a phone number, rang it. Her call was picked up.

'Hello, this is PC Judd from West Midlands Police headquarters. Could I speak to Carly Driscoll, please?'

'Hello, this is Carly's mother. I'm sorry, she went into work this morning, because it's quiet on a Saturday. She wants to get her life back, although her father and I weren't very happy about her going. Can I help?'

Judd had wanted to speak with the young woman directly, ask her if she had recalled anything more about the physical interactions between herself and the man who abducted her. Frustrated, she went with a more direct enquiry.

'The jacket Carly brought in to us has been examined. Are you able to confirm the specific hair-colouring product Carly uses?'

'I'm sorry, but she doesn't use anything like that.

'Can you suggest a way in which a product like that might have gotten onto the jacket?' There was a short silence.

'Maybe it came from one of her friends. They're always having something done at the hairdressers.'

Thanking her, Judd looked down at her note of what Adam had said to her and sighed.

'Come on Mr Locard, give us a break, yeah?'

Picking up the E-FIT, she took it to the window, looked again at the depiction of a man suspected of killing five women, her thoughts drifting to the dark figure Julian had seen disappearing down the alley towards the rear of her house, after which her gate, always secure, had swung free, waking her. She dropped the E-FIT, looked out at Dennis's never-moved car in its usual parking place.

'He's a bit odd, but I don't think he misses much.' She frowned. 'Didn't he say that he was going to be away that night? If he wasn't, I need to ask him what he saw or heard . . . and it might stop me talking to myself.'

Reaching for her keys, she headed out of the house, pulling her door closed. Stepping over the dividing wall, she knocked his door, knocked a second time. It slowly opened, Dennis framed in his doorway, his dark hair lank, dressed in a baggy cardigan, joggers and new-looking black Nike trainers.

'I need to talk to you, Dennis.'

For a moment, she thought he was going to refuse. He stood aside.

'. . . Come in.'

She went inside, waited as he closed the door then followed him, noting what looked to be newish carpet on the stairs, the same for what was visible of the sitting room.

'You're having new floor coverings, Dennis?'

Getting no response, she followed him past a solitary framed poster of a knickerless tennis player and on to the kitchen. To Judd's eyes it looked like little had been done to it since the house was built. He hadn't said how long he had lived here. He indicated chairs at a small table. The whole place was cold.

'Have a seat. I'll make a—'

'Dennis, I need your help.'

'Why? What about?'

Judd got straight to the point. 'Something happened in my back garden a couple of nights ago.'

He looked away.

'I don't know about it—'

'There were noises, Dennis. Your security light came on. Whoever was there got in through the rear gate which he left open.

The noise of it banging woke me up. If you were home, you *must* have heard it.'

His closed face told her that he wasn't about to volunteer anything. She went with what she had already decided to say, without revealing the nature of her job.

'I'm thinking about reporting it to the police. They'll probably want to speak to you—'

'No.'

'And they'll ask you to tell them what you saw.'

'I didn't.' She looked directly at him.

'If you did see or hear anything, you'll have to tell them.' Getting no response, she said, 'What I know about you, Dennis, is that you're very security conscious. You take a lot of interest in police activity in this area.'

'It's what we need,' he monotoned. 'Stop people getting hurt.' She frowned.

'Exactly. If you were here that night and you talk to the police, something might occur to you—'

'I don't want to – get involved— I don't know anything.'

He *was* home that night. She was sure of it. She caught his evaluative look. A loner he might be, a bit odd certainly, but he was no fool. She went with a change of tone.

'You're right in what you said about the need for more police presence. Do you remember telling me about the police vehicles with flashing lights you saw quite recently? Very early one morning? There's a really big investigation going on right now and—'

'Brampton.' She stared at him.

'What do you know about that, Dennis?' She watched his face shut down, knew she wasn't about to get more from him.

She stood, left the kitchen and moved along the hall, picking up his soft footfalls directly behind her. She reached the door, tried to open it, tried a second time, starting at two expressionless words in her ear.

'It's locked.'

Her heart sped. His hand appeared over her right shoulder, a key gripped in it. He inserted it into the lock, slowly turned it. The door swung open. On a rush of relief, she stepped outside, over the low wall and reached her own front door without hearing the sound of his door closing.

Same day. 5.45 p.m.

Julian came into Watts' office, where Traynor was sitting alone. 'Hi, Will. Sorry, I'm a bit late I've been busy with data searches.' He looked around. 'I thought Bernard was going to be here?'

'He's been called to the scene.'

'Oh? A development?'

'I don't know. Julian, I want us to make a start on constructing a list of investigative facts. Once we have those facts assembled and agreed, we'll use our respective theoretical knowledge to see what they might tell us. It could help us move from what we agree we know to further possibilities. At the least, it could increase the clarity of what we have.' Julian sat, looking keen.

'That sounds like a good plan, Will.'

'We'll start by looking into his inner life.' Julian's brows rose.

'His—? I'm not entirely sure what you mean.'

'People anticipate a monstrous inner life to be reflected in some way by outward physical appearance and behaviours. Yet, none of the "monsters" I've ever met revealed that kind of inner self. Not to their victims until it was too late. Not to me. I've had to infer that inner life from what they actually did.' He looked intently at Julian.

'That's what we're here to do. Look at the behaviours. Go beyond the façade. *See* the savage, the grotesque abomination that he *really* is.' Julian stared at him.

'Will, I'd better admit right now that I've never done anything like that. To be honest, I wouldn't know where to start.' Traynor looked at the troubled young face.

'We start by discussing *him*. A character in his own story, starting with what we know of his physical presence, then on to his various behaviours as indicated by what we know he has done, and finally what it all has to tell us about his inner self.'

'But how—?'

'By looking at and using the known facts about him.' Julian's face cleared.

'You mean, like what's shown by CCTV footage?'

'That could be a start. How about I make notes on my iPad as we go, then send you a copy for us to work from tomorrow? That way, we can refine our ideas as we progress.'

'I'm up for it, Will.' Traynor reached for the iPad.

'I'll start. What do I know of this killer? He's someone familiar with both Manchester and Birmingham, but that's all I can say on that issue. It's possible he lives in either place, or neither.'

'If it is neither, we're talking about an individual with no backstory in either city.'

'Exactly,' said Traynor. 'Which might explain the lack of leads coming from the local populations. We've already discussed the timings of his strikes, that they indicate his being in employment which allows him significant mobility.'

'I've considered that,' said Julian. 'Initially I was thinking lorry driver, but that just doesn't fit with him moving around a campus, locating victims. A large vehicle would be too memorable. I'm now thinking sales representative, something of that order. That in turn suggests somebody with an easy, confident manner, a gift-of-the-gab type, who's able to get along with people on a superficial level.' Traynor tapped iPad keys.

'That makes sense. What else might we conjecture about him?' Julian frowned.

'. . . We're pretty sure he's stalking his victims prior to killing them. If that's right, what if part of his reason for stalking is to gather additional cues about them, I don't mean those about their routines. He's also looking for cues on their interpersonal behaviour.'

'Examples?' Julian leant towards Traynor, his face keen.

'We all people watch to a degree, yes? I think what *he's* doing is watching how these young women move around, how they make social decisions and judgements about other people, how they interact based on those judgements. He's learning how socially open, how confident or otherwise they are.' He looked at Traynor. 'While he's stalking them, he's gathering what he can about their personalities. He's doing it because he's no risk-taker. He can't afford a misjudgement and choose the wrong victim. He needs to be as sure as he possibly can be that he's selecting one who's likely to accept his overture, be compliant in her response. If he observes a woman who is not just confident but is also openly challenging during social interaction, he would steer well clear, don't you think? We know he has a physical type, Will, but I'm suggesting he also chooses them according to their character, their interpersonal behaviour.' He met Traynor's gaze, his eyes widening.

'You know, this is the first time I've really thought it through like this. It's how he managed to abduct them with zero fuss. Whenever he is out and about, he's actually collecting *data* on how potential victims are likely to respond to him. He's selecting them on the basis of their openness, I suppose you would call it. Given that openness, he knows that they're likely to be disarmed for when he does strike.' He gave a slow headshake. 'Jeez, he's smart. What he's doing is going for what he knows is the easy take.'

'Well said,' responded Traynor. 'Every abduction smooth, every victim taken without the slightest resistance.' Julian rubbed his hands together, looked at him.

'I suggested he possibly works in sales, do you think he's likely to have that kind of analytical way of thinking?'

'The role of a salesman requires precisely those kinds of evaluations.'

'Which suggests that while he may not have higher education, what he does have is a hell of a lot of nous, where people are concerned.' Traynor nodded.

'What else is he?' Julian's phone rang. He reached for it.

'Yes, sir. OK, give me a couple of minutes and I'll be with you.' He ended the call.

'Sorry, Will. Brophy wants to see me. Something about paperwork he needs to complete to extend my time down here. I suspect he also wants to use me to get ammunition about the investigation's slow progress. He'll get zip from me.' He stood.

'Can we continue with this, Will? This is the first time I've felt really "up" since I got here.'

'How about Monday some time? What I'd like to do is discuss this killer's motivation, his M.O. We already suspect that it involves him acting out sexually, post-mortem.' Julian looked doubtful. 'It's a paraphilia,' said Traynor. 'There are many you've probably come across, theoretically.'

'That's a yawning chasm in my forensic psychology training. I don't recall it being referred to during my courses.'

'It's a not uncommon aspect of serial cases.' Julian shrugged.

'My work since I graduated has been restricted to lecturing.'

'If you have the time, read up on it between now and Monday.'

'I'll do that,' Julian smiled, 'so I can hit the ground running.' He gathered his things, then, 'We're agreed that his personality type is antisocial, so wouldn't there be some reference to him in the system? Say, as a teenager, for theft, fighting, animal cruelty, all the usual shtick?'

'If he did exhibit those behaviours, it's possible he was too young for an antisocial diagnosis. It's also possible that those kinds of offences were regarded as minor with the likelihood that they're now "spent" in police terms, leaving no indication on file.'

'Should we at least check it out? I can do it.'

'It's a big task, Julian.'

'Once I've seen Brophy, I'll get onto it. Josie Miller's working a late shift, so I'll ask her for some help.' At the door, he looked back to Traynor.

'Any other ideas for our next meeting?'

'We focus on what his victims can tell us about who killed them and how he thinks.'

'How do we do that?'

'By putting ourselves at those events.'

'I've never actually done anything like that. I don't have your level of experience.' Traynor stood.

'Don't sell yourself short. We know what happened to Amy Peters and Erica Trent. They will provide some insight into how he thinks.' Julian looked suddenly upbeat.

'I was thinking about that last night. I see him as a sharp, efficient planner who might have picked up his forensic aware-ness by watching TV crime shows, yes? The big question remaining for me is, how does he find the time to plan, watch, select and stalk, *and* have a job, a life? The Manchester media dubbed him "the Phantom". It exactly sums him up as far as I'm concerned. A killer who keeps well within the shadows. Makes no waves. That's quite an achievement, Will.' They left the room together.

'One of my jobs in Manchester was supposed to be the evalu-ation of witness statements. It didn't take long. There weren't any of investigative use.' He looked at Traynor. 'After, say the first two homicides, why weren't his subsequent victims on their guard? Why didn't they sense that they were being watched? I discussed it very generally with my girlfriend. She agreed that women develop that kind of awareness as self-protection. I suggested to Boulter that I follow it up by looking at campus security records for possible complaints from female students. I did. It yielded nothing.' They paused at the stairs.

'What about the other three victims?' asked Julian. 'Do we include them in what we're doing?'

'No,' said Traynor. 'Without their remains we don't know for certain what actually happened to them.'

'He's a real enigma, this killer, isn't he?' Traynor looked at the keen, young face.

'Julian, my direct experience of repeat killers is that *every* single one of them has been a banal, self-obsessed nonentity.' Julian stared at him.

'Really?' Traynor nodded.

'It's the fictional portrayals we have to thank for leading us to expect something other, something melodramatic. By the way, I'm planning a visit to Manchester in the next few days. Depending on what I learn there, I might consider suggesting to Bernard that we make a direct appeal to this killer via the media. What do you think?'

'You mean, to entice him out of the woodwork?' Julian looked doubtful. 'Based on our discussions, I think he's way too sophisticated for that. What do you think the chances are of him being a police officer?'

'I've considered it because of the forensic acumen in what he does. Does any officer in Manchester come to mind?'

'Not a single one. Maybe it's somebody based here in the Midlands.' Julian grinned. 'How about a forensic officer? *Igor?*' He laughed. 'That's more believable than any of the officers we're working with here. Kumar is a rule-follower who's desperately short on imagination. Jones is a sexist yob with all the sophistication of a bacon sandwich, but I can't see him having the analytical approach necessary.' He became serious. 'This killer doesn't want to get caught so I doubt appeals to him would help. While you're in Manchester, try asking Boulter about any recent developments he hasn't bothered reporting to us down here.'

'Boulter would probably prefer to keep such information to himself. Like most officers, even those who are struggling, he wants to be the one who's investigation breaks the case.' Julian's phone rang again.

'I'd better go.'

'Same time on Monday?' Julian nodded.

'Suits me. Most of what I've said today has been off the top of my head, so I'd like to give some real thought to what we do then.'

Same day. 8.15 p.m.

Traynor was driving home, the meeting with Julian in his head. The over-riding impression gained was that Julian knew very little about paraphilias, essentially emotional disorders which influenced an individual's sexual choices and were often present in sexual homicide. It had come as a surprise to Traynor. Thinking about it now, a possible explanation was that all of us qualify, then tend to focus on specific areas which interest. Julian had chosen university lecturing. He frowned. Maybe that explained it.

He arrived home to an empty house. Jess and Em had gone to the theatre. He went directly to his office, emailed research papers he had promised to a couple of his students, then looked at the notes he'd made on his iPad during his afternoon meeting with Julian. He had read them several times when he heard sounds from the direction of the front door. He went into the hall. Jess was removing her coat.

'Was it a good play?'

'Very.' She squeezed his arm. 'You should have come with us.' She followed him into his study.

'I didn't get back here until gone eight.' He paused. 'Em hasn't come back with you?'

'No. Did you know she has a steady boyfriend?'

'. . . No.'

'Third-year physics student. He was at the theatre.'

'I see.'

'If you're "seeing" someone massively unsuitable, think again. He's very pleasant.' She gazed down at his notes.

'I got drawn into work,' said Traynor. 'I've decided to go to Manchester in the next couple of days.'

'I thought your brief was the two young women whose remains were discovered here?'

'It still is.' She came to him. He held out his arms and she sat in his lap. They stayed like that for a few minutes, Traynor's hand stroking her thigh.

'Tell me you're not working too hard on this case.'

'Don't worry about me, Jess. Julian Devenish, the psychologist, is now working on it with me.'

'I'm glad to hear it. You're bound to make progress working together, sharing the load.'

Hearing her optimism, watching her leave the study, he glanced down at the notes he had made, his eyes moving over the lines of words. He reached out, switched off the desk lamp and followed her from the room.

'How long will you be in Manchester?'

'I'm not sure. I might go to Stockport as well.'

'What's in Stockport?'

'Again, I'm not sure. That's why I'm going. I'm hoping it might rule out a possibility I'm considering.'

TWENTY-SIX

Same evening. 9.30 p.m.

In the relative quiet of West Midland Police headquarters, Watts was unsettled. What Traynor had said about the killer's post-mortem behaviour towards his victims was the cause. Not the actual behaviour, although that was unsettling enough. Something else was bothering him. After a few minutes, he stood. Some time going through old files might be well-spent, if it stopped this nagging uncertainty.

Leaving his office, he crossed the relatively quiet reception and went down the stairs to the basement. Tapping a code into a pad beside the door, he pushed open the heavy door and walked inside. This was where the physical case files were stored. He hadn't been down here for a few years, but the smell came back to him. Old paper and dust. He knew what he was looking for. He switched on lights which flickered on ahead of him as he moved to the far corner of the vast underground storage and a particular archive.

Reaching it, he knelt, examined the labels on various hefty storage boxes. All of these cases predated Will Traynor's involvement with headquarters. His colleague back then, Kate Hanson, was an equally sharp psychologist. He wanted to look at one case file in particular. He slid one of the boxes all the way out, carried it to a table where he read the label on each file, getting a rush of recognition and memories.

He looked at the details inside, the kind he never liked reading about. The things done by individuals he regarded as sick, regardless of Hanson and now Traynor telling him they were sexual anomalies indulged in by those with emotional difficulties. He closed the last file and stared down at them. Fetishes. Paraphilias. Loads of others. Forensic psychology was big on them. To Watts they were distasteful, sickening, yet he knew about them because his job demanded it. How could anybody who had worked on such cases not be aware of them? He gathered the files together, slid them back into the box.

The answer he got to his own question was something inconceivable.

Monday, 22 April. 3.35 p.m.

Traynor was alone in Watts' office once more, preoccupied with his planned visit to the north, the answers he needed from Boulter and a fast-diminishing optimism that he would get them. He looked up as the door swung open and Julian came inside.

'Hi, Will. You want an early start today?'

'Yes.' Traynor went straight to the question at the forefront of his mind. 'In confidence, do you have anything to add to what you said before about Adrian Jones?'

Julian sat across from him. 'OK. You should know about something that happened a few nights ago. It was late. We'd all been at the site until late. I took my usual route home which passes Chloe Judd's house. As I reached it, I saw Jones on foot. I recognized him straight away in the streetlights by his swagger, his dark hair. I slowed, watched as he disappeared down an access path to the rear of Chloe's house. He and Chloe aren't an item and I couldn't think of a legitimate reason why he was there, so I parked and followed him. He had her gate open and he was inside her garden. As soon as he was aware that I was there, he took off by climbing into the next garden. I still don't know what he was doing there.'

'You reported it?'

'Much as I dislike Jones, I wasn't sure what it meant and anyway

Bernard's got enough going on. I mentioned it to Chloe, so she might have taken it further.' Traynor made a brief note.

'Shall we make a start? I want to focus on this killer's behaviour, what he actually does. Get some ideas about how he thinks.'

'I've been thinking some more about what makes him tick. It relates to our discussion of his motivation.' Julian paused, his eyes on Traynor. 'I think his entire motivation is in the actual planning.'

'The planning?'

'Yes. That's his focus. His "reason for being". He spends hours, *days* on it. Think about it, Will, and what we know about him. To me, he's obsessively thorough. He takes account of every single aspect of a planned attack, the time, the weather, where to park his vehicle, the minutiae of his own physical presentation, probably down to decisions such as whether to wear aftershave. He rehearses his actual contact with a victim, knows *exactly* what he needs to say and how she is likely to respond.'

'You're thinking this is planning-as-compulsion? That kind of behaviour doesn't arise out of nothing. Any theories as to why?'

Julian sat back, shook his head. 'That's where I run out of road.'

Traynor read from brief lines of notes.

'Amy Peters: May 2016. Melody Brewster: October, same year. Claire Walsh: August 2017. Marella Ricci: March 2018. Erica Trent: November, same year. If he and his planning are driven by compulsion, what happened during the gaps between these dates? Is he actively stopping himself from abducting and committing homicides? Why would he do that? *Could* he desist, if it's compulsive behaviour?' Julian reached for the A4, frowned at it.

'He must constantly monitor his own behaviour. Keep a tight grip on his thoughts. Try to stay on an even keel.' Traynor shook his head.

'Keeping a grip on such invasive thoughts would be a difficult proposition for him.' Julian looked up at him.

'Is this experience talking, Will?' He watched Traynor's face change. 'Sorry, I heard what happened to your wife from one of the officers here.'

'Yes, it is. Thoughts about what happened to my family sometimes impact on my current life. When they're insistent, I often can't stop them. I don't see the individual we're discussing here as having that kind of problem. The thoughts inside his head are a source of anticipation, pleasure and, eventually, gratification.' It was Julian's turn to look surprised. Traynor continued.

'As I've said, he's likely to self-soothe with alcohol, have recourse to pornography and, like you say, spend much of his time thinking and planning. I doubt he tries to control or resist them. He revels in them. And another young woman dies.' He watched Julian chose his words.

'As part of my PhD, I conducted a survey on pornography. The results left me in no doubt that it's a scourge. I believe it's at the basis of a lot of sexual crime.' Traynor shook his head.

'Sorry, Julian, but I don't agree. Pornography does not *cause* sex crimes. *People* cause sex crimes.'

'You don't believe that it inspires them, in this case: him?'

'His deviant thoughts, his sexual aberration, they're all his own and the foundation of them lies years back in his development. Pornography merely reinforces his thinking. It doesn't make him do what he does.' Traynor paused. 'He made a mistake.'

'How's that?'

'Remember our conversation yesterday, about his painstaking analysis of his future victims? Carly Driscoll was his mistake. She fought him, to the point where she was able to escape.' He waited as Julian absorbed this.

'Know what I think, Will? I think she met up with some guy, they struck up a conversation, she got into his car and she wasn't averse to his coming on to her. When things stopped being to her liking, she resisted and had to come up with an explanation.'

'You're saying hers is a false allegation?' Traynor shook his head. 'Her statement is convincing and what we know of her is that she's a responsible young woman – a little naïve, maybe.' Julian grinned.

'*Naïve?* To the point of being unbelievable, if you want my opinion.' Traynor slow-nodded, decided to change tack.

'Do you have a theory as to why he brought two of these five young women to the Brampton site?'

'Not a clue, sorry. Maybe it was to get away from the heat in Manchester?'

'But there was no heat, was there? You've told us how slow the police were up there to realize what was happening. He used that slowness to his advantage.'

'How's that?'

'He approached Carly Driscoll as a police officer. What if he did the same with Amy Peters and Erica Trent?' Julian shrugged.

'Anything's possible but we'll probably never know for sure—'

'I think that's exactly what he did. I also think he was stalking Erica and gradually, very gradually, allowed himself to be seen by her.' Julian gave a quick headshake.

'That goes against what we've already said. Why would he do that?'

'Because by the time Erica became his focus, she, like most female students, would have been aware of the police presence and she accepted that he was an officer.'

'Why would she do that? By then, the faculty itself was issuing warnings.'

'Because of what Chloe Judd has discovered. She followed up a potential lead, spoke to the tutor who was possibly one of the last people to talk with Erica. She confirmed that Erica was contemplating extending her social life. I believe Erica left that tutorial and she met *him.* She accepted he was an officer because she had seen him around that campus, probably guessed from his appearance that he wasn't a student. He had only to identify himself as an officer and he was halfway to achieving what he wanted: Erica inside his vehicle.' Julian gazed at him, gave a slight headshake.

'Sorry, but that's speculation, Will.'

'What we've learnt about her indicates her to be a very intelligent, level-headed young woman.' Julian shrugged

'Aren't they all? Until somebody like *him* comes along.'

'This case is about control, Julian. Total control.'

'If you want my opinion, Will, we can speculate all we like but it doesn't take us anywhere.'

'Not all cases are built on theory. Creative speculation is sometimes all we have. How about this for one: he's a sadist.' Julian's head came up.

'No *way.*'

'Of course he is. It fits with control and possession.'

'I don't see it like that. I think he probably wanted to avoid violence. Unless he was forced by circumstance—'

'There's evidence of pre-mortem beating.'

'I don't know what to say about that . . .'

'Our professional knowledge allows us to speculate on the likelihood of events.' Julian was looking restless.

Traynor asked, 'Are you OK?'

'I feel like I'm yet again reaching the edge of my professional expertise.' Traynor studied him.

'Now you've thought about the case, did you come up with any ideas as to why he chose the Brampton site?'

'Probably, the most prosaic of reasons. It's lonely there. Ideal for the "possession" thing he's after, which I can't comment on because I don't have any theoretical insight into it—'

'I think there is something very specific about *that* particular place which *he* knows and which draws him there.'

'. . . Sorry. I don't have a clue what to say about that.' Julian glanced at Traynor. 'Are we making any progress here, given my ineptitude?' Traynor gathered his papers together, went over to the coffee table.

'We're two professionals exchanging views and I need coffee before I drive home. Want some?' Julian raised his arms, stretched.

'Please. You know, I've been thinking about this – this voyeur-stalker-necrophiliac business. I just don't see him as some base, animalistic type. There's more to him than that. He's more cerebral.'

'Because?'

'What I'm saying is, this guy is no slave to some sexual compulsion or we would have him by now. Like I said before, it's all in the planning for him, then onto a smooth abduction and a perfectly orchestrated *finale*.' He paused. 'He's a master class in homicide, Will.' He stopped, face flushed, looked up at Traynor, took the coffee he was offering. Traynor sat on the edge of the table.

'That's where our opinions really diverge. To me, he's exactly like every repeat killer I've met. No finesse. No genuine emotional engagement with the victims. *Watch. Wait. Take.* The kind of killer newspapers will label "sick", once he's caught.' There was a lengthy silence. 'I know how he managed to achieve control over his victims, as if I were there. What you said about his being "cerebral" might apply during the first five or so minutes he's interacting with a victim. Before he shows the creeping horror that he really is.' Julian looked up at him, surprised.

'That's a really dramatic pronouncement from "Dr Cool", aka Will Traynor.' He grinned. 'It sounds scary and real. Better be careful, Will. Brophy wants a quick arrest and he's not fussy who it is.' The grin disappeared. 'Sorry. Bad joke. All we know for sure is that he abducts without confrontation, gets them into his vehicle and he's motoring, no pun intended.'

Traynor was silent, eyes fixed on low cloud forming beyond the window.

'My theory has always been that he drinks prior to each abduction.'

'Yes, and I think you know that I really doubt that. It would interfere with his focus. He wouldn't do anything to compromise the smoothness of an attack. You're not suggesting he's drunk when he abducts these women?'

'No.'

'How about a theoretical compromise?' Julian smiled. '*If* he drinks, it's just enough to take the edge off? Improve the smoothness of the whole operation but still remaining sharp.'

'Carly Driscoll stated that she smelled alcohol on him.'

'Can we trust what she says? As I said, I'm not sure about her reliability.' Traynor sipped his coffee.

'Something I learnt early on in this work, Julian, is that we have to value victims' words. Where are the other victims?'

'. . . What other victims?'

'Melody Brewster. Claire Walsh. Marella Ricci.'

'Oh, I see. That's anybody's guess. We'll probably never know. He's too good.'

'You're right, he is good. But in the midst of all that planning and watching and learning there's a tragedy.' Julian waited.

'I give up. What's the "tragedy"?'

'He finds every single killing a disappointment.' Julian regarded him for a few seconds.

'How can you know that?'

'Because he *keeps* on doing it. Because it *never* matches up to his fantasy. It *fails* him every single time. He knows it and it adds to his fury against women. It's a lethal cycle. *That's* where he sees his own lack of control. He has no way of stopping that relentless, problematic cycle.' Julian got slowly to his feet, looking worn. He yawned.

'I've just about had it, Will, but I want to thank you for asking me to do this. It's really got me thinking now.' Traynor also stood.

'There's a lot there to think about. Are you staying?'

'No. It's getting on for five o'clock so I'll head home. Let me know if you want another discussion, Will. I'm up for it.'

'Of course.'

TWENTY-SEVEN

Same day. 5.10 p.m.

Carly Driscoll stopped her car, lowered her window and looked across at the police station. She had managed her first full day back at work. Despite struggling to concentrate during some of the afternoon, she counted it a success. Her parents had been against her going. They had wanted her to take her time, make it a gradual process. She was pleased now that she had insisted. She was reclaiming her life. It was the reason she was here. She had had one call from the police since she was last here, from the young, blonde policewoman she had talked to, asking how she was. She was back because she wanted to know if there had been any progress with the investigation into what happened to her. She had considered phoning but suspected she might be fobbed off. What she wanted, what she needed, was a response which would tell her that something was being done. Now she was here, she would try phoning the number the young, blonde officer had given her. She got out her phone. If there was no reply she would go inside, ask to see her—

Voices and movement took her attention back to the massive building beyond its metal railings. Several men were coming out of it, heading across the car park. It had happened before when she was here. They probably worked shifts. This time she wouldn't allow it to get to her. As they moved across her line of vision, she opened her car door, her eyes widening, chest tight. That odd, floating sensation was back, but this time she knew why. It was because of what she was seeing. Voices drifted towards her.

'Meet you there around half eight!'

She watched three of the men turn to a tall, fair-haired man emerging from the building, the same voice saying something about a drink.

'Come *on*—' It sounded like 'Bill'. 'Tell the ball-and-chain—'

The next words were blown away on a stiff wind. She watched, transfixed as one among several others continued on to a row of parked vehicles. He wasn't exactly as she remembered, but it was him. It was all there, in the face, the way he moved—

The sound of car doors slamming and engines starting up made her jump. Several vehicles were moving to the exit, just metres from where she was parked on the road. Flustered, scarcely breathing, she pulled her door shut, her palms slick. She started the car, got it into gear on her third attempt. It stalled. The cars were coming closer. On a wave of dizziness, she accelerated. Engine roaring, she pulled away, tyres screeching.

Twenty minutes later she was home. Her father had some meeting and her mother— She couldn't remember what her mother had said. She got out of her car on a sudden gust of wind. Pushing her hair from her face, she ran to the house, unlocked the door, slammed it, deactivated the alarm and stood, gasping, in warmth and silence.

After a couple of minutes, she went up to her room, removed her coat and work clothes, let them drop to the floor. She lay down on the bed, pulling the duvet around herself, staring at nothing. He had *told* her he was a police officer. She thought back to her interview. The big man and the blonde woman hadn't seemed to believe it. They were wrong. She had just seen him. Her heart flipped over. The day she had made her statement, she had been asked for her contact details. She had given them. Watched them being written down. If he had seen her earlier, he could get her address.

Panicked, throwing the duvet aside, she ran from the bedroom, leant over the banister to reset the ground-floor alarm then backed away. She had told them what had happened, what he had done to her. And all the time he was there. Inside that building. The police couldn't help her. He was one of them.

She lowered her head and sobbed.

Same day. 5.50 p.m.

Julian parked the Mercedes and got out. Preoccupied, he aimed his fob and walked to the apartment block's entrance. The evening security officer who had just come on duty looked up as he came in.

'Evening, Dr Devenish.'

Getting no response, he watched him wait for the lift then take the stairs. Day staff had a lot of positive things to say about the occupier of apartment 2B. As far as the man on duty was concerned, he was just another rich git.

Same day. 6.00 p.m.

Traynor looked down at all of the investigative information he had accumulated. He also had research papers and open textbooks in front of him. He had interrogated every single fact known to the investigation. He also had a separate list. One containing his personal suspicions. He stared out at darkness. It had taken him hours to assemble what he had. It was too risky to keep his suspicion to himself. Watts had to know. He got out his phone, tapped a number. His call was picked up.

'Hello, Will.'

'Connie, is Bernard there?'

'Yes, I'll call him—'

'I'm on my way. I need to talk to him face to face.'

After forty minutes of debating how to deliver all that he knew, Traynor was inside Watts' house, refusing offers of drinks. Still standing, he faced them.

'The individual responsible for the Manchester abductions, the attempted abduction of the two young sisters and that of Carly Driscoll is part of your team.' Watts was on his feet, his eyes fixed on the criminologist.

'You'd better be one hundred percent sure of that.' Chong moving to his side.

'Listen to what Will has to say, Bernard.'

Traynor delivered all of it, the facts he knew, the suspicions he had.

'Before you act on what I've just told you, I'm on my way now to Manchester and Stockport where I'm hoping I'll get the clarification I want.' Reaching the door, Traynor turned to him.

'The minute I have it, I'll ring you and confirm it.'

Same evening. 9.45 p.m.

Judd was busy reading everything she had pulled together. Her phone rang. She reached for it, got Jonesy's voice and some background noise.

'I'm busy, Ade. What do you want?'

'I need you to come here—'

'Get lost.'

'Just listen, Chlo!' She did.

'I'm on my way.'

She was at the pub within fifteen minutes, saw Jones outside, Kumar waiting with him. She got out of her car and went to them.

'Where is he?' Jones jabbed his thumb at a slumped figure at a nearby table. She looked back at him.

'If I thought for a single minute that you had made trouble for him, spiked his drink—!'

'Behave, will you? Posh Boy's had two-and-a-bit pints, which for him is probably a skinful and he was being a pain in the arse—'

'And you want to take advantage of the situation to cause trouble!'

'Just take him away, will you? He can't drive in this state. What you do with him after that is up to you. Where d'you want him?'

Ignoring the heavy innuendo in Jones' tone, she went to her car, yanked open the front passenger door and waited for them to bring Julian to it, watched as they dumped him on the seat. Julian's head lolled forward. Jones pushed the door shut.

'He hasn't had enough to make him sick—'

'If he has and he is, I'll send you the bloody bill!' Jones watched as she opened her door, got inside, closed it and turned the ignition. He knocked on her window.

'Wait!'

She got out, watched him walk back to the table, pick something up and head back to her.

'His jacket!' He patted it. 'Keys in the right-hand pocket. You could always take him to your place. Have your way with him. If you decide to dump him at his place and you feel lonely later, ring me. I'll be straight round!'

Snatching the jacket from him, she dropped it on the rear seat, got inside, pulling the door hard. Julian didn't stir.

She drove him to his apartment complex. Parking close to the entrance, she hurried inside to where a man was on duty at the desk.

'I need some help. Dr Devenish is in my car.'

He followed her and together they got him out and into the building, where they put him down on a chair close to the lift. She left the man to it.

The security officer eyed the tenant of apartment 2B who was stirring and getting to his feet. He managed to encourage him into the lift.

'. . . This is . . . very, *very* good of you. Lis'n, I've got a bottle of Chateau— wine in my fridge. You can have it for being so helpful, yes? I'll let my father know jus' how good . . .'

He listened to the words. He already knew that his tenant's father owned most of the apartments here. He just wanted rid of him so he could get back to what he was doing on his iPad.

'Sorry, Dr Devenish. We're not allowed to accept gifts or gratuities, but thanks all the same.'

His hand against the tenant's chest to steady him, he opened the door of 2B with his pass key, flicked on a light and led him inside. Guiding him towards the bedroom, the tenant broke free of his grasp and blundered to the living room sofa where he dropped down and lay on his back. The employee looked down at him, uncertain. Drunks could choke after a skinful. He didn't want this one's dad coming after him for neglect. He reached for a large cushion, lifted the tenant's head, pushed it underneath. That looked better.

About to turn away, his attention went to something caught between the sofa cushions. Something small and shiny. He reached for it, held it up, watched the small gold crucifix swing from the fine chain. He looked down at the tenant who was now asleep then back to the crucifix lying on his palm. Very nice. Small, but heavy, something engraved on it. He narrowed his eyes at it, studied the tenant's face, the closed eyes, weighing up the risk of taking it, aware that anything with a name on it might present problems. He didn't need that kind of aggravation. He dropped it onto the tenant's chest and left him.

'That's for Amy whoever-she-is, not you.'

After dropping Julian at his apartment, Judd parked, got out and saw Julian's jacket on the rear seat. Sighing, she reached for it then slammed the door hard. Looking up, she saw Dennis lurking at his front door, his mouth already open.

'I've got something to—'

'Sorry, Dennis. Another time, OK?'

Inside her house, door closed, breathless, thinking of the time she could have been working, instead of bloody *messing* about— She brought her breathing under control, wondering what might have happened if she had brought Julian back here? Probably nothing. But what about in the morning? After he had spent the night in the narrow bed in the otherwise empty spare room? She looked at her watch.

'It's wine o'clock. Sod it.'

Going into the sitting room, she dropped his jacket over the back of the chair next to the table she used as a desk. Walking from the room, she was stopped by a soft thud. Sighing, arms hanging, she turned, went back, picked up the wallet that had fallen from it, dropped it on the table and headed to the kitchen.

Returning, glass in hand, she sank onto the armchair, took a mouthful of wine, looked at her watch. Slinging her legs over the arm of the chair, she leant back, wondering if she had the energy to do more work. Another mouthful of wine. There would have been complications if she had brought him back here. And anyway, he didn't live *here*. He had somebody in Manchester who had a daughter and—'

She rubbed her eyes, frowned. Putting down the glass, she got up, crossed the room and reached down for something lying on the floor. She brought it back to the soft light above the armchair. A photograph. She gazed at it. It must have slipped from his wallet. She should put it back. It was Julian with his arm around a woman. A woman with long hair obscuring much of her face. She brought it closer, studying their side-by-side configuration. Julian's wide smile, the set of his shoulder suggesting he was the photographer. The woman in his life? She had to be somebody who mattered to him. She studied the woman some more, now seeing the generous mouth, lips parted in a half-smile. Stylish-looking. She let the photograph drop to the table. It slid off, fell to the carpet.

She left it there, turned away. She had had enough of this whole *sodding* day.

TWENTY-EIGHT

Tuesday, 23 April. 3 a.m.

Judd had given up on sleep. She was downstairs, her eyes fixed on the E-FIT. It had been bothering her for some days. It was bothering her now. She didn't know why. E-FIT man looked back at her, giving her nothing. Headquarters' resident E-FIT expert, Gavin, was praised for his expertise. She shook her head. It still looked to Judd like a face knitted together from scraps of random features. She went back to the list of questions she had made, was halfway down the A4 when her concentration wavered. Retrieving the photograph of Julian and his girlfriend from the floor, she looked at it. The obvious happiness on his face made her heart constrict.

She switched her attention to the girlfriend, wanting to see everything about this woman who made him so happy. Her eyes absorbed the clothes that were visible, a tasteful mix of white and shades from cream to camel, a French manicure. It always paid to know the opposition. Judd sighed, shook her head, her eyes still on the tanned woman. They were clearly on holiday together somewhere. Where was the child Julian had told her about? On a sudden wave of envy, she realized that this woman came from money. So did Julian.

She dropped the photograph on the desk, covered her face with her hands. Why was she prying into his life, giving herself nothing but bad feelings? She picked it up, slid it back inside his wallet. She leapt as her phone rang. It was Watts.

'Where are you?' he asked.

'At home, where else at this time?' she snapped, flustered. 'Where are *you*?'

'At headquarters.'

'Something's happened! What's going on? Is Will there? If Will's there I'm coming in—!'

'He's on his way back from Stockport.'

'*Stockport*—?'

'Stay exactly where you are. Lock your doors. Don't open them to anybody. I'll get back to you—'

'Wait! Ade Jones' family lives in Stockport. If this is anything to do with the investigation, tell—'

'Just do as I *say*! Check your doors. I'll be at your place, soon as I can.' He was gone.

She was exhausted, her head filled with questions without answers. She went to the kitchen and made an instant coffee.

Fifteen minutes later, it sat forgotten, cooling on the floor close to where she was sitting. OK, she had been uneasy about Jonesy being in her garden that night, but what possible connection could he have to the investigation, beyond working all hours on it like they all had? She sighed, rubbed her eyes. It was now four thirty a.m. Nothing from Sarge. She reached for her phone, knowing that he would be riled at her calling him, but just waiting around was— The phone vibrated in her hand. She leapt up.

'Sarge?' Julian's voice came.

'It's me, Chloe. Bernard's asked me to check you're OK.'

'I'm fine. What's going on? Where are you?'

'Outside your house.'

Going quickly to the window, she saw his car. She rushed to the front door, pulled it open, watched as he got out with a small wave. The Mercedes' lights flashed as he walked the path towards her and came inside.

'Sorry for showing up like this. Did I wake you?'

'No, I haven't been to bed.'

'Listen. I owe you an apology for that business at the pub. Ade Jones kept buying halves, but it was me who drank them so – I'm sorry.' He came inside, followed her into the sitting room.

'Forget it.'

She went to the table, picked up his wallet, held it out. 'Here. It fell out of your jacket pocket. Your jacket is over there.'

He took the wallet from her.

'Thank you.'

'What's going on at headquarters, Julian?' He looked at her.

'Bernard hasn't told you? Adrian Jones is about to be arrested.'

'*What?*' He sat on the chair next to the table. He looked exhausted.

'I don't know any of the details but it's obviously connected to the deaths of Amy Peters and Erica Trent.' She stared at him.

'No, no. That's not possible.'

'Will is at headquarters. It's really crazy there, but it seems he brought back some information from Stockport, gave it to Bernard, who is now planning to arrest Jones.'

'How—? What information?' He looked down at his hands holding his wallet.

'All I know is that they've checked him out with his police colleagues and friends up there.' He studied her shocked face. 'He's your friend. I understand that, but I've seen another side to him. He's got a thing about women—'

'No, no. That's not true. OK, he's full of chat, but he wouldn't *harm* a woman.' She watched him stand.

'You asked me, Chlo, so I'm telling you what I know. Bernard has gone to the Brampton site. I'm on my way there—'

'Not without me! Give me two minutes.'

She left the room, ran upstairs, returned wearing jeans and a fleece.

'This is *all* wrong. I'm going to ring Sarge.'

'Obviously, he knows more than we do, so we need to accept—'

'I don't care what he knows or *thinks* he knows! This is making no sense.'

She went quickly to where he was sitting, searched through the papers on the table for her phone, saw the E-FIT, held it towards him.

'Tell me that *that* looks like Ade Jones! It's nothing like him.'

She walked away, phone in hand, eyes fixed on the E-FIT. Suddenly, it was there. In the eyes. The brows. The shape of the mouth. How had it taken her so long to see it? It was the eyes. She had been thrown off by the dark hair. She turned slowly to face him, her heart dropping inside her chest. He had his wallet open. He was looking at her. His voice when it came was soft.

'Are you OK, Chloe?'

She tried to form words. They wouldn't come. The tune he had hummed when she was at his apartment was back inside her head, a song she hadn't heard since she was small. Suddenly she remembered the words from an old record Moira used to play.

You fill up my senses . . . She stared down at his hand, held out towards her, and thought of the photograph she had seen of his girlfriend. She looked Italian. She looked like—

She stared up at him, her brain trying to compute the impossible.

'Come with me, Chloe. Let's go and help Bernard bring this investigation to an end, and once it's finished, we'll talk about the future. I *promise* you'll never want for love or anything else ever again. We can live anywhere you like. You can choose . . . As long as you're with me, I'm happy and, erm, we're meant to be together . . . We'll be happy. I'll make you great food. You'll never want for anything, Chloe, not while I have breath in my body to look after you . . .'

She listened to the superficial, repeated words sliding between his lips, his face expressionless. Now she understood what Will meant when he said that people like him talk about emotions, fake them rather than feel them. That their lack of understanding of others' emotions make them strangers in a strange land because they don't feel like everyone else does. He knew *exactly* the words to say to her. He knew what she needed. Because she had told him. Shown him her vulnerability. And now he was using it—

Like a night in the forest—

The forest. The trees around where Amy Peters and Erica Trent had lain. The other young women they hadn't yet found. She knew now the true nature of that photograph. He had his arm around one of those dead girls. Marella Ricci? Inside Judd, shock and fear gave way to white-hot anger. She had been a victim once. Never again. Ever. Her words came on an explosive sob.

'You . . . *liar*. You've lied to me, to Sarge and everybody else since the first day you arrived at headquarters all those years ago. Played the part of the professional and all that time you were manipulating us, *using* me, but Will's onto you!' She saw his face change. With two steps he was in her space.

'Shut the fuck up!' His saliva hit her face. She looked beyond him then back.

'I've *seen* it! The photograph! You with Marella Ricci and she's *dead*, you heartless, sadistic, *murderous* bastard—!' He had hold of her, his mouth open, lips drawn back from his teeth, veins visible on his forehead, his temples.

'You bought into it!' He shook her. '*Didn't* you? You *liked* what you saw! Me!' His hand tightened on her. 'For the sake of clarity, you're really not my type. I prefer the tall, the long-limbed with a hint of sophistication and learning.' Both of his hands were at her throat, her face on fire, her lungs screaming.

'Let her *go*!'

She staggered against the table as Traynor's fist made contact with Devenish's head sending him senseless to the floor. Officers filled the room. Jones knelt by him.

'Hello, Posh Boy. How're you feeling?' He looked up at Traynor. 'That's a serious hook you've got there, Will.'

Judd opened her eyes on hearing Watts' voice. He was giving her a once-over, pointing at her face.

'You look like you're getting one or two dodgy blood vessels in that eye—'

'I don't care,' she whispered.

'You will, in a day or so. You have Dennis to thank for calling us.' He went to the door.

'Kumar!' The officer sped to him.

'Sarge!'

'Go round to Mr Adams' house and get his statement. Take it nice and steady with him.'

Judd swallowed, her voice ragged.

'Who's Mr Adams?'

'It's Dennis. He knows how to be a good neighbour. Incidentally, he was a chemical engineer before some low-life took a fancy to his belongings as he left work and hit him on the head.' Judd bowed her head and sobbed. Watts raised his hand, patting air close to her shoulder.

'Come on. He's been telling me how much he's improved since he's started having occupational therapy.'

'It's not just Dennis, it's . . . everything.'

'I know. Is there anything you need?' She shook her head. 'Right, stay here. I've got a few things to do.'

'How did you know it was – him?' she whispered.

'From Will. He never believed it when Devenish pleaded ignorance about that post-death behaviour with the victims. Necrophilia. Something any psychologist would at least have heard of.' He paused, not looking at her.

'It didn't make sense to me either. When I headed the cold case unit at headquarters, one of our reinvestigations featured a case which involved breath play' – he shook his head – 'don't ask. It's similar to what happened to the women in this investigation. At eighteen years old, he was part of that reinvestigation so it didn't make sense that he wouldn't know about necrophilia. By then, Will was following his own suspicions.'

'. . . How does Dennis fit in?'

'He saw Devenish arrive in your garden that night and pull on a ski mask. Dennis admitted he felt reluctant to say anything at the time, but we've got the mask. It's with Chong, a lot of pine needles stuck in it. It's probably what he was wearing when I went after him at the site.'

'Where did you find it?'

'Inside a red Mini parked in the apartment garage, property of the actual tenant of the apartment who confirmed it by phone from San Francisco.'

'. . . My head's splitting,' she whispered.

A long time later, Judd was sitting in her quiet house looking at Watts, who had come back to see how she was. She shook her head.

'I can't stay in this house. I'm going to sell it. Try and find something else I can afford.' She was crying again. She raised her arm to her face. He was on his feet.

'No, no, not on your *sleeve*. Here.' She took the neatly folded handkerchief, pressed it to her face. He waited for her sobs to quieten.

'I'll tell you what I think, Judd. What you don't do is let what's happened force you into anything you might regret.' He looked around.

'If you want my opinion, this place suits you down to the ground. You're a bit light on furniture, but when you're more yourself, Connie's got some nice stuff she doesn't need any more. Only a suggestion, mind.' She looked at him.

'We're amalgamating.' She laughed, wept again. He waited, not knowing what to do.

'Come on, bab. Get a grip, yeah?' She looked up at him.

'I'm an expert on how it feels to be let down. *He* didn't come close.'

After Sarge left, she went to the kitchen. The bright red flowers grabbed her attention as soon as she entered. The pot plant that had arrived with the Chinese food. She walked to it, reached out and lifted it from its place on the windowsill. Looking down at it, she knew it had to go. She took it into the garden, feeling her heartrate climb. She couldn't have it in this house. Her childhood thinking that every single thing had feelings was still there. She looked down at the flourishing little plant, swallowed hard.

'Sorry, but you can't stay.'

She carried it to the end of the garden, unbolted the gate, placed it by the side of the rough path some feet away, then walked back to the house.

TWENTY-NINE

Early June. 10.10 a.m.

Traynor, Watts and Judd were in a meeting room inside the Queen Elizabeth II law courts, discussing the case with the Crown Prosecutor, Kevin Osborne. Traynor was immaculate in a mid-grey suit, Watts aware of his own, which had seen a fair number of hearings. He had caught Chong's frown at his suede shoes as he left the house and responded, 'This is no beauty contest.'

Here, now, that was how it felt. His eyes moved to Judd. He had jerked awake at three a.m., mithering that he hadn't reminded her that physical presentation meant something in court. His eyes moved over the neat, smoothed, blonde hair. When he first saw her this morning in her crisp, white shirt, dark suit and heels, it had occurred to him that she could easily be mistaken for one of the young solicitors about the place. Watts breathed. He wanted this over. Done.

The prosecutor was looking serious.

'He's charged with the murders of Amy Peters and Erica Trent, but he's pleading not guilty. Be in no doubt that we're facing a fight.' Watts gazed at him.

'What about the evidence? The Mini—'

'It belongs to Oliver Stephens, the man who is leasing that apartment from Devenish senior. Yes, the ski mask you recovered from inside it has the defendant's DNA on it. It also has Stephens'

DNA. It's *his* mask. We're anticipating that the defence is going to raise doubts about its direct relevance to this case.'

'What about the photograph he had in his wallet?' asked Judd. 'The one he couldn't bear to get rid of because of what it meant to him?' She looked directly at the prosecution barrister.

'Isn't it enough that he attacked *me*?' She looked away, the barrister's sympathetic voice coming to her.

'The difficulty we have is that his defence is going to place its own construction on whatever occurred between you and the defendant at that time. As for the photograph,' Osborne looked to Chong, 'my understanding is that there is no conclusive proof that the young woman shown in it was deceased at the time it was taken?'

'That's correct,' said Chong, 'although my examination of it suggests that she was and scene of crime officers will also testify that they've matched the configuration of trees to those at Brampton.' The barrister nodded, looked around the table.

'The defence is going to make a lot of the fact that these two young women are believed to be part of a series of five abductions.' Osborne paused. 'Yet we can't prove that those other three missing women are even deceased.' Watts' face heated up.

'Oh, come on, Kevin! There's no indication of their bank accounts being accessed, there's *nothing* to suggest that they're still alive.'

'I hear what you're saying and I shall present that view to the court. What I'm saying is that the defence will almost certainly focus on the fact that, as of now, there is no proof as to what actually happened to them.' Osborne paused. 'How confident do you feel as Senior Investigative Officer about the case you're putting forward?'

'Very. His DNA was on Carly Driscoll's jacket.'

'If I was for the defence, I might suggest cross-contamination within police headquarters.'

'What about the other evidence Adam's got relating to the marks on her jacket?'

'We'll have to wait and see, but my concern is that the defence will attack it as circumstantial. None of his DNA was found on the two victims—'

'Which makes sense! Devenish first got involved in police investigation as a student. He's *savvy*. Forensically aware.'

'That's an opinion, isn't it?'

'What about PC Reynolds' statement about his experience at the site when Devenish appeared to find a coin—'

'Reynolds is a young officer but he's sharp. He thought about what he saw: Devenish with *both* his hands in the earth, then offering him that coin, his other hand still buried.'

'There's no evidentiary value in that.'

'There should be. He'd found the crucifix. Devenish is crafty. He was *desperate* that day to be the one to go over there and start searching!' Watts eyed counsel. 'I hear what you're saying, Kevin, about proof, but I see more than enough to convict him. As a trusted member of my investigation, I asked Devenish to make several data searches. For every single one, he reported having found nothing. On one occasion, I asked him to check juvenile records for any individual who might fit the type of suspect we were developing. *Still* nothing. You know what we've since found. J. Devenish, fourteen years old, arrested for breach of peace, namely, looking into the bedroom window of a neighbour's daughter whose room was on the ground floor. Try this. Prior to Carly Driscoll's first visit to headquarters, I asked Devenish to be present during that interview and he backed off, saying he was ill—'

'He *knew* she might identify him.' All eyes turned to Judd.

'The second time she came to construct the E-FIT, she came into my office looking unwell. She said that seeing a group of police officers coming out of the main doors had disturbed her. You've seen the headquarters' CCTV footage we recovered showing Jones, Kumar, a couple of other officers involved in the investigation – and *him*, Devenish, right there with them. Carly Driscoll *saw* him. *That's* what upset her and she's made a statement to that effect.' The barrister looked at each of them.

'I share your frustration but you're aware that his father has secured the best defence team. What I'm doing is presenting you with a realistic picture of the potential fight we have here to secure a conviction – and the very real possibility of an appeal if he is found guilty.' Osborne looked across the table.

'Is there anything you would wish to emphasize from your knowledge of the defendant, Dr Traynor?'

'Yes. The question as to why these young women with long, dark hair were chosen to be victimized. My research on Devenish's family background has indicated a very likely reason. Far from the positive picture Julian Devenish gave to Police Constable Judd about his mother, my research indicates otherwise. She was a physically attractive woman with long, dark hair. She was also a chronic alcoholic, often physically and emotionally unavailable to him due to her many stays in residential facilities to address her addiction. She was also emotionally unavailable to him during those times she was at home. She died several years ago.'

'I shall be raising all of these issues in court. Dr Traynor, we are planning to call you last because your dual professional and investigative roles in the matter are likely to lead to lengthy examination and cross-examination. I apologize now for the wait you will have.' He looked to Watts.

'We'll hear your evidence before that of Adam Jenner and Dr Traynor.' He shifted his gaze to Judd.

'I shall be calling you first.' Judd stared at him, looked at Sarge who clearly wasn't expecting this either.

'Why PC Judd first?' The barrister looked down at the papers in front of him.

'Our understanding is that the defence is planning to make an issue of the nature of the relationship between PC Judd and the defendant. We plan to soundly refute and dispense with it as an issue as soon as possible.' She gave him a direct look.

'We were colleagues.'

Osborne nodded. 'We know the value of the evidence you've produced. It's part of my job to ensure that you're aware of potential challenges to it.'

Traynor spoke. 'This was a rigorous investigation which led to Julian Devenish's arrest. Part of my testimony will be my professional opinion that if he is freed, he is almost certain to kill again.'

'I've read your statement, Dr Traynor, and I'm in no doubt that you're right, that we're dealing with an extremely dangerous individual. Your views and those of your colleagues will be presented to the court to the best of my ability.' Osborne got to his feet. Watts looked up at him.

'How has Devenish been so far?'

'Cool to the point of cold. As though the whole process has no relevance at all to him. Let's see how it goes today, shall we?'

Thirty minutes later, her colleagues still in the side room, Judd was sitting alone near the door of the courtroom, thinking of other times she had given evidence. Times when it had gone well, when she had emerged with a metaphorical fist raised, a resounding 'Yes!' inside her head.

Her name was being called.

Chest tightening, she stood, followed the usher into the court-room. Heads turned in her direction as she walked inside, the usher leading her to the witness box. She avoided looking in the direction of the dock as she was sworn in. Whenever she came into a full, expectant courtroom, it felt as if it was the very first time. Her heart was hammering. Somewhere in this large, crowded room were the parents of Amy Peters and Erica Trent. The usher left in a flurry of black. Judd waited, shoulders back, head high, glimpsing movement from the prosecution bench. The wigged-and-gowned man who had spoken to them earlier now stood, conferred briefly with still-sitting colleagues, nodded and turned to her.

'Police Constable Judd, I'm Kevin Osbourne and I act for the prosecution in this matter. I'm going to start by reading your state-ment which is fairly short, for both the court's benefit and yours. When I've done so, I shall ask you some questions relating to that statement.' She listened attentively as he read it, then asked, 'Can you confirm that that is your statement?'

'Yes, it is.'

'You and the defendant were colleagues, both of you part of the police investigation into five truly shocking abductions which occurred in Manchester, which latterly proved to be—' The judge intervened.

'Mr Osbourne, there's no need to air the very basic aspects of this distressing case. We have already heard them. Let's proceed.' The lawyer looked at him, nodded.

'Of course, Your Honour.' He turned back to Judd. 'Would you provide for the court a brief outline of your role in that investiga-tion, Officer Judd?'

She responded to this standard question by outlining the recovery of the remains of the two missing women and her several visits to the site.

'During the course of the investigation, I read all of the evidence made available by Manchester police and conducted necessary data searches to extend our knowledge of what had happened to the missing women.'

'What was the defendant's role in that investigation?'

'As a forensic psychologist, he provided psychological opinion on the abductions and murders, firstly to the Manchester force and more recently to West Midlands Police.'

'So, professionally speaking, your two roles were entirely separate.'

'Yes.'

'Thank you, PC Judd. Remain where you are, please.'

She waited as Osbourne sat. The lead barrister for the defence stood, yellow hair just visible beneath her wig, her facial colour high. Judd had come across her before. She had a nickname: Rhubarb-and-Cream. Her eyes fixed on Judd.

'Police Constable Judd, I'm Yolanda Sittard and I act for the defence in this matter. Is what you have just said to my learned friend about your role and that of the defendant being separate entirely accurate?' Judd's thinking ground to a halt. She looked away from the counsel's plump face and bright lipstick, to the judge.

'Your Honour, I've already explained it. I'm not sure as to the meaning of that question, so I need—'

'Just answer, please!' snapped Rhubarb, her sharp eyes on Judd's face. The judge frowned.

'Ms Sittard, much as I am committed to maintaining the pace of this hearing, the witness has requested guidance and it is my duty to provide it to ensure that she fully understands what is being asked of her.' The judge looked down at Judd.

'What you are being asked, PC Judd, is whether your professional role and that of the defendant were *entirely* separate and unconnected.'

'Thank you, Your Honour. Our work roles were entirely separate, although at times there were joint meetings and activities at the site from where the remains of the two victims were recovered.'

'I'm obliged to Your Honour for that clarification,' said Sittard. She turned to Judd.

'Your response to my question is satisfactory as far as it goes. What it does not clarify for the court is whether there was any, shall we say, *additional* contact between you and the defendant.'

The judge sighed.

'Please make your point, Ms Sittard.'

'I certainly shall, Your Honour.' She looked across at Judd. 'It is the defence's stance that in fact you and the defendant worked *very* closely together at times during the police investigation.' Judd knew she was being led into slippery territory.

'We were colleagues. We pursued much of our separate roles within the same building at police headquarters which occasionally led to some collaboration between—'

'Come, come, Officer Judd. There's no need for coyness. You are a young woman. The defendant is a little your senior but a young man.' Judd stared at the florid face, looked to the judge who was waiting, brows raised.

'As I have said, we were colleagues. We shared information, shared our views of investigative developments.'

'I see.' Sittard's face was indicating her enjoyment of this exchange. 'According to the defendant, there was much more to that "collaboration". He has stated that you and he were involved in a sexual relationship.' The vast room was silent. Hearing the words, Judd was in freefall.

'. . . No.'

'He has also stated that when *he* ended that relationship, *you* became extremely angry. You vowed to "make him regret" that decision. Even more to the point, he states that you were determined that suspicion would be made to fall on *him*—'

'That is ridiculous *and* a lie.' Sittard turned to the jury, one hand on her hip, pencilled brows raised, her tone lightly mocking.

'Are you telling this court, and I remind you that you are under oath, PC Judd, that you and the defendant *never* had contact outside of the parameters of the police investigation?' Seeing where the defence was heading, Judd knew she had no choice.

'I did visit his apartment once at the request of Detective Chief Inspector Watts who was in charge of the investigation, to deliver some documents.'

'What time did you arrive and leave?' There was little Judd could do but tough it out.

'I arrived at around six and left at nine thirty or thereabouts—'

'I see. Was it a *large* number of documents you were given to deliver? Were you required to *read* them to my client?'

Stung by the sarcasm, Judd responded, 'He *invited* me to eat, so I did.'

'Was that the only time you and the defendant had— how shall I phrase it, "extracurricular" contact?'

'If you mean, was that the only time I saw him outside of work hours, no. He came to my house, uninvited a few days later with Chinese food—'

'And what time did he leave on that occasion?'

'At approximately midnight or thereabouts.' Seeing Sittard's gratified glance in the jury's direction, she added, 'I did *not* have a sexual relationship with him.'

Sittard turned slowly back to her.

'I'm very obliged to you, Officer Judd, for anticipating my question. Are you categorically denying *all* physical contact between you and the defendant?' Judd was furious with herself.

'. . . He kissed me once, possibly twice, on the cheek. I did not—'

'Thank you, Police Constable Judd. Remain where you are, please.'

As the barristers conferred, Judd took her first direct look in the direction of the dock, at the expensive suit, the neat blond hair, the tongue appearing and moving slowly, deliberately over his lips. Furious, nauseated, she glanced quickly around the courtroom. No one had seen the tiny gesture, all eyes fixed on the barristers engaged in a lively discussion with the judge.

Hearing words excusing her from further questions, she left the witness box, head up, walked to the door and out.

THIRTY

Same day. 11.40 a.m.

The prosecution took Watts through the items of police evidence, after which Sittard stood and covered similar ground, presenting the defence's interpretation of that same evidence.

'Detective Chief Inspector Watts, allow me to go back to two items of evidence you have described for this court: the red Mini which you say was used in the attempted abduction of two teenage females who, I understand, were never inside that car, and Carly Driscoll who is to give evidence claiming that she *was* inside it.

My client's response is that that car has no connection to him, that it is the property of a tenant to whom his father is leasing an apartment. The defendant's position is that he never drove that car. In fact there is no forensic evidence to indicate that he was ever inside that car, is there?'

'We have evidence that it had been thoroughly valeted inside and out.'

'Thank you for that interjection, Detective Chief Inspector Watts. I was about to go to the relevance of a ski mask which was found inside it and which you have indicated in your statement was worn by the defendant at the recovery site.'

'Yes. It was dropped there by him as he ran from me—'

'Were you able to categorically identify the defendant on that particular day?'

'No.'

'That ski mask is in fact the property of the tenant I just referred to, who has stated that he lent it to the defendant for the purpose of skiing. What is your response?'

'That ski mask bears the DNA of both tenant and defendant. What you've said doesn't exclude the defendant from using that ski mask to conceal and protect his face from scratches when he was within thick tree cover at the site as I pursued him,' said Watts flatly.

'You did not actually see the defendant's face on that occasion.'

'. . . No.'

The to-and-fro continued. Like Chong, he was also unable to be categorical that in the photograph depicting the defendant and the young woman at his side, that same woman was deceased, although he landed a blow to the defence's case by pointing out that Miss Ricci's parents had confirmed their belief that it was their daughter. Muffled sobs drifted around the courtroom, evidence that Ricci's family members were also present. Sittard turned to the jury.

'The defendant has admitted that he and Miss Ricci dated briefly early in 2018. Moreover, he has produced a statement expressing his sincere regret that he did not admit to that relationship earlier in the investigation.'

Sittard's suggestion that the defendant's DNA on Carly Driscoll's jacket was due to cross-contamination at headquarters was another step too far for Watts.

'That's your interpretation of our evidence. As the officer responsible for this investigation, I have submitted clear chain-of-evidence records.'

'But not complete records, in respect of the whereabouts of one item, a length of black masking tape recovered from the scene, which is still unknown?'

'It is my belief that the defendant removed it from—'

'As you well know, Detective Chief Inspector, courts operate on *evidence*, not *belief*.'

Five minutes later, Watts emerged from the courtroom. He had done what he could. There were always competing constructions to any case. He knew that if Devenish was found guilty, he would derive much pleasure from thinking about those small items. Watts was hoping for a long sentence, but there was no telling what the outcome was likely to be. As he walked away, he heard Carly Driscoll's name being called.

The young, slender woman with rich swathes of brown hair stepped into the witness box to a ripple of whispered comment. She gave her evidence in such a quiet voice that the judge twice had to ask her to speak up.

Sittard rose, smiled at the young woman, and launched a blistering attack on her evidence, suggesting that her identification of the defendant as her abductor was mistaken. Driscoll dealt reasonably well with that, not quite so well with the defence's other suggestion that Driscoll knew her abductor, which would account for why she had so meekly gone with him. It brought Driscoll to tears, but she stood her ground and was then excused.

Her place in the witness box was taken by Adam Jenner, head of the forensic team. The prosecution reminded the jury of the presence of the defendant's DNA on Driscoll's jacket then turned to another matter, that of the marks on it.

Asked to comment on them, he said, 'Those marks were subjected to chemical analysis which identified them as hair dye. Microscopy indicated minute flakes of it from which I was able to identify specific particles. Following a search of the apartment complex, an empty hair dye container was located in a waste bin outside the building—'

Sittard was on her feet. 'Your Honour, this is *very* unsatisfactory evidence, given that it was not found inside the defendant's apartment.'

She was overruled and he continued. 'The remaining contents of the container were also microscopically analysed and were shown to be chemically indistinguishable from the marks found on Ms Driscoll's jacket.'

Responding to a prosecution query, Jenner confirmed that the defendant's fingerprints were found on the external surface of the container.

He was excused, the defence choosing not to question him.

THIRTY-ONE

Same day. 2.30 p.m.

All eyes were on the witness box and the tall, fair-haired man waiting there. In response to the prosecution's request to confirm his full name and professional title, he responded, 'Dr William Brodie Traynor. Lecturer in Criminology at Central University, Birmingham.'

He confirmed his doctorates in forensic psychology and criminology, along with details of his theoretical expertise relating to personality development, aberrant sexual behaviour and homicide. He also confirmed his assistance to major police investigations within the UK. The prosecution barrister nodded, smiled.

'And you are recognized by the West Midlands Police Force among many others as an independent expert.'

'Yes.'

'I would appreciate it, Dr Traynor, if you would briefly outline for the court the nature of two most recent homicide cases in which you had both an investigative role and that of an expert.'

'Of course. One of the cases involved a young woman who was murdered while out jogging, the other the shooting of a married couple inside their car.' Murmurs of recognition drifted from the public gallery.

'Both high-profile West Midland cases which you assisted the police to resolve.'

'Yes.'

'I should like to go to the matter before this court and for you to outline for this hearing your professional role in it, including your contact with the defendant.'

'I was invited to participate in the investigation following the recovery of human remains in an area known as Brampton, just beyond the city boundary. I visited the scene several times. I also read all of the available documentation relating to all five victims.'

'After viewing both the site and the remains which were recovered, what conclusions did you draw, Dr Traynor, as to what happened to these two young women?'

'That both victims had been transported to that area alive. On viewing the remains of the first victim, there was no indication that an attempt had been made to bury her, although they had become covered by natural vegetation over time. There had been minimal effort to conceal the remains of the other victim.'

'Did your observations inform your opinion as to what occurred to those remains?'

'Yes. The availability of Amy Peters' remains indicated to me that that was a purposeful choice made by a killer intent on revisiting the bodies of those young women for the purposes of post-mortem sexual activity.' Above the horrified gasps of observers within the court came the judge's voice.

'Most shocking and distasteful, Dr Traynor.'

'Yes, Your Honour, it is.'

The prosecution barrister asked, 'As the investigation progressed, did information come into your possession which strengthened your professional opinion regarding that behaviour?'

'Yes. Towards the end of the investigation, I was shown a photograph of a young woman who looked very similar to a student who is also suspected of being abducted from the same university. More recently, her identity has been confirmed by family members as Marella Ricci.'

'Would you describe for the court a second person in that photograph, please?'

'It is the defendant.' Whispers started up, increasing in volume.

'*Quiet*, please,' said the judge, adding, 'Continue, Mr Osbourne.'

The prosecution barrister gave a small bow.

'I'm obliged, Your Honour.' And to Traynor, 'Did you formulate a theory as to what was being depicted in that photograph.'

'Yes. In my opinion, at the time that photograph was taken, Miss Ricci was either incapacitated or already deceased.' There were sounds of two or three people quickly leaving the court. Traynor saw that they were Ricci's family members.

The barrister continued in the now leaden atmosphere. 'You have provided a statement in this matter, item number 341 in the file in front of you, which indicates that as the investigation unfolded and you and the defendant were working together, you became increasingly confused by the quality of the defendant's participation in discussions with you. Could you expand on this for the court's benefit?'

'Yes. I noted that the defendant appeared extremely reluctant to engage in discussion of certain aspects of the case. At one stage, he denied any professional knowledge of the kind of post-mortem behaviour I referred to earlier.'

'And that struck you as unusual?' Traynor nodded.

'Very much so. While a layperson might be anticipated to have zero knowledge or even awareness of such behaviour, it would not be credible in a graduate such as the defendant, with an honours degree in forensic psychology, particularly one who had worked alongside the police on cold murder cases during his time as a student.' The barrister paused, gave members of the jury a direct look.

'I understand that Detective Chief Inspector Watts came separately to a similar conclusion.'

'Yes. He searched archived cold cases which he himself had worked on with the defendant, Julian Devenish, and found one dating back to that time which featured very similar sexual behaviours to those I described earlier.'

'For the sake of clarity, Dr Traynor, there is no suggestion that the defendant had criminal involvement in that historical case?'

'No. The issue is that while assisting the investigation under discussion here, his stance that he was ignorant of such behaviour is not credible.'

'Dr Traynor, would you tell the jury what that professed denial by the defendant suggested to you?'

'That he wished to avoid or distance himself as far as possible from awareness of such sexual activity.'

The barrister then asked Traynor to describe two professional meetings between himself and the defendant during which the murders were discussed. Traynor outlined the first meeting, during which the defendant showed reluctance to offer his views on the kind of individual responsible, or comment on the post-mortem sexual behaviour. 'Which I found confusing and also difficult to accept.'

'And what transpired during the second meeting, Dr Traynor?'

'His presentation was very different. He appeared confident in his views of the personality of the killer of both young women, indicating agreement with my earlier suggestions that the likely suspect was a user of pornography and also a stalker, but he took that view much further, stating his belief that pornography was a *causal* factor of sexual crime. Such a view is not supported by modern psychological research, although it is regarded as having an influence.'

'Would you kindly explain that for the benefit of the jury?'

'Of course.' Traynor looked towards the jury, all of whom gazed attentively back at him.

'Research indicates that for those individuals who use pornography and also sexually offend, it is the *personality* of the offender which is much more relevant than the material itself. To put that in context, if pornography were a direct *cause* of sexual offending, the anticipated rate of such offending among, say, teenage boys who are known to be attracted to that type of material, would be extremely high. But that is not borne out by offence statistics. Research also indicates that individuals who are high-volume users of pornography are also likely to have pre-existing problematic aspects to their own behaviour, such as impulsivity, sexual dysfunction and personality traits of an antisocial nature. Given those preconditions of impulsivity and so on, such individuals tend to experience difficulty in controlling their sexual wants and desires.' Most jury members were making notes.

'Did the defendant's expressed views indicate anything else to you, Dr Traynor?'

'Yes. I believe he was attempting to create a future defence, should it be needed.'

Osbourne continued. 'Thank you, and now, familiarize us if you would, with the key features of the psychopathic personality,' he glanced at the jury, 'keeping in mind that many of us in this courtroom lack psychological knowledge.'

Aware of an unwavering gaze on him from the dock, Traynor said, 'Fictionalized psychopaths are often presented as extremely deviant in their presentation to others. In reality, it is not an easy task to identify a psychopathic personality, at least in the short term. They can present as extremely agreeable, with an easy charm and a ready wit, yet with sufficient awareness not to overplay those qualities. The reality is that those features are a sham. Behind them lies an overblown sense of self-worth. This is an individual who is able to cause distress and pain to others because he lacks the ability to empathise. He feels zero remorse for all that he does. In my opinion, the two young women whose remains were found at Brampton were killed by an individual with psychopathic traits, plus those of impulse-control and so on that I described earlier.' Traynor paused.

'I regret to say it, but it is my professional opinion that Marella Ricci met a similar fate, as did the two remaining victims abducted from Manchester—'

'*Objection!*'

The defence barrister was on her feet, eyes blazing at the judge. 'This witness must stay within the known facts of this matter.' The judge gazed at her.

'Miss Sittard, this witness is expressing a *professional* opinion.' And to Traynor, 'Continue please.'

'The individual who killed them has a deep hatred of women, which is skilfully concealed behind a pleasant, even trustworthy façade. However, when he chooses to show his true self, he strikes suddenly and with unbridled fury.'

'Thank you, Dr Traynor. I want to ask you about psychological tests for identifying personality disorders such as psychopathy—'

'The defence objects to this avenue of inquiry, Your Honour.' The judge was looking irritated.

'I shall hear this witness's response on similar grounds to that which I outlined barely a minute ago. Proceed, Dr Traynor.'

'There is a widely used and valid test which identifies psychopathic traits.' The prosecution barrister nodded.

'Was it suggested at any time following the defendant's arrest that he engage in such testing?'

'Yes. He refused to do so under advice from his legal team.'

'What did that refusal indicate to you?'

'Given the defendant's knowledge and familiarity with such tests, it indicated that he was extremely concerned as to what the test might reveal about him if he responded in an open, honest way.'

'And, if he had engaged in testing in a dishonest way, what might that have indicated?'

'The test is structured in a way which identifies untruthful responses and it would inevitably have raised significant concerns about the quality of his participation and speculations as to why he was being avoidant.'

'You're suggesting that in your opinion, if he had participated, his responses would have raised concerns, whichever stance he chose?'

'Exactly.'

'Thank you, Dr Traynor. I'm aware that my colleague for the defence is becoming extremely restless, so may I quickly return to your second discussion with the defendant and ask you to give this court your observations of the defendant's behaviour during it?'

Aware of movement in the dock, Traynor responded, 'When discussion turned to the likely progression of what was done to the two victims located at the Brampton site, the defendant's physiological responses were observable extremely quickly.'

'Please be specific for the court.'

'My observations of him at that specific time were that his face reddened, he began to perspire and his pupils became noticeably dilated. Pupil dilation is known to occur in response to arousal. Given that this was a professional discussion with no overt fear factor, the alternative explanation is that the defendant was sexually aroused by his own description of what he was suggesting happened to the victims in the case.'

'Liar! *Liar!*' The voice from the dock ripped through the almost total silence of the courtroom.

It erupted in pandemonium, all eyes fixed on Devenish, now resisting the two officers close to him, both arms raised, his hands fisted, the veins at his temples bulging. Traynor looked at him and knew that what he was seeing was the face Devenish's victims had seen in their final moments. He looked away.

Gowned ushers headed towards the dock, the defence barrister and her junior counsel gazing open-mouthed, the jury watching the defendant's violent resistance, their eyes wide, some with hands pressed to their mouths, several now on their feet as the court doors flew open and uniformed security officers rushed inside. Devenish continued to scream at Traynor as he was surrounded, his arms pinioned.

'Here's a *promise*, Traynor! When my father hears the outright lies you've told this court about me, he'll *crucify* you, do you hear?' He continued to struggle as he was removed, his voice fading. 'He'll investigate your wife's death! Find out what *you* did. You'll never work again!' His voice was increasingly obscured by the tumult in the courtroom. '. . . I'm *innocent* . . . love women . . . My father . . . make sure . . . you'll *pay* for this!'

Watts and Traynor left the court building together, went to a nearby coffee shop where they each ordered espresso and waited without speaking for it to arrive. When it did, they sipped it in silence. After a minute or so, Watts said, 'Woah, I'm getting the caffeine hit.' He looked across at Traynor. 'Brodie?'

'My mother's choice.'

'You were right about him, Will.' Watts spooned sugar into his espresso. He shook his head. 'When he was part of the cold case unit, a nicer lad you couldn't have met. Something I only recalled yesterday: when he joined my cold case unit, he was under a bit of a cloud. He'd hacked into the university's financial records.' Feeling Traynor's eyes on him, he said, 'The university knew about it. They told us he hadn't stolen any money. It was regarded as an escapade by a computer-mad kid, and he was open about it to me and my boss at the time. I never for a minute thought he was weird and neither did Kate Hanson. I'll have to break the news to her. She probably already knows by now.'

Traynor nodded. 'You saw a young, fresh-faced student, a computer nerd, keen to hone his forensic skills and knowledge. He was all of those things you believed he was, Bernard, and he was none of them. What we saw is the self he created. He didn't fool everyone. Adrian Jones didn't like him. He found it difficult to say why and I'm guessing he attributed it to what he saw as a difference in background. Ray Boulter told me that he thought Devenish lacked sympathy for the families of the missing students. I assume he meant empathy.' Watts frowned into his espresso.

'Josie Miller wasn't keen on him. I should have picked up on that because for Josie, it has to be a first.' He gave his face a vigorous rub. 'How the hell are we supposed to pick up on people like him without wading through a load of theory?'

'We listen to them. Be attuned to their lack of empathy, the lack of word discrimination.' Watts waited, looking uncertain.

'Door. Shoe. Axe. Glove. Love. Corpse. Car. Maggot. Laugh.

Strangle.' Traynor tapped the table top to a steady rhythm. He nodded. 'Bernard, your face is testimony that those words do not carry equal emotional weight. For Devenish and all others like him, that's what they are: just words lacking any emotional significance because *he* is an emotional desert.' Watts stared at him.

'That's one of the worst things I've ever heard. On the plus side, just as we left the court building, I got a whisper that his father left the proceedings early to go back to Canada.' They were silent for a couple of minutes, then, 'Any ideas where his other three victims are? Why we didn't find Marella Ricci at Brampton?'

'Having taken her there, I don't know why he didn't leave her. Only he knows. I'm not anticipating that he will tell anyone. As for where she, Melody Brewster and Claire Walsh are buried, I can tell you only what I think: when Chloe and I talked recently, she recalled Devenish playing music when she was at his apartment. One of the tracks was Elgar. It seems he spent some time during his early years in Worcestershire with his father.' He looked at Watts. 'And also his mother. Remember when he looked from Brampton to the Malvern Hills on the horizon?'

Watts' face said it all.

'It's possible he took them there.' There were some seconds of silence, then, 'You and I have a responsibility for ensuring that Devenish stays wherever he is sent.'

'Amen to that.'

After twenty minutes Traynor left. Watts ordered another espresso, knowing he would be wired for the rest of the day and probably half the night. He stared out of the café window at people rushing past to buses, others climbing into taxis. Everybody on the move. He had thought of mentioning to Traynor who the prosecution barrister was. He hadn't. It wouldn't have meant much to him. Holding the loaded spoon above the espresso, he gently tilted it, watched brown sugar slowly fall into blackness and disappear. Kevin Osbourne, barrister, ex-husband of Kate Hanson, forensic psychologist, Watts' one-time colleague in the Unsolved Crime Unit. They and Joe Corrigan, the US police officer also assigned to the unit back then, had worked well together. She and Corrigan were living in Boston now. He hadn't heard from them in a while. As it happened, neither had they heard from Watts. His phone rang. It was Connie.

'I'm at home, wondering where you are.'

'I'm on my way. I stopped off and had coffee with Will.'

'How are you feeling, now that it's more or less over?'

'It'll never be over till the other three young women are found.'

A silence formed between them. 'You arrested him, gave evidence against him. You've done all you can, Bernard. It's time to come home.'

He left the coffee shop, joined the throng hurrying along. He went to the multi-storey, got inside his vehicle. After pushing through forty-five minutes of heavy traffic, he had reached home when his phone buzzed. It was Kevin Osbourne.

The verdict was in. Guilty. The sentencing would come later. Osborne indicated that he anticipated it being life with no chance of release.

THIRTY-TWO

Mid-June.

A single ring of her doorbell brought Judd into the hall. Reaching the door, she paused, looked through the small aperture, smiled and opened it.

'Dennis! Come on in. Did it take you long to get here?'

A while ago, when she'd first said it to him, he'd looked adrift, pointed to his house next door. Now, it was a set joke between them. He shook his head.

'You wouldn't *believe* the traffic!'

He walked ahead of her along the hall, glancing into the sitting room.

'Nice curtains. And the desk, and—'

He continued on, his gait still a little off, but improving. He was back at his job now and wearing his hair shorter. A friend who had regularly taken his car for a drive to keep it running had finally persuaded him to sell it. Dennis had made quite a thing of positioning his cones in front of her house, since when she had never had to search for a parking space.

She followed him into the kitchen, saw him look around at the new window blind, the tiled floor and shiny brushed steel stove.

'Very nice.'

'Have a seat, Dennis and I'll get some drinks organized.' He sat down at the small, modern dining table she had been given by Chong, along with several other items.

'Only soft for me. On medication.'

'I know— Now, who's that? No, stay where you are,' she said as he got to his feet.

At the door she checked her caller then opened the door to a slim, brown-haired man in glasses.

'It's Jake,' he said. 'Jake Petrie?' She smiled up at him, nodded.

'I remember.'

'I hope you don't mind me dropping by?'

'No. Come on in.' She led him through the house and into the kitchen. He stopped on seeing Dennis.

'I'm sorry. Is this a bad time—?'

'Not at all. This is Dennis Adams, my next-door neighbour.' Dennis was on his feet, one of them jostling the table, his hand held out.

'I remember the name Petrie from the court hearing. I wanted to give evidence but I didn't have to.'

'Sit down and join us, Jake. We're having quiche and salad.'

'That sounds great, if you're sure it's not inconvenient?'

'I'm sure.'

She opened the oven, removed the quiche, set it on the hob and reached for the salad. Drizzling dressing, she glanced at them now in conversation. She gazed out of the window, past the large, vigorous pot plant and its bright red flowers. Life is full of learning about all kinds of things. Sometimes, it came the hard way. Sometimes, you got it wrong. She looked back at the splash of green and red on the windowsill. She had thrown it out once, then brought it back inside again. It was just a plant.

Removing garlic bread from the oven, she nudged it from its tray onto the glass worktop protector and reached for a knife. Following the trial it happened very rarely, but he was back inside her head. He had fooled all of them for a while. It had been different for her. He had fooled her in the way he probably had his victims. How skilful he was at it, she thought, and how he must have hated us women. They had talked and ate and laughed together and she had wanted him from the first time she saw him and he *knew* it. She had allowed him an insight into her life, her background, her vulnerability and he had seized on it, drawn her to him and she had allowed that too.

She took the bread to the table, came back. Julian Devenish was never a real person. He was a construction, a façade beyond which there was nothing but a chilly void. Will's words. She began slicing the quiche, glanced back at Dennis and Jake sitting at her table, their conversation easy.

Nice men. Good men. Her friends. She carried the quiche, an extra plate and the salad to the table.

'Let's eat.'

ACKNOWLEDGEMENTS

This is where I express my grateful thanks to all those who have given their professional support to me: Camilla Bolton, my agent, and Jade Kavanagh at Darley Anderson. Also, to all at Severn House (simply, the best!).

There are two more names I must add: Chief Inspector Keith Fackrell, West Midlands Police (Retired) and Dr Jamie Pringle, Senior Lecturer in Geosciences at Keele University.

Both have given their valuable time and professional expertise in responding to my queries during the writing of *A Dark, Divided Self*. They have done the same for previous books and their generosity with their time is very greatly appreciated.

A big thank you to both.

There is yet someone else who deserves my unreserved thanks for responding to my queries with typical zest: Dr Colin L. Graham, Honorary Lecturer in Analytical Chemistry at the University of Birmingham.

As ever, I take complete responsibility for any errors in my interpretation of the information they so generously gave me.